Simon the Elf wants to tell you the true story behind Jolly Ole St. Nick. Yeah, he's a vampire. But that alleged gift giver and lover of children hides more than that fact from you. And what about Mrs. Claus and Rudolph? Venture into a world of enslaved elves, enchanted animals, and death wrought by Santa himself. With his sharp wit, Simon will lead you into the darkest realms of Christmas. Warning: Simon cusses a lot. But you would, too, if Santa held you captive.

SANTA IS A

VAMPIRE

A Simon the Elf Novel

Damian Serbu

A NineStar Press Publication

Published by NineStar Press
P.O. Box 91792,
Albuquerque, New Mexico, 87199 USA.
www.ninestarpress.com

Santa is a Vampire

Printed in the USA
First Edition
November, 2018

Print ISBN: 978-1-949909-45-6

Also available in eBook, ISBN: 978-1-949909-42-5

Warning: This book contains graphic violence; murder of adults and children; mention of past rape; mention of past child sexual abuse; homophobic comments.

To John Lauro and Scott Williams; no two people better embody love and friendship in all the world.

Chapter One: Introducing the Blood Sucking Legend

JOLLY OLD ST. Nicholas. What a laugh.

If you only knew the real story behind Santa Claus. He keeps it buried for a reason, after all. Because you'd hunt him down up there in his North Pole ice castle if you even had a remote idea regarding his real identity.

Mrs. Claus and Rudolph too. Well, maybe not the missus. It's complicated. But more on them later. Back to Santa.

Let's peek in on this esteemed man who brings gifts to children and represents the blessed holiday of Christmas, shall we? He would kill me if he found out I leaked this information. Well, I intend to leak it, no matter the consequences, because I'm keeping this in a journal. If you're reading it, I probably succeeded. Which means dead Simon the Elf, for sure, if he discovers me telling people any of this information. But death might improve my situation since this enslavement sucks big ones. I started this secret blog and will release it without concern for my well-being.

So, if you're reading it, I'm probably dead.

This first little story will tantalize you, get your feet wet with everything I want you to learn.

It's late November, so Santa moves around a lot more freely because everyone expects to see him out there, greeting the children and gathering their Christmas orders. A lot of fools dress up like him to please the little kiddies or earn a buck. Everyone sees these fake Santas everywhere they go. Good enough for the real Santa Claus, because it hides him. He appears as another of the fool Santas walking about during the holidays.

That and his silly outfit disguise him—What a costume he picked!—but again it serves his purpose well. The ridiculous beard and red outfit mean Christmas cheer, presents, and a happy fat man coming to spread joy. Of course, he manages a real beard and authentic outfit to intensify the experience when people meet him.

Do you know why he wears red? I do. It hides the blood stains better. Okay, confession time. I'm throwing out my theory, but don't ask for proof. He never said that or explained the red. It just makes sense to me. Even though he usually cleans the blood up. Oops. Getting ahead of the story again. Let's take a deep breath and refocus.

By the way, in case you require my credentials, I'm an elf. Trapped against my will to do Santa's bidding. More later.

Okay, focus. Late November. Turkey Day's come and gone and Santa enters prime time. He creeps out of the ice palace, chains the poor reindeer to the sleigh, and speeds away, with a couple of elves, including me, enchanted in the sled against our will. We never know, until he issues a command, what he intends for us. Sometimes we ride along to keep him company; sometimes we get clean-up duty; sometimes we have to help.

We fly over various parts of the world, almost land in Germany until Santa spies one of those Secret Hunters. "Dangerous. Let's go someplace else."

"Scared, are ya?" I glance over at him. "Ouch!" Santa backhands me. It's another curse of mine, but one I came to elfdom with. See, I'm a bit of a smart-ass and can't hold my tongue. Gets me in trouble a lot.

"Let's find someplace more hospitable." Santa instructs the reindeer to change course and never answers my question. But I suppose the slap upside the head could be considered an answer, of sorts.

To America, the land of advancement and scientific reasoning. I recognize the coastline right away. Why, even the hardcore Christians dismiss Santa as a legend based on an alleged saint from the past. Saint, indeed. But such thinking helps hide his true identity.

We swoop over New York, but Santa seldom likes to hunt there because it doesn't really present a risk. Masses of people living on top of each other, often killing and dying without his assistance. Where's the challenge in hiding a body in that mess?

Moving right along, the reindeer glide over the little town of Wilmington, Ohio. It offers Santa everything he desires. I know from experience. Remote. Tranquil. Peaceful for the most part. Until a dead body materializes right in the midst of the holiday cheer. Santa's way of taking a dump on Season's Greetings in a happy little community.

So Santa guides the sleigh over Wilmington College and sets it down in the town cemetery. We can't land on roofs yet, without people wondering if Santa's calendar got all out of whack. Few people enter a cemetery in the midst of a cold November so we can hide out here.

He orders the reindeer to shut up, except Rudolph, who gets to run and do his own thing. He trots off with his bright-red nose high in the air. The other reindeer stay here. I often wonder if anyone questions the sudden appearance of reindeer manure where no reindeer exist. Of course, even if they thought about it, no one would come to the conclusion that Santa hid his sleigh and reindeer in the cemetery for a spell. Because most over the age of seven don't think he exists.

Once he gets the reindeer squared away, Santa tells a couple of my fellow elves—two I think are big assholes, so you know—to watch the sleigh and get the hell out of Dodge if anyone shows up. Santa can summon us from afar, so no worries there.

Me? I get the distinction of tagging along with him. He makes me his personal assistant on these sublime missions because he knows how much I despise it. The killing. The secrecy. And his perfect disguise of being Santa. Well, this pains me to admit, but I think he also enjoys my company for some twisted reason, especially my mocking of him and constant chatter. We have a complicated relationship, to put it mildly, compelling him to keep me close, no matter how much I detest it.

My compadres snicker as I run along to keep up with Santa. I take a second to stop, turn around, and give them the bird.

We saunter right down Main Street and wave at the passing cars when they honk. I almost puke every time he lets out a jovial, "Ho! Ho! Ho!" Little kids run up to him and say hello, followed by asking for presents. He feigns delight and interest while holding back an inclination lurking beneath the surface. Sweet little kid blood.

We get far enough away from prying eyes to meander down a residential street. Then we wander around while Santa scouts the houses and makes an assessment of our target. This goes on for a couple hours, until most children lie sleeping in bed. Even most adults are passed out by now.

One car zooms past. I wonder what they think, seeing Santa amble down the road amidst these houses, lit up for the holidays. Do they think it's someone's dad, surprising the kids in disguise? A hired dude going to a party? Maybe it's a stripper, dressed for the occasion until the ladies (or men) demand the pants and coat come off?

Nope. It's the Real McCoy. And the lady behind curtain number one, alone in her house as she waits for her husband to get home from the night shift, just became dinner. Okay, I have no idea if a husband on a night shift exists. I lied to make the story better. But the woman sits alone in this normal-sized house. Looks like she's dusting or cleaning something.

Sometimes Santa walks right up to the front door. Knocks or rings the bell, and the fools open it for him. Listen, even without Santa's hidden reality, who opens their door for a dude in a Santa outfit unless you're expecting the stripper I referenced?

Anyway, no front door this time. Or back door. Instead, he touches the side of his big-ass nose, grabs me by my neck, and yanks me along as we fly through the air, land on the roof, and plunge into the chimney. He could get in the fucking house any way he wants, by the way. He does the blackened chimney thing for two reasons. One, for effect. You know, back to living up to the legend and playing by the rules. Despite the fact the sleigh and reindeer remain hidden among the dead in the cemetery and not up here on the roof with us. No one will question a big guy in a Santa costume plopping into their fireplace and shouting out a "Yo!" It may startle them, but since it conforms to the legend, people tend to go with it. Idiots. Two, he does it tonight because I hate it. I hate heights. I hate flying. And I hate when he touches me.

We hit the fireplace grate and roll out onto the carpet in the living room, where we stand in triumph before the poor woman, who gives a yelp. Actually, she screams bloody murder.

"Shh, my dear one. Shh!" Santa puts his finger up to his lips and winks at her. "Nothing to fear. I imagine you didn't believe in good ole Santa anymore? Adults so seldom do these days. But as you saw from my arrival through your chimney, I do, indeed, exist!" Santa sweeps his arms out with a flourish, to indicate his body and presence in the flesh.

The woman stops screaming, thank God, before my eardrums rupture.

"And this here is my worthy assistant, Simon."

"I'm not here because I want to be—" Santa clamps his hand over my mouth and glares a warning. Right. I'll stop, because getting locked in the ice dungeon when we get back to the North Pole totally sucks.

"Is he all right?" she asks him and points to me.

This is what gets me so pissed off. Stupid fucking people. I want to shout back at her. Hey! Lady! Wake up! A big fat ass plunged down your chimney with a little elf under his control. You scream, but because he wears a red suit and laughs and has a crazy beard, you relax and engage him? Trust me. You do not want to engage him!

Instead, I shrug my shoulders and smile. Self-preservation ranks over saving her stupid self. So I speak to make it right. "Sometimes I forget myself. Coming down the chimney got me dizzy and all. Everything's cool."

Santa pats my back, signaling I recovered well enough he'll lighten my punishment.

Too bad nothing will help this poor woman. Glancing around the living room, I deduce my inaccurate take on the husband thing. She lives alone, because I only see pictures of cats, herself, and a few of large family groups.

Yet she looks normal enough. A little heavyset. Pretty smile, long black hair that flips up into curls at her shoulder. Her clothes leave little to desire, with the baggy sweatpants and Cleveland Browns sweatshirt. But she was cleaning, so who the hell dresses up to tidy up?

Santa grins and does his "Ho! Ho! Ho!" laugh at her.

She giggles back at him. Fool.

"Tell me, dear, what's your name?"

"Samantha." She bats her eyelashes.

What is wrong with her? Seriously, most victims at least get a little skittish at this point. An internal wiring signals danger, even if the Jolly Ole Elf seems harmless enough.

"Samantha!" Santa laughs. "Delightful! Of course, I knew your name already." If I forgot to mention it, Santa lies even more than I do. "Come here, and give Santa a hug."

She hesitates a bit. She dips her chin, smiles as the red spreads across her cheeks, and wiggles back and forth.

"Come, come!" Santa opens his arms wide.

Samantha falls into them more than she comes to him. He hugs her close, rubs against her, and finishes with releasing her. Usually he would spring into action now and force me to help. Her compliance gives him other ideas this time.

"Listen, it's too early in the Christmas season for people to see me. Do you have a private place we could go? I need to ask you a few questions about your gift requests and enlist your help in making the holidays special for needy children."

As she leads us up the stairs and down a hallway, I snort by accident. Santa pops me upside the head, so I turn my near laugh into a sneeze.

"Gesundheit." Samantha turns after she opens a door and motions for us to enter. "I converted this spare room into an office." Santa goes first; I follow.

"What a delightful space! What do you do in here?"

Santa's lying again. I almost hurl at the state of this room. Crammed full of papers, boxes, an old computer dumped in a corner because a newer version sits atop the desk, and other crap. Books strewn across the floor. And it reeks because the closet houses a cat's litter box, long overdue for an empty.

"Well, I work from home for my job sometimes, when the lawyers have editing and stuff for me to do. Otherwise," Samantha glances around, as if gremlins lurked nearby to hear her secret. Actually, they might. I arrived with Santa down the damn chimney, so who am I to insinuate gremlins can't exist? "I'm writing a novel."

"Ho! Ho! Ho! What a pure delight! May I read it?"

She hurries over to the computer and sits in front of it. She clicks around and opens a document. Reading the first page, I surmise this here office is in a better state than the writing. A corny romance, with the sex scenes represented by dot dot dot. You know: "Kellen grabbed her around the waist, pulled her close, and engulfed her mouth in a sensuous kiss......" Figures she'd fear typing out the words penis, vagina, clitoris, and cum, or even climax of throbbing. So represent them with dots.

Santa has enough with playacting to live up to his reputation. I thought it odd he let this continue for so long.

Snap! One handcuff around her wrist. Samantha whips her head around, but not before he grabs her other arm and clicks the cuffs on the other wrist. Hands behind her back, sitting in her chair. Poor Samantha will soon learn Santa's true nature.

"Santa?" Samantha whimpers when he spins her around to face us.

"Sorry, dear." Santa holds out his hand to me. Ugh, I know what he wants, so I give him the handkerchief. He shoves it into her mouth, and now I get the reaction I expect.

Panic. Her eyes go wide with terror, and she struggles to free herself from the chair. Santa pushes his weight against her, and they both go toppling over with the chair smacking hard onto the floor.

I step into the background. Nothing I can do.

They wrestle around a bit until he has her tied up.

"Oh, my lovely. I wish I could do this a different way. Truly." Santa pets her head as she sobs into the rag in her mouth. "It has to look like a burglary or something gone wrong. Understand? That's the reason for this." Santa motions his hand over her body, ripping her clothes.

By the way, another FYI—he lies through his teeth again. He conceals his crimes in a lot of different ways. For some reason, he feels compelled to try to pacify her this time with his nonsense or make himself feel better perhaps. He ties her up and stages a burglary for extra fun, not necessity.

Back to the situation at hand. Oh, one more thing. At least I never witness any rapes. I don't know about every vampire, but this fat jolly one has no appetite for sex. Only blood.

Santa stands up and takes off his hat, handing it to me. He stretches out his neck, cracks his knuckles, and then allows the transformation.

His eyes go coal black, the color of the stuff he puts in the stockings of naughty boys and girls. His round cheeks turn pale. When Santa opens his mouth, his fangs descend.

The bloodlust takes little time to take over. He peers down at Samantha, as if seeing her for the first time, and falls to his knees before her tied up and shaking body.

Right to the jugular, he sucks at the blood until poor Samantha lies dead on the floor.

Santa gets up, wiping the blood from his face. He smears it around. Licks what he can off. His beard looks disgusting. Drops of blood run down onto his coat. He holds out his hand for his hat, placing it back on his head after grabbing it.

So picture the image of Santa you have in your mind, with his hat cocked at a slight angle, the red suit, the black belt with a big gold buckle, the leather boots, and him smiling down at a camera. But turn the twinkling blue eyes to black pits and smear the bushy white beard with blood. Creeps me out, too, even after all this time.

"Stage this scene while I tidy up in the bathroom." The fangs ascend, but those scary eyes still stare right through me. Pits of hell.

I hear Santa in Samantha's bathroom, with the water faucet on and him scrubbing away. The whole time, he sings at the top of his lungs, "Jolly Ole St. Nicholas." Even I smirk this time. I mean, come on, he's twisted, but that's funny.

While he makes himself presentable, I get out my little kit. Santa carries a small tin with supplies imbued with the sort of magical properties we elves use after he finishes up, so the authorities see a typical murder scene or natural death.

Such as this little vial of green powder, I sprinkle over her neck. The fang wounds heal, the blood evaporates, and any sign Santa touched her disappears. Next, red powder— a dash I rub into my hands. I lean over and grab her around the neck, and without so much as squeezing, strangulation marks appear and her windpipe gets smashed in.

I move shit around and get out the multicolored bubbles. They operate similar to the bubbles in the pink little bottle little kids blow, except they come out in a rainbow of colors and twinkle in imitation of the multicolored lights on a Christmas Tree. More of Santa's humor. Or comparable to the bubbles people use at weddings now instead of rice, so a bunch of birds don't croak. When I blow, tiny bubbles fill the room. Kind of as if a thousand Glinda the Good Witches float into our midst, looking for Dorothy.

This magic gives no visual evidence of its effect. The bubbles sparkle and float through the air, like a normal day at the beach. Which is the point. No sign of Santa or his demented and captive elf left in the room for anyone to see, even with the CSI crap police will try to employ to find the murderer. These here bubbles expunge any sign we did our thing.

By the way, before I continue telling you this tale, which is for your benefit, stop judging me. It irritates me. See, I can read your mind. I know you're wondering why I do all this without protest. Why not stand up to the fat man or try to run fast as hell away?

Not possible. The most I can do is razz him and annoy him, to a point. But he can track me down. And then he'd whip my arse. Not kill me, which I might prefer. But torture me and force me to do even more grotesque and awful things along with him. I told you, I'm a slave. And I'll give you a little more of my story later. For now, stop the judgment.

On the other hand, I can't stop him. I have no power over him. He controls me.

Still, I sense you contemplating. Even my slavery and fear of punishment can't explain my comments and base sense of humor. *That* came with me before I ever met Santa or got hooked into his demonic life. Smart-ass. Sarcastic. Used humor to cope with the macabre and unusual. It transferred over into my elf life, and now you get to experience it by reading this here tale.

Santa barges into the room again, scratching his buttocks, and surveys my work. He nods his head. "You're a little shit. The shittiest little shit among the elves. But you do your job well."

When he peers down at me, I moan. Yeah, the blue eyes returned and no more blood. Looks like good old Santa again. No, I want to faint because he twinkles, not because of his love for good little girls and boys getting presents. It's about the fact Samantha and her blood donation failed to sate him. Sometime I'll have to ask him why we can't steal blood bags from the Red Cross and be done with it. No death, just a little theft to keep him going.

"What shall we have for dessert?" he asks me.

"Pudding. Or cheesecake. I bet she has some in the fridge."

Santa picks me up by the neck, which hurts, badly. "That's your problem. You do what I tell you because you're afraid and because you can't escape my enslavement. But still, you pop off. Your mouth won't stop."

"Yeah, but you like it."

Santa shoves me into one of the big back pockets on his rear and starts out the door. Before he jumps out the second story window and moves on to his next victim, he rips a big fart to humiliate me further.

I puke in his pocket. Funny right now, as it oozes into his pants. Not so funny in a little bit when he finds it.

Back to walking down the city streets, Santa on parade! He reaches into his pocket and pulls me out by one of my feet and drops me on the ground. Makes my head hurt hellaciously when it cracks against the cement. I get up and brush myself off and follow after him.

A car full of teenagers passes by and honks. One young man hangs half out the passenger-side window and hoots at us. I can imagine what it looks like to their tender little eyes. A dork in a Santa outfit. And the only little person living in Wilmington, dressed up as an elf since he failed at midget wrestling. Assholes. And my friends wonder why I hate teenagers.

We get to a small park when Santa halts. "Son of a bitch. You lousy little fuck!"

I spot his hand in his back pocket, which he pulls out with vomit dripping off his fingers.

Time to run. I dash over to the slide and scurry up, but stop halfway because a tube covers it and conceals me. No way Santa would fit in here. When he's mad, sometimes he forgets he can go down chimneys and shit, so that will delay my capture too. This is a temporary hiding place, sure, but delaying his wrath softens the blow when it happens. You never want to catch his wrath two seconds after he explodes.

"Get out of there!" he roars from down below. First the red hat with its white ball dangling from it appears, followed by the blue eyes glaring at me.

Instead of obeying, I pull out the little kit and let the green powder slide down. I see his hand pick it up and hear him unscrew the lid. He knows. A dash in his pocket and all my puke goes away. Nothing more than a harmless prank. Unless you do it to a badass Santa vampire.

A moment later, my blood begins to tingle. At first it feels good, the final buildup to orgasm an apt comparison, only this shoots through my whole body. Problem being it lasts for about a split second before it starts to hurt. A slight ache overtakes me, like if you get too close to a hot frying pan. I either move, follow where it wants to lead me, or in another minute it will burn. As in, I caught on fire. This shit immolates an elf if we resist.

So, little me swoops back down the slide into Santa's waiting arms. He picks me up and dangles me in front of his face, holding me with his fingers by the back of the collar. He drops me, and right before I splat on the ground, he grabs hold of me by my hair. "Don't ever do that again. You've experienced the ice dungeon, but not for an entire year."

Fuck me. The ice dungeon sucks big Santa balls. You can't even imagine. Most I got locked down there, because of my mouth, of course, was a week. I barely survived.

To make sure I understood his point, Santa takes my ear in his other hand and pinches super hard, until I let out a slight scream and feel the blood trickle down the side of my face. He glances at his fingers, licks the crimson stuff, and drops me into the pile of sand at the slide's base.

Ouch. I landed right on my butt. It takes me a second to believe nothing broke in the fall.

"Much better, elf. Perhaps you can have a cookie when we get home."

In addition to being sadistic, mean, deceitful, and a vampire, Santa has mental issues. I know, sadistic, mean, and deceitful implies something psycho going on, made worse when said person needs to drink human blood to survive. I'm referring to the fact he gets a little too much into his role as Santa. Not Santa, the real-guy-come-vampire behind this mess. I mean, Santa the image he created to disguise his reality. One minute he draws blood out of my little ear, which still hurts like hell, by the way, and the next he wants to give me a cookie. I must have just turned three and will work for sweets.

Lucky for me, time to move on. Santa spins around and starts toward the street again, assuming I follow behind, a good little elf obeying Santa. I learned the line not to cross a while ago. So I have my fun, tweak him or whatever, but make sure I stop before I send him over the edge and become one of the dead elves. He does enjoy killing us from time to time. Though I enjoy pushing it as far as possible too.

He leads me down a winding road, up a slight hill, and right to a nice-looking modern home. Big. Red brick with white columns. Long circular driveway up to it. Nice fountain in the middle of the whole thing, I'd guess, except they wrapped it in a blue tarp for the winter. A pretty grand home compared to a lot of what I viewed as we toured Wilmington. The middle of the night has arrived, so other than teenage hooligans and a few assorted fools, most of Wilmington went to bed. Including everyone in this house.

Thank God, because it means no chimney. We walk up and go through the front door. Locks be damned, Santa can enter any dwelling he wishes by turning the knob or pulling on the handle. No key required. More of his damn magic. I drop these tidbits to remind you if Santa sets his sights on your precious blood, nothing can stop him.

Beautiful living room and exquisite formal dining room, right out of a best homes magazine, but not much time to appreciate it as we head upstairs. I spy the Christmas tree in the front window, with all-white lights, already decorated and beautiful for the holiday season. No presents yet, but they will come. Maybe not. Not for this family, with Santa having arrived. Garland runs up the banister, also with lights woven into it. Pretty. A perfect Christmas scene.

I almost laugh out loud again, because halfway up the stairs they hung a Christmas picture. Pretty big. Of Santa. A nostalgic drawing of Santa scanning his list of naughty boys and girls as the elves at his feet fill brown bags full of assorted goodies. How could I not at least giggle a little? It's called irony. In fact, one of the painted elves kind of looks like me. But not as cute.

Looking to the top of the steps, I jump out of the way and my heart races when an animal comes barreling my way. A cat runs fast as hell back down the stairs and spins around at the bottom, toward the back of the house. Smart animal. Get the hell out of the way. Unlike people, animals know to get the fuck away from Santa.

People should pay heed to their pets more often. A Tsunami gives a good example, right? Folks hanging on the beach and—Wham! Enormous wave engulfs a town. Where were the animals? Running for higher ground because their lives literally depended on it. Back to the cat. Santa walked through the door uninvited, and Cat thinks, "Nothing good can come from his being here. I'm gone." I should have hitched a ride on him.

Back to the task at hand. We walk right up the grand staircase, down a hallway, and toward the room with a nightlight shining out. Even the upstairs seems grand. Pretty wide baseboard and a gigantic chandelier hanging in front of a window, which looks into the front yard. White reindeer, with little clear lights covering them, stand in the yard, one moving its head back and forth. Not the same as the real creatures waiting for us in the cemetery, with their putrid asses and pooping everywhere.

Another, smaller Christmas tree sits up here. Ornaments made by the kids or something adorn it.

Santa stops in front of it with his back to me. I hate when he does this. No reason, other than a power trip. Santa needs a psychologist. Soon enough, I hear him peeing on the Christmas tree. Zip. He tucks everything away and spins around again.

Back toward the light. And dessert.

A little boy, around six-ish, lays sound asleep in his bed, made to resemble a race car. The room is a complete, youngster in charge, hell of a mess, with an assortment of cars, a couple Barbies, and action figures flung all over the place.

Good thing I've been at this long enough I stopped feeling deep emotional pain for the victims a while ago. You saw it with Samantha. Her behavior annoyed me more than generating any sympathy for her dying. I hate that Santa runs around killing and shit. But I have no control over it. Right? I hate the torture part. Wish I could stop him. At the same time, life demands that you accept what you must, act where you can, but otherwise muddle along. At least, Simon the Slave Elf adopts this life philosophy.

What's the prayer, ending with having the wisdom to know the difference? Between what you can change and what you have to accept? That's me. Can't change it, so I found the wisdom to accept it.

Also seldom fazes me if Santa goes after an old geezer, middle-aged fool, or kids. See, by the look of things, this kid will grow up a spoiled brat. Hateful little thing. Become an adult a-hole, like his parents. Samantha added more goodwill to the world than this little one.

Jaded, right? You want to throw this book across the room, you're so disgusted with me. I get it. I understand. But at the same time, I'm trying to survive here. To cope. You sit there all judgmental because life seems grand to you. Try a dose of my reality and we can talk.

Thankfully, no long drawn out scene this time. Santa's eyes turn black. The fangs come out. And Santa kneels beside the bed, tilts the little tike's head, and drinks away. I do cringe at the subtle slurping sound coming from his lips. More because it's gross than because the kid's dying.

A minute later, Santa lifts his head, his eyes closed, his face a vision of contentment as he savors the taste.

When he looks my way, the eyes are already changing back to blue. "Blow the bubbles."

Quick and easy, this one. Santa takes care of the powders while I do the rest. I leave him for a moment, going out to the Christmas tree to blow magic around there, too, except the wretched smell and piss remain.

Santa joins me, his beard already cleaned up, and down the stairs we go. I glance real quick at the Christmas tree and see a cat, possibly the same one, maybe a different one, hiding in the branches.

Once outside, Santa takes a deep breath. "Feel this cold air in your lungs. Come on, my boy. Time to get back to the reindeer." Sometimes he treats me how Dorothy treated Toto, which annoys me too. Better not push my luck right now with a comment.

"Do I look like Lassie to you?" Ah, damn, I spoke out loud, didn't I?

Santa nods. "Yes. But Lassie's cuter."

We head toward the cemetery. This time a cop car drives by as we move down a main drag. Seriously, shouldn't he at least pull over and see what's up? It's got to be three a.m. Nothing good can come from Santa and an elf, whether you think them real or not, sauntering down your city streets at this hour.

NFL coaches say it a lot. "Nothing good happens after midnight." I think Herm Edwards said it first, but true dat.

As if reading my mind, Santa speaks. He often chats with me after feeding.

"That's the genius of the disguise at this point, don't you agree?"

I nod. No use bickering with him. Sometimes I do for sport, but I'm worn out. And on the edge of getting in enormous trouble if I push it.

"So few believe in me anymore. Many, of course, never did. Kids do. And have." Great. Philosopher Santa. "But adults use rational thought. Scientific. Anything mysterious, they either assign to their religion or to the fact science has yet to discover an answer. There's so little wonder left in the world. Which is to my advantage.

"All these folks think Santa doesn't exist." He waves his arm in the air with a flourish. "Once I created the legend, they went with it as a quaint children's story. Thought it nothing more than the legacy of a former saint." He laughs. Then belts out a big "Ho! Ho! Ho!"

Oh, yeah. The legend. He's always referring to it, but I want to know how he did it. The real story, behind the scenes. He always refuses to tell me. Maybe I'll try again when we get back but before I have to move on to my next task. Not toys, but you guessed as much already.

"It's so safe now. So easy."

"I thought that was the point?" Oops. Those words flew out aloud too.

Santa peers at me, annoyed. But no punishment. He keeps walking along. "Yes, I wanted the disguise to make things easier. But this has become ridiculous."

The town square also has a big tree lit up for the holidays. So festive. A manger scene decorates the yard of the church across the street.

"Go get it. I know you want to." Santa points toward the church.

Okay, so my sense of humor gets the best of me again. Santa started it. Never even crossed my mind before he did it. True, I laughed at him. The first time, at the absurdity of it. Santa goes around killing people, has this whole ruse of a Christmas saint, to disguise that he's a vampire. He comes out at night – no problem, because people expect Santa at night. Wears red to hide the blood. You get it.

So why does he steal Jesus from the manger scenes? He takes the little babe and throws it out at random as we fly back to the North Pole. Sometimes he weighs it down and drops it in the ocean. Other times, he plops it into a lake so a boater will find Floating Baby Jesus come spring. Other times he tosses it at random, no idea where it will land. Or over a specific town or area, hoping someone will discover this random Jesus having plummeted from the sky.

I thus find myself walking down the street and contemplating the theft of Jesus. Any time Santa figures out he made me chuckle, he revels in it. I probably have Stockholm Syndrome, where you come to sympathize with your captor? Anyway, I do enjoy snatching up Baby Jesus.

I hurry across the street, make sure the cop didn't follow us, which he should have done, and have Jesus in my arms in no time. This church bought one of those realistic dolls, looks the same as a real baby. Creepy.

Santa, Jesus, and me now walk a little faster toward the cemetery.

Santa and I walk in silence for a block or so until Santa decides to chat. "Why don't you embrace what you've become? All the comments." Santa twirls his finger in the air. "Pretending to dread it. Lashing out so I have to punish you. Doesn't it ever get tiring? There are darker parts to you than you acknowledge. Dig deeper and find them."

I hesitate to respond. Not sure what he wants. The truth, or for me to stroke his ego? Remember, I did enough already tonight to get myself in deep doo-doo. Maybe even a sentence to the ice dungeon. Better be careful.

Plus, I recognize my dark side, even admitted it to you with the whole, who-gives-a-shit-who-dies rant. But who wants to engage in a deep psychological discussion with creepy Santa?

"I march to my own drum." Whenever I have to lie, I revert to saying the dumbest fucking things. Especially using ancient phrases, making me sound a century old. Funny. I get lost in thought because my brain sticks on the truth but warns, *Don't say it.* Another part of my brain says, *Hey! Say Something! Silence breeds suspicion.* Inner panic ensues until I blurt out something to do with marching and my own drum. I never even owned a drum. Only bad nutcracker soldiers own any drums.

Santa chuckles at my old-school retort. "You're full of crap. Tell me the truth."

Glancing down at Jesus in my arms serves as truth serum. "I don't like being a slave, you know? How hard is it to understand?"

"Right. I get it." Santa nods. No anger, so that's good. Of course, he won't free me either. "But we're avoiding the heart of the question. Given your slavery, why not own the evil-elf image? You're crass. Jaded. Sarcastic. You don't care too much about people. Of all the elves, you react the most flippantly after I feed. But still the defiance."

I see the cemetery gates up ahead. We can't reach them fast enough. Soon as he sees the reindeer, our conversation will end. Still, I gotta say something.

"The killing thing, I guess. Well, the slavery pisses me off, no matter what you say. It's a shitty thing to do to people. I was happy, you know. Before you came and captured me. So don't brush my former life under the rug so fast. But there's the killing. Jaded and sarcastic does not translate into massacring innocent people."

"I don't massacre. Just a person here and there when the need calls."

This time I laugh at him. "What's an innocent person here and there, right? They die eventually. Besides, you do more in this world to off people than feed off them, and you know it. You thrive on creating death and destruction."

"It's called population control."

"Or, in my case, sarcasm."

Almost there, so as predicted, Santa halts our conversation and turns his attention to what's next. We hurry past the headstones as Santa gives a silent call for the reindeer to return. This also alerts my elf compatriots to prepare the sleigh. We hear this signal from Santa, matches a dog whistle he tunes to our ears. Except no one else can hear it. And it's not the come-forth, burn-my-blood, angry calling from Santa, simply an audible way to get us going so he can avoid boiling our blood to move us into action.

"We had to stay in this creepy cemetery," Bobby tells me as we hook up the reindeer.

Bobby always whines about shit. Everything. I try to stay away from him because it gets old and irritates me beyond belief. I know, I bitch a lot too. Most slaves probably do. Bobby takes it to another level. Besides, he only sees what happens to him and nobody else.

Santa sneaks over to the woods, to take a dump or something grotesque. I always wonder why he has to shit if he drinks nothing but blood.

"Yeah, well, fuck you." I try for eloquent when I talk.

"You're such an ass. Simon the Asshole. What's up with you? Why do you thrive on being a shithole?" Bobby asks.

"Because while you suffered so fucking much in the Silent City, I had to go help him create a couple more residents. And clean up his piss again on a Christmas tree. Smells like toxic acid mixed with vinegar and bug shit."

Bobby tilts his head. "Do bugs shit?"

"For fuck's sake—"

"Stop bickering." Santa half shouts behind us. "Get in. We're leaving."

Soon enough, Rudolph and his stupid red nose lead the way out of Wilmington toward the North Pole. I hear tell Santa slapped the ugly sucker on him when he went rogue in the 1930s. Wish I knew more of that story so I could make fun of his prissy ass.

"Get up here, and bring Jesus with you," Santa barks at me.

I had tucked myself in the back, with Santa's bundle of toys and other sadistic accouterments, holding Jesus in my arms as if a real baby. I prefer it by myself, but Santa orders me to move. Always wants me up front. At least I get farther away from Bobby this way.

Not sure what to do here, because moving scares me to death. Literally, if it goes wrong. Imagine moving around on an airplane. But remove the lid. So one wrong bump and you, the flight attendant, everyone's drink, and all assorted and unsecured stuff flies into the atmosphere with nothing to catch it.

I crawl through the bags, toward the seat, keeping as low as possible. Behind Santa, I peer up at the top of the seat and almost pass out, seeing the open sky above me.

"Simon," Santa warns with a growl.

I reach up and dump Jesus next to Santa, pulling myself up with both arms once I free them. With one leg over the top and almost there, I almost piss on myself when we hit a bit of turbulence and I bounce in the air. I clutch at the seat and struggle to hold myself in the sleigh. See, one wrong move and I fly out of this thing. You think Santa would swoop down to save me? Not. Dead elf, crashing into a home in Toledo. I got lucky this time and plop into the seat.

It takes me a bit to settle down and breathe without hyperventilating.

"Here we go! Ho! Ho! Ho!"

Santa drives the reindeer down over Michigan, past Essexville and toward Midland. Without warning, he snatches Baby Jesus from me and drops him onto Wixom Lake.

It's frozen solid this time of year, so either an ice fisherman will find JC and think it a teenage prank, or he'll sit there in the cold through the winter until the thaw comes. Then Jesus would float in the water and a boater will find him. Wonder if they'll recognize Jesus after so long? Depends, because underneath he seems like any old doll from a toy store.

I glance back and wave goodbye to Jesus.

Over the last couple minutes of flight time, I enjoy the scenery. Shit will hit the fan soon enough. For now, the sky is so clear and beautiful. The stars peer down at us. I see my breath, but Santa uses wicked magic to keep the elements from killing us up here at thousands of feet above the earth. Similar to what he uses to make reindeer fly. No need for a pressurized compartment or emergency oxygen masks.

Millions of people stare at those same stars at this very moment. They may wish upon them or stop to enjoy their beauty. An astronomer probably discovered a new one and named it after his great uncle, or one of his cats. Maybe after a pet gerbil from his childhood. I try to burn this memory into my mind, the grandeur of space, so I can recall it when things get bad or scary. It reminds me of happier times. Free times.

Too soon we begin our descent. I start slipping toward the front of the sleigh and kick out my feet to prevent landing in the footwell.

"Ladies and Gentlemen—" I have a hard time keeping my mouth shut, in case you didn't notice. "—as the captain begins our descent, please turn off all electronic devices and return your tray tables and seats to their full, upright and locked positions—"

"Simon, stifle." Another Santa reprimand.

"It's FAA regulations."

"Enough."

Here it comes, the moment of transformation, from the seen to the unseen.

If you flew over Santa's ice palace in your own plane, even a lower flying fighter jet, you would see nothing. Nothing but desolate North Pole ice, snow, wind, and misery. You need to travel with Santa to get in here.

Wish I knew how he conceals the whole thing. It might help me escape or expose him. No such luck. Only Santa and a very select few get the real dirt. Rudolph knows. He and Santa are good pals. I told him to escape and go join the circus, become one of the freaks. He bit me.

I'm not even sure if Mrs. Claus knows how to get out of here. Could be Santa and Rudolph alone know.

The point being, he has this hidden fortress, right up here in the North Pole where you expect Santa to reside. At first, even sitting up here next to the man, I see nothing but snow and ice.

With a whooshing sound, we pass through an invisible force field. We enter either a new realm or, as I said earlier, a veiled vampire castle in the ice. Hard to believe no human has ever caught on, but I think we've established so far that humans aren't cracked up to be as all-knowing and smart as everybody hopes.

Let me explain. So, ignore everything I said so far. No Santa vampire. No enslaved elves and flying reindeer. No drained and dead bodies littered across the world because of Jolly Ole St. Nicholas.

Because I want you to see the stunning beauty of this palace before we get back to reality.

Made of solid ice, picture something appearing as a cross between the castle at Disneyland, a medieval fortress, and the grand presence of Buckingham Palace. Spires reach into the sky, flags flutter atop every turret, of green-and-red stripes, of course. A couple of banners proclaim this Santa's realm.

If relocated to an urban city, it would take up at least six city blocks. I have still only seen parts of it, even though we get pretty free reign to wander up here until called to work, to duty, or onto a journey. The place goes on endlessly.

A moat surrounds it, with running water flowing in a constant circle. No one could cross this river: first because it flows rapid, next because it would freeze you to death in seconds. It's as wide as the Mississippi River. No idea how he keeps it from freezing over, other than the fact the whole place operates on his magic from one end to the other.

A short stretch of land gives an outdoor appeal, followed by the ice bricks to provide more security. Santa controls the climate around the castle, too, as he does when we ride on the sleigh. He prefers it cold, thus our choice of residence in the North Pole. Maybe because of his weight and the asinine outfit he insists on wearing even up here where no one sees him but captured elves, entrapped animals, and Mrs. Claus. Feels to me as it did in the dead of winter, when the wind whipped off a frozen lake or river and smashed you in the face, taking your breath away.

No need for a drawbridge or anything over the moat, since we always fly home. It also acts as a security measure, in case by chance an elf does manage to escape. Dead in the water. Only thing missing are alligators, but I'm not bringing that one up or I'll become the official gator keeper around here.

Above the main entrance, Santa carved into the ice an ironic palace name: Winter Wonderland. Makes me chuckle every time. So I despise the man and everything he does, but I still manage to appreciate his twisted humor from time to time.

Peering into a castle window and catching a bit of a chill, I long to get inside. You see, inside, this place acts like a grand hotel. Luxurious rugs. Beautiful chandeliers sparkle against the icy backdrop. And plenty of portraits and photographs of Santa.

Despite Santa keeping the entire castle frigid, I think so it won't melt or because again he gets so freaking hot, the same magic used to keep us cozy enough in the sleigh protects us in there too. Not because Santa gives a shit about our comfort, mind you. Because he wants us able to work hard and focus. Unless you get in trouble. He might strip the temperature control from your body for a while, so your nuts freeze off, as punishment.

The grandeur still stuns me. Too bad I live as a slave here.

Ever visit one of those ice bars or hotels? The one in Vegas, or other countries? Imagine that atmosphere and intensify it by ten but add more luxury and less of the biting cold.

I never understood wanting to pay money to sleep in such a place, or even grab a beer. Never made sense. "Hey, I'm on vacation and having fun, so I think I'll go try to freeze myself to death while throwing back a beer with the hope being drunk will warm me up!" Confounding. People spend their hard-earned money on such nonsense, going to a place that has to loan you a huge coat and extra warm mittens. Only polar bears should seek such climes.

Well, until you see Santa's palace. It helps me see what these ice bars and hotels aim to do, without the magic and means to pull it off like a Christmas-loving vampire.

The huge ice doors creak open and allow us entrance into the back part of the palace. I called it the garage once and got hit upside the head. Santa failed to offer a better name. Barn? Carriage House? Who knows. Once inside, this area alone seems enormous.

Okay, back to reality because it's time to land.

"Why do you need this much space?" I ask Santa. I always wonder but keep a lot of it to myself, no matter what you think of my big mouth. Since we became so chummy on this trip, I let it rip.

"Because I want it."

I nod. Makes sense. What did I expect, a philosophical rumination of the merits of living in a gigantic ice palace with the missus and him to enjoy it alone? I keep forgetting the difficulty of reasoning with a serial killer.

Although, do vampires count in the serial killer category? Yeah, they kill on a regular schedule and often in the same pattern. But then, they need it for survival. Still, it seems a relevant category. I should write the FBI to recommend it. Vampire serial killers. Its own categorization.

The sleigh lands and elves come rushing out from everywhere to unload the bags we never used this time and unhitch the reindeer. Except for Rudolph, who undoes himself and trots off toward his private wing of the palace. Asshole.

I spot my best friend and walk over to her. "Hey, Trixter." She defies all the rules around here as much as I do. For example, she keeps her hair almost buzzed, Demi Moore style in her army movie. Santa hates it. Girl elves are supposed to have long hair and look pretty, at least as far as elves go. But Trixy shaves it off every week. For whatever reason, Santa gave up and allows it. Kind of like how I get by with being a smart-ass a lot more than the other elves.

"It's Trixy." She slugs me in the arm.

"Whatever. When are you going to tell me your real name? We've been friends up here a long time. You're my best pal, and still you lie when it comes to your name."

Trixy laughs at me as we head to unload a bag together.

"Tell me the truth." Whoa. This one's heavier than I expected. "If you were a drag queen or porn star, I'd go with Trixy. Stage name and all. No need for a real name. Or maybe if you had a history as a cheerleader, it might make sense. But independent and assertive lesbians, even when captured into elfdom, do not name themselves Trixy."

Trixy laughs again. "That's my point. It must be my name."

I almost give up on the names conversation when Hedgehog, Trixy's girlfriend, trots over to help out.

"See, now she makes sense." I point to Hedgehog. "Muscular black lesbian woman goes by 'Hedgehog.' For an online-dating service, her profile would get tons of hits. And the accuracy would appeal to everyone. But a lipstick lesbian looking for a petite, anorexic hotty would see Trixy and get excited, until Demi Moore shows up."

"Demi's hot. Not as hot as Trixy. But hot." Hedgehog lifts a sack by herself, while Trixy and I struggle to carry one between the two of us.

I nod. "No argument from me. I'm commenting on the name, not standards of beauty."

Finished, the three of us head over to the fridge to grab a beer. As far as slavery goes, Santa does offer certain perks. When not working, we can mill around and hang. No need to worry the slaves cavort to plot an uprising or threaten to run off, because we can't do either while trapped within the magic North Pole realm. I suppose this acts as a way to keep us a little pacified. Stave off an elf insurrection. Again, no need to worry about uprisings. He can kill us with ease. I've seen it happen.

Right here, in the—okay, not garage but another place that houses sleighs and transportation modes—Santa installed three refrigerators and stocked them with a large assortment of beverages, including beer. Come to think of it, he may enjoy us inebriated, pliant, and content with specially made Santa beer, brewed right here by other elves in the Santa Ice Palace.

Trixy and I go for the darker stuff, while Hedgehog throws back a light version in two seconds and grabs for another. Never try to keep up with Hedgehog. She could drink Santa under the table.

"Anything exciting happen while I was gone?" I ask.

Trixy laughs. "Yeah, reindeer mutiny. They ate Mrs. Claus, shit in Santa's suits, and set up an animal kingdom before enslaving penguins."

She's funny. It takes me a while to stop giggling. "Why bring the poor penguins into it? Did he make you work, or were you chilling?"

"Hedgehog and I got a new assignment to work on a new potion."

"Major suckoid." I have nothing better to say.

Trixy and Hedgehog have chemical engineering backgrounds. In fact, Santa targeted them for their skill. Even though he knows magic and can do all sorts of sorcery, he makes them take it to a new level, or overcome something he can't figure out. Even Trixy and Hedgehog admit working on magical chemical schemes excites them. Santa infuses this whole place with a mystical sense that either doesn't exist anywhere else or has been lost to the scientific revolution. So they experiment on the universe in ways never imagined, which helps keep them from going nuts from the awful enslavement. Kind of like I use sarcasm to cope, they put their energy into brilliance. Lesbians are more practical than most of us.

"Totally sucks. Big balls." Trixy opens her mouth wide, as if getting ready to suck them in. "A new way to induce otherwise normal people into serial killing."

Still another thing I have to tell you about later. Santa's little bag of tricks. The things he creates by changing and manipulating folks.

Hedgehog cracks open her third beer. "We did hardwire it to go after conservative Republicans in America."

I spurt my beer across the floor. Being a good elf slave, I run and get stuff to clean it up. Well, it has nothing to do with being a good elf. More to do with keeping out of trouble. I'm still waiting for a punishment for the shenanigans and my mouth on the trip.

"What did you do?" Trixy asks me.

"Same ole, same ole. Kind of boring actually. Little creativity. He fed on two people." Up here, you need to watch your language. Santa erupts, a volcano exploding on up your ass, if you say he killed, murdered, sucked the life out of someone, or any such negative take on it. "Pissed on a Christmas tree. We did get to steal another Baby Jesus and toss him in a lake in Michigan. Too bad the Christmas tree lights don't conduct electricity through Santa's pee and fry his pecker."

Before we get much of a laugh out, Santa meanders from around a corner, in his more casual Santa outfit, the red onesie pajamas. He barks out my name, but of course, he already knows where I am. "Simon!"

Trixy and Hedgehog fade into the background. No need to take anyone else down with me. Whew, I think he missed the electricity and pee comment.

"Yo! Yo! Yo!" I bellow.

Santa glances at me out of the corner of his eye. "Do you amuse yourself?"

"Kinda."

"No one else finds you funny. Least of all me. Which brings me to the point of calling for you. You'll need to grab a six-pack for what's coming next."

That can't be good. I have no idea what it means, except even Santa acknowledges this will drive me to drink. To be on the safe side, I grab two six-packs and walk over to him.

He moves away without a word, expecting me to follow. We pass the sacks of crap, now being emptied and placed back in their appropriate locations. Here's another elf slave annoyance of mine. Santa makes us pack those bags for every journey, but he only uses the stuff inside them at random times. Inconsistent. But he must have a clue what he intends to do before we head out. So why make us do that every time? Punishment? Because he can? Maybe in another life Santa was a Boy Scout, what with always being prepared. He goes toe-to-toe with them in his homophobia, or at least their previous position on it from when I was growing up.

A few elves toil away polishing the sleigh, while others scrub the floor where the reindeer let it go after their arrival. Oh, shit. I figured it out. Literal shit.

Santa kicks open the swinging doors into the reindeer stalls. Reeks like hell in here.

"Um, before we get this going, I have a question." I scratch the top of my head as I survey the room and choke back the inclination to vomit.

Santa whips around, his eyes black, his fangs descending.

"I thought you already fed for a while." Why, oh why, do my lips keep flapping in the breeze?

Santa grabs me by the collar and lifts me up, eye to eye with those pits into hell. I stare into my own death, pissed, mostly because I ended it on such a bad joke. I at least wanted to die with something over-the-top funny, not a lame jab at a vampire.

But the eyes fade to blue, the fangs disappear, and Santa almost smiles. "I confess a problem with you."

My shirt starts to choke me from Santa dangling me up here for too long. "Just one?" I squeak out.

"You amuse me. At times because you're funny. And other times because you think you're funny. Either way, the amusement also gives me the opportunity to punish you, which I also very much enjoy. So many of the elves never do a thing. Always compliant. Always afraid of me. You're different. Go ahead, ask your question."

Santa sets me back on the ground. It takes a second before I breathe again. I gag a couple times and claw at my throat, like something still chokes me, until I take a deep breath and calm down.

It hits me. Did Santa give me a compliment? In his "I'm a killer vampire" kind of way? Who would have guessed such a thing? I need to concentrate on keeping it under control, not going overboard and forgetting he can still kill me if I piss him off.

Still, he invited me to ask my question. "I was going to ask why you don't use magic to clean up the reindeer shit and piss and stuff. Everything else around this abode sparkles nice because of magic. Why not in here? Don't the reindeer deserve better? I think it makes them sad to live here in the smell for too long. They'd fly better if they were happy. It's already a lot for them to get used to flying since it's not in their genetic code or anything." I have more to say but think it best to stop at this point.

Santa kneels in front of me. Not smiling, not pissed off. "I'll answer your question this time. Because I need a tool to use to punish naughty elves. Torture works from time to time but gets mundane after a while. Worst case, I execute the culprit. The ice dungeon contributes to the options, too, but I witness those scenes on a television screen, not live, which can ruin the fun. What of an elf who crosses the line but perhaps falls short of needing torture or the dungeon? Let's say an elf has a sharp tongue and a big head. Torture may knock it out of him, but end the fun. Instead, bring him here to play in the muck. It will remind him I'm master, without breaking him too completely." He stands back up. "Get to work."

Message delivered. It almost makes me salute him and get excited to do my job. Almost.

Santa walks away without another word. As usual, and without having to tell me, he'll give me two hours or so to get this place into shape, so it matches the rest of the palace. He'll return to Copy Editister a full and complete inspection. And if I fail, well, not good. Last time he had me clean out each of the reindeer's anal glands. Better hit the deck when shit comes flying out. Literally, I mean. When we talk reindeer and dung, remember it's always literal.

I grab the broom, a shovel, and the elf wheelbarrow and head to stall one. I do them out of order. Having done this a few times, I know which reindeer put out nice round pebbles and who has incontinence issues. And so I stand before Vixen's home first and foremost.

I'll spare you the gory details. Suffice it to say, he could use more fiber in his diet. It takes me longest here, because I gag, vomit a couple of times, and otherwise wish I were dead. You'd think this would keep my mouth shut, right?

I manage to survive that experience and head to the next stall. One down, fifteen more to go.

Everyone except Rudolph lives here in their own personalized reindeer suite. Rudolph lives in an exclusive wing of the palace I mentioned earlier. One all to himself. He has a toilet, so no cleaning his place. Most of the reindeer act as reindeer, except Santa enchanted them to fly. Rudolph is a whole different story.

So sixteen stalls must become manure-free. Why sixteen? You went through the names and came up with eight reindeer, right? Nine if you count Rudolph, but he has a hissy fit if you lump him in with the other creatures. Well, think about it. Unlike Santa the eternal vampire and Mrs. Claus, as well as the enchanted elves Santa needs, oh, and Rudolph, every other creature up here dies. Well, come to think of it, that means only the reindeer die. Wonder why he lets them expire but nothing else? Strange. Vampire logic. So Santa needs two of every reindeer, so there's always a backup. Plus, they tire if you fly them two nights in a row. It gets confusing as hell for the poor creatures, because they each have a doppelganger. Call for Comet, and two glance your way.

Some are female, some male. Not always balanced; it changes around. I never got to go with Santa to pick a new reindeer, but no doubt he has criteria he employs for picking the best-suited ones. Maybe based on whether or not they get motion sick in flight? No idea. But Santa travels out to Canada or a remote wooded area after one of the reindeer drops dead and comes back with another one who gets named after the one who croaked.

I dump the last barrow of shit into the river outside and wipe my brow. I got it done in record time tonight, and it only took one six-pack. Still, I grab a seventh beer and my eyes swish around with the water in front of me.

No rest for the wicked, so off I trot to finish. Tidy up the hay, put things in order. Donner already relieved himself again. With fifteen minutes and three beers to spare, I complete the job.

I lay back in the hay to rest, realizing my last beer sent me over the top. Reclining next to my favorite reindeer, Blitzen, I pat her leg and drift to sleep.

"Perhaps I should give you a stall out here." Santa's voice lurches me out of my sleep. I pop up, so scared I think it sobered me. Nope. Good buzz still going. "You behave as one of the beasts most of the time."

I stand in the center of the aisle as Santa walks around the room, inspecting.

Even with his back to me, his likeness stares at me with venom. He has a ten-foot portrait of himself hanging in here with the reindeer. He commissioned one of the elves to do this one. Most of the time, it humors him more to buy the commercial versions of himself and place them about the ice palace, so he smiles at you wherever you go. Here, the reindeer and their visitors get the real Santa. Black eyes burning into you, fangs pointing at your throat, and blood dripping all over him.

I think I figured it out. He uses cleaning the reindeer home to punish, so put this image of him in here. Smart man.

"Unfortunately, even in your inebriated state, you did well."

Santa storms off, perhaps disappointed my punishment for the night has ended. I saunter after him, petting each reindeer and giving them an extra carrot.

I walk down the grand hallway, running my finger along the ice wall and watch it melt a trail that disappears behind me as I go. The elf recreation room hops with activity, but I don't feel chatty tonight.

I sway around a bit and turn toward my little room. I picked a place at the very top of the palace, in one of the turrets. Very small, space for my little bed and a small dresser. The wind whips through here a little more, but you don't feel it once under the covers. My solitude is important to me. Much as I love Trixy and Hedgehog, and have a few friends among the other elves, life up here at the North Pole gets me down sometimes. It's lonely for my kind. My room reflects my forlorn reality.

At least during my sleep, I dream a lot about life before Santa, before enslavement, before I shrunk to three feet tall.

Chapter Two: On Elfdom

I PROMISED TO tell you a little of my history. No elf pun intended. Simon, pre-elf. Same smart-ass. Same tongue that gets me into trouble. But taller and even happy. I'll get to my story. But first, you need to learn the general state of elves up here at the North Pole.

Imagine the ability to seize anyone you see and take them against their will to do your bidding for the rest of their lives. Sounds similar to the Old South history you learned in school, right?

Now, add magical properties, so the people have no means of escape and you can summon them at any time, from anywhere. A dash of Harry Potter mixed in, right?

Take people of any height, short, tall, average—it makes no difference, and the second you enchant them to your command, they all shrink to about two-feet to three-feet tall.

Bam! You have yourself a gaggle of enslaved elves. That, my friends, is what the Jolly Ole Elf creates for himself. Enslaves individuals of his choosing, shrinks them down to size, and controls them with Santa magic no one has figured out how to undo. The few who tried met an untimely demise at the hands of Santa himself.

Except for Trixy and Hedgehog. No one knows except me, but they try to figure it out from time to time. Even with their smarts, and even with the bad stuff they concoct for Santa, they gained no better clue than the rest of us.

Back to the poor fools he caught trying to undo the magic. Back to the Old South again, after the slave insurrections when they mounted the heads of the perpetrators along the road to warn other slaves against rebellion. Santa crucifies elves in the middle of the castle, so we have to pass them every day as they die of malnourishment. Ever study Vlad the Impaler, the late 1400s ruler in present-day Romania? Same damn concept. Except at least Santa doesn't dine in the midst of it. Or Jesus and bad guys in the Roman empire, hanging up there to die in front of everyone. Whether you like being up here or not, those images will keep you in line; trust me.

Even so, others have tried in secret without success. Not even Trixy and Hedgehog. Nothing comes close to freeing us or revealing the deepest secrets. If those two can't crack the code, none of us will.

Next question. Because I can see it in your mind. Why the hell does a vampire need elf slaves? Or for that matter to dress up in a ridiculous outfit and capture poor reindeer and make them fly? Well, I'll get to the outfit and persona, plus more on the reindeer and Rudolph, but this here chapter focuses on the elves. So why enslave them, right? Seems as if he could accomplish everything he does with his magic and vampire mojo. No need to drag us into the fray against our will, right?

I wish I had an answer. You saw what happens if I ask Santa questions. Most of the time, I get in trouble and forced into a punishment. He answered why he makes elves clean up the reindeer stalls, but that was one in a million, and in part, because he could humiliate me with the answer. Put me right in my place.

So no one knows why he enslaves us. I can take stabs at it, from having dealt with him and living up here for so long. Strictly guesses, mind you.

Best guess has to do with sadism. You know, the quickest answer to why he enslaves us—because he can. You saw it already: he enjoys torture. He played with the poor woman before he offed her in her own office, pretending the real Santa had arrived and then all of a sudden cuffing her. Still pisses me off, she went along with it to the extent she did before it dawned on her something was fucked up. Anyway, he could slide down the chimney, nuzzle up to a victim without their knowing, and suck their blood. But, instead, he tortures them.

Same with the little boy. But he had a bit more compassion there. Found the kid sound asleep and drained his life from him without a fuss. But let's think about it a little more. Don't think for a second the implications escaped Santa. A family, waking in December in anticipation of the approaching holiday season, only to find their son, brother, friend, dead in bed. Santa knows he left carnage in his wake. Otherwise he could prey on murderers and rapists. You know, like the twenty-first century concept of vampires who only kill the depraved. Nope, Santa is a badass. Add to the mix, pissing on the tree, so the family knows a foul act happened, but the police, coroner, and everyone else will find no other evidence and rule it a death by natural causes.

So if Santa can do that to innocent folks around the world when he wants to feed his fat belly, why not enslave elves? No explanation needed, other than the control he has over the hundred or so of us living with him at the North Pole. He can order us around, punish us on a whim, and expand his sadistic empire with our assistance. So ends my first theory in answer to why I think he enslaves us. Because he has the power to do it and relishes the evil control.

The softer side of me wonders if he also keeps us around to give him company. I know, what kind of company do you get from miserable, enslaved people? But Santa seems to appreciate having me around. I even made him chuckle a few times.

Back to the Stockholm Syndrome, if you're psychoanalyzing me—thinking that I would stoop to considering a more palatable explanation for the entrapment of elves against their will only out of a delusion. So go to town, if you want. I don't dwell on my own psychology. Never did, but especially not up here in the Ice Palace Christmas Wonderland. Too depressing.

I'm saying the idea of his needing company has merit. Santa has a past of a sort. He was human at one time, followed by becoming a vampire. You'll see when I get to more of his story. For now, I mean it gave him a connection to humanity at one time in his history, before he became a vampire and created the Santa ruse as his particular stunt and manifestation of the past. So perhaps he clings to a notion of empathy and compassion by surrounding himself with the elves. Or needs our company.

In that case, he still has to enslave us so we can't escape or rat him out. Couple it with the sadism creeping into everything about the fat man, and you get a volatile combination of needing love but getting it through ultimate control over others.

Like abusive people. They love their spouses, kids, dogs, or whatever, but something wrong in them breaks and they beat the shit out of those same creatures and people. It's evil but a part of our world. So maybe Santa has a dash of abuser in him.

Finally, and again you could combine this theory with the other two, or get the three of them to help make sense of enslaving elves, but I wonder if he has limitations we don't see? So he needs us to help him. He appears all powerful to us. A vampire who can fly around the world and execute on a whim. An entity with a hidden kingdom no one has found for decades, despite the advanced technology, radar, and exploration of almost every inch of above water surface the world over. Elves who have tried everything to free themselves but have no power against him. The list goes on and on and on indicating infallibility.

Yet everything has a weakness, right? Seems like even the greatest of plans comes with a limitation. Ask the folks on the maiden voyage of Titanic how it worked out to assume their eventual tomb could never sink.

Santa must come with chinks in the armor, too, that limits his ability to do everything he desires without the enslavement of elves up here in the frigid cold Winter Wonderland of Santa's creation.

You know, this got me wondering about the effects of global warming on Santa's future. Will this place survive, if we keep heating up the earth, melting the ice caps, and tempting fate with the disappearance of the north and south poles? It might get so hot as to even melt Santa's magical palace here at the tip of the world.

Whoa. I got way too deep. Must be the beer I drank, cleaning out the reindeer stalls. I gotta cut it out. I'll run this global warming theory by Trixy and Hedgehog and let them gnaw on it for a while. That is, after they stop laughing their asses off at me.

In fact, I need to cut out *all* the philosophical bullshit. Because bottom line from the get-go is I can't answer why Santa enslaves us. I know he does and gave you my best guesses. Someday he could enslave a person, Socrates or Kant or even Freud, and said elf will write the determinative philosophy on why Santa enslaves us. Not me.

So back to the general notion of enslaving the elves, to get to my story. Whatever the reason, capturing and choosing the elves functions much as it does when Santa picks a new reindeer.

I never counted the exact number of elves up here. Around a hundred, near as I can tell. I recognize almost everyone, but not everyone's name. A few I know well, Trixy and Hedgehog the best, others I know because we work together too often, whining fucking Bobby comes to mind, and others I know because I think they're hot or funny or exotic. But a lot only exist in my mind, nothing special to report.

So an indeterminate number of elves slave away at the North Pole for Santa. The only cool aspect of elfdom comes with the protection Santa offers from death. Unlike our counterparts, who age and die, we don't. However, sometimes we get sick. But other times we're immune. Makes no sense, but I know we need an elf doctor up here, except at times Santa can cure us with magic, other times we have to wait out a virus, and sometimes the doc performs surgery or performs a cure. It's way above my pay grade to figure out the difference between the three. It does go back to my earlier idea: Santa can't do everything he wants.

Elves die when Santa decides to off them, for whatever various reasons. We perform a quick ceremony, then as with the other trash and dead stuff, we work our way out to the moat and dump the body in. I have no idea where it goes or how it disappears, but it does.

So we need a new worker. This gets fuzzy with the math too. Because sometimes we end up with a couple new elves. Or a new elf shows up, even when no one died. Or we lose an elf, maybe two, and Santa never replaces them. A process goes on in Santa's brain to figure it out without revealing any logic in the madness to the rest of us.

When the time comes, Santa goes out, chooses a victim, and one day this fine individual had a normal life, the next day finds herself or himself at the whim of a vampire-come-Christmas-legend. He never picks a down and out kind of guy, to my knowledge. Always a content and happy individual. And from all over the world.

Makes me wonder how we communicate. I speak English. Only language I know. But Trixy came from France. And others from every continent and numerous countries. Yet we get here and chat away without any language barrier. Everyone I speak with sounds to me as if they speak English. Although I know Bobby knows Russian, nothing else. Huh. Never wondered how the language thing works before.

So Santa chooses a victim at random, whose life he can ruin.

Okay, enough with the general introduction about enslaving us elves up here at the North Pole. I think you get the gist. So back to me. What did Simon the Elf do before Santa came uninvited into his boudoir and captured him? Let me tell you.

First, you should know I have no intention of going into the nitty-gritty details regarding my entire life before Santa showed up. We're skipping my childhood altogether and moving right to adulthood. Because it's depressing to remember my family, and this here tale focuses on exposing Santa and his real nature, not me. I'm just the vehicle delivering the goods.

Still, I get you have curiosity and want to know what the fuck I represent. Seriously, I do. But I don't feel like dragging my mom and brother into the whole scenario. Let's leave them out of this, with a kind of peace and quiet.

Though I do often wonder what they think now. We had a close family, with my mom, brother, and me growing up after my dad skedaddled out of town right after my brother was born. Lots of love and good times. Nothing ever tore us apart.

So when I get melancholy or too morose over my Santa beer, I wonder about them. How are they doing? Do they still search for me? Do they think I ran off and left them in the lurch? Or even more depressing, do they fear every day something dreadful and violent happened to me? Think I got captured and taken into the sex trade? Or locked up in a serial killer's basement, where he removes a digit once a week and cuts off my scrotum until I bleed to death? Who knows what awful thoughts run through their heads. Because I figure all they know is one day I was there, Simon doing his thing, and the next I vanished.

So back to my story, or at least the part I intend to tell you.

After high school, where I did pretty well, thank you very much, I got a swimming scholarship to attend a university. I went off and did pretty well competing, winning a few races here and there and setting up a life for myself.

That's when I came out of the closet and started dating, but nothing too serious. Plenty of guys threw themselves at me, with my swimmer's build. Don't get me wrong, I never maintained an angelic status. Uh, no. I enjoyed my share of one-night stands.

But I hate the thought of disease. It terrifies me. One wrong face suck and you get herpes living on your lips. Fucked up. Let alone something worse, which might kill you. Which is why I always advocate condom use.

I still don't get barebacking. I know, you could compare it to fools who climb a wicked steep mountain to get a thrill, never worrying that every once in a while someone plummets right off the rock to their death. Part of the excitement, right? You could off yourself at any minute. Same with racing, fast boats, all sorts of strange stuff people do for adventure necessitating risking life and limb. Or bungee jumping off a fucking bridge. Is barebacking any different? I suppose it's riskier. And high up on my dumb-ass meter. But still, seems comparable to me. And don't start in with the bullshit it feels better. I'm sure it does, but it also increases the death-risk thrill to mountain climb without safety ropes. Stupid.

This tangent gives you a good sense of what my friends thought when we went out together. See, I started the smart commentaries long before Santa and I rode around together killing people.

Back to college and my self-limited sex life. To avoid nasty fungus or bacteria growing on my genitals, I spent most of my time practicing my swim moves or studying. Because I knew, come the end of college, I better have something other than my charming good looks, smoking body, and smart-alec attitude to get by in life.

I majored in accounting, figuring I could make my skills work for good once I graduated. On the one hand, I often wondered what the fuck I could do as an accountant that wouldn't put me to sleep every day at work. On the other hand, in the good ole US of A, anything facilitating capitalism had to come in handy. It's money, right? So do something involving money, and you'll always have opportunities. At least that was my deep philosophy when picking a major.

I graduated with a solid reputation as a swimmer, no debt, and an accounting degree in hand. Second one in my family to graduate college, after my younger brother. Still pisses me off he did it in three years, while it took me five because of swimming, but what the hell? He deserves it.

Who the hell knows what he's doing these days with his degree in history? Boring the shit out of people a lot, I suspect, like I started my career counting money.

You're now up to speed on Simon until he graduated from college. Now I play the role of Bob Dole or one of those monarchs from eons ago, talking about myself in the third person. Weird. You learned everything I want to tell you, from birth until I earned a college diploma.

Here's a spoiler: I had two years between that moment and my enslavement.

I got a job pretty fast. Not a good job, mind you. But a job in a market where a lot of my peers moved back home and bitched because they lived with their parents again.

They groused especially when they had to follow rules. "I'm an adult now," they'd argue. "Free to do what I want. Screw them if they can't handle my boyfriend or girlfriend or other friends in the house. I can drink what I want, when I want. They should get off my back."

You've heard those rants before, right? Here's the thing. I used to respond with logic, which pissed them off. Their soliloquy when it came to independence and adulthood sounds all fine and dandy until you plop them back in their parents' roost, with the old high school posters on the wall and relying on mom for dinner every night. And this came rent free, unless they had smart parents who charged them at least a small amount so they'd get the hint.

Moving back in with the parents is kind of like renting a motel room for a while. You put yourself in a situation where certain rules and regulations apply to you, even if they don't when you're in your own place. Middle of the night naked walk down the hall for ice? Cool if you're at home. Not cool in a hotel. Hang the ugly picture of you in Italy pretending to hold up the leaning tower? Okay in your own funky living room, not okay in a hotel room. But intensify it in your old home, because Mom and Dad expect to control their property a certain way and manage their lives on their own terms. Remember, they got accustomed to your sorry existence living at college.

Get it? Move back in with Mom and Dad and they have say over your life. How hard is it to imagine they don't want to know how loud you scream as an adult when you cum? Or to know their little girl brought home the fifth guy to bang in two weeks? Or even to realize you took to wearing dirty underwear because you can't be bothered to clean them?

So I avoided live-at-home misery with my stupid little accounting job at a local bakery. The owners were sweet, no pun intended. I made a decent living but started to grow a little around the waist because the major perk of working there happened to be the free goodies.

I worked there for a year, until a major company downtown hired me away at twice the salary and in a kickin' skyscraper. Even had my own small office with a window. I moved to a new apartment downtown too. Small. As in, a combined living room-kitchen area, small bedroom, and bathroom. But right in the heart of the city.

I loved it. The nightlife. The people. The constant energy. I made a ton of friends and had a good thing going. Even had a boyfriend for about five months, before he wanted a commitment for life. I adored him enough. Had grown to love him, even. But he demanded rings, a civil union, and a huge wedding. I worried we should take more time together before jumping in whole hog.

I'll spare you the drama. Still makes me cringe.

You don't need to know any more. I told you too much already. That captures my life in its basic essence at the time that Santa entered it.

We need to get back to the focus of this here tale, which has nothing to do with me and everything to do with a fat-man vampire that everyone reveres and loves.

I strolled home one night in late January, my scarf tight around my neck, my fingers bitter cold despite my gloves. My ears hurt from the chill because I refused to wear a hat. It messed up my hair. Vanity will kill you. I suppose I should have lectured myself, what with being a moron, worried my coifed hair looked perfect as my ears fell off from frostbite.

I remember the walk home, ten minutes from where I worked, not because I was so cold, but because I almost fell over that day in the office when my boss handed me my bonus check. Holy shit. I had never seen that much money collected in one sum and dished out to me.

If you can "see" money on a pay stub. I mean, it's not like he forked over bills and had me carry them home. Direct deposit avoids the fear of being robbed with a bundle of cash in your pocket.

I vaguely remembered that he told me I would get a once-a-year bonus when he hired me but pushed it from my mind. No bonus at the bakery, unless you counted free cookies. Plus, I made enough not to need a hunk of money in January. They could have robbed me blind, waiting for me to ask when my bonus was paid out, because I'd never remember.

I pondered the whole way home what to do with it. Put it away? Smart, but boring. Vacation? Where? Take my family with me? What about a down payment on a car? But who needed a car in the city? Maybe invest it to see if I could upgrade to a bigger condo?

I decided to wait for a while to do anything, except call Mom the minute I got home and tell her. She still reveled in our successes, so I wanted to share the news.

I entered the lobby, got my mail, and threw it all in the trash. At the elevator, before I even got in, I sensed something wrong. The instant I stepped off on my floor, the hair on my arms stood straight up. I owned a condo at the end of the hall, so could not even see it yet, but the vibe felt amiss.

Important note! I did not meander along as if nothing was wrong at this point. I did not invite a stranger up to my office, or sit there frozen with my life at stake. This explains why so many of Santa's victims piss me off. People should pay attention to their surroundings and obey their senses. Not that it saved me, but still.

Despite my misgivings and slow, cautious steps down the hall, I got to my door with nothing out of the ordinary going on. Quiet hallway. Door locked. Nothing. Little Max, the terrier who lived next door, did his usual bark as I walked by.

I put my key in the door, warning be damned, and pushed it open without stepping into the room. Then I got a jolt of fear. Still, nothing looked amiss. Dark. Everything in order, except for my cereal bowl I left out in the morning because I got behind in the shower. But I chalked it up to annoyance at the messiness, not an omen of danger lurking inside.

Still, for an unknown reason, I stood frozen in front of my door, the hair on my arm raised, a bad feeling in my gut. The rational part of my mind tried to shove me into the condo, because it made no sense to fear anything, with the security in my building, the fact my door was locked when I got home, and nothing looked amiss. The survivalist in me screamed to go down two floors to get Kate, my buddy in the building who sat around the pool drinking with me, and go in together.

The rational part said, "What the fuck will a hundred-and-ten-pound woman do?"

She knows karate, I thought. One better than me in the self-defense category. Plus, two people screaming in total fear might get more attention than my lone voice.

I jumped when the elevator opened down the hall. Whoever came up went the other way, but it scared the shit out of me.

Still no clue what to do. Enter the dark but normal looking condo, or head for the hills? Thankfully, a perfect solution hit me square in the face. Go to the neighborhood bar around the corner for an after-work drink to celebrate the big fat bonus in my bank account. That would give me time to make a plan. Maybe drunk I could resolve the inner conflict about whether or not to enter.

I reached to pull the door closed when a black-gloved hand and red sleeve grabbed me by the wrist and yanked me into my condo. Before I could even begin to shout an alarm, I flew across the room, slammed into the coffee table, and hit my noggin hard against the side of an end table.

Who knows how long I was out. I never thought to ask Santa, even after a couple conversations with him about why he chose me. Of course, he never answered any of the questions, anyway.

I came to, tied up and lying on my couch in nothing but my underwear. My blurred vision saw a red blob sitting across the room in my favorite chair, with his feet kicked up on the side of the couch next to me.

"Ho! Ho! Ho!" he said.

"Fuck me. Just my luck. Instead of a swift killer, I get a kinky pervert who will butt fuck me before leaving me to die a slow and painful death as I bleed out from my anus."

I think the head trauma from him throwing me across the room caused my smart-ass remark. Because it borders on stupid, same as the people who infuriate me by inviting Santa into their midst without a fight. Why say anything? Take it, because you will, whether something comes out of your mouth or not.

I do think it better to spew forth with the sarcasm, rather than plead for your life. Bad movie scene, when faced with a clear killer. They always cry and beg for mercy, even when everyone watching knows it won't work. Or, if it does, it represents bad Hollywood writing. So at least I avoided the pathetic attempt to convince Santa to spare me.

My comment, of course, made Santa laugh. Looking back, I think it saved my life. It would take a lot of contemplation and a lot more Santa beer to figure out if throwing my opinion out there was for the best. At times I wish he had offed me.

He stood up, still laughing, and came over to the couch and sat on my calves. Hurt like a mother fucker. Santa reached over and snapped my underwear band.

"Nothing kinky. Don't go that way, even if you do. But getting a person naked keeps them in place and reluctant to try to run. Strange, isn't it, how people would rather keep a peculiar form of dignity and not appear naked in their hallway rather than live."

Santa had a good point. I would loathe to crawl out of here in my skivvies, nice body or not, but public humiliation should beat death, right?

"So no perverted stuff, good. Because I'm not into bears."

Again Santa laughed, reached over, and snapped my underwear even harder than the first time. "Do you know who I am?"

This time I chuckled, despite my impending doom. Funny question. "Not really. A fat guy with a Santa fetish. But straight. No idea how I play into the equation."

"Dinner." He said it without emotion, as if announcing he would stroll down to the local pizza parlor for a pie.

"You're a cannibal?" I squirmed, getting more nervous. "Do you eat your victims alive?"

Laughter again. "Why aren't you screaming for help? I had it all planned to tie you up, wait for you to wake, see you struggle against the ropes and yell bloody murder, so I could pounce across the room and have my meal. But you didn't scream."

Another good point by the Sanster. Why no shriek for help? Plenty of people around to hear me. I suppose a part of my brain, maybe the dumb rational part guilty of trying to convince me to come on into the condo, resolved I had no chance of survival. By the time I came around, he had me tied up on the couch in my underwear and could have launched at me and shoved my socks down my throat to shut me up. Shouting would use up energy without helping out. Instead of a long answer, I shrugged.

Nothing regarding his true nature hit me yet, however. The shock kept me from getting too deep with the whole situation. I never pondered how the dude got into my place. I accepted he broke in. Instead of thinking about ghouls, zombies, or vampires, I assumed deranged killer.

I did yelp a little when I looked at him again. The Santa blue eyes I first looked into had turned to those black pits. And I got to see the last few seconds of transformation as the fangs made their final descent and his face contorted.

I passed out.

Classic. Passed out like someone bopped me over the head. I came to again, assuming I died until I felt my wrists behind my back and the cool air on my semi-naked body. Santa had moved to sit on the floor in front of me.

"Oh, you're back." He turned his head to look at me and turned off the television.

I chuckled, which made him frown.

"Something funny?"

"You watch 'Dora the Explorer'?"

"You're lucky you're even alive to see my viewing habits."

Or not. Still wonder if I might be better off had he killed me instead.

"What, Dora gonna come through the television and attack me? Or are you going to torture me to death with endless episodes of it until I go batshit crazy?"

Santa got up, frowned down at me, and slapped me hard on the face. He burst into hysterics. The pain from his hit shut me up for a while. I remained quiet and had no idea what to expect when he turned around and lorded over me again.

He unzipped his red pants and pulled out his jolly red pecker. Short, round, and fat, like him.

"I thought you weren't into guys?" I asked.

"Just need a bit of relief."

Piss shot out of his dick and all over my face. I pressed my eyes shut and clamped my lips together. The smell alone made me gag. When it ended, I still refused to look because the pee would burn in my eyes.

But I had to open them when he grabbed my shoulders and yanked me into a sitting position. At least he put Mr. Happy away.

Santa collapsed onto the couch next to me and patted my leg. "I think I came to a decision about you."

"What? You're going to take a crap on me now?"

He squeezed my knee until I screamed in pain, laughing the whole time. "Nope. You've taken well to my being a vampire."

I jerked my head and stared at him. "Um, I wouldn't say that."

Santa nodded. "Yeah, it's true. You're handling it well."

"No. I'm not." I shook my head.

"Trust me. I'm an expert on these things. You're doing well. So it's decided!" He clapped his hands and got to his feet.

Santa walked over to his little sack of goodies and rummaged around in it, throwing boxes here and there, whistling "Jingle Bells" the entire time.

"I'm thinking it over and want to talk to you." I squinted to see if he even heard me, but he kept searching. "Death seems better than whatever you've got planned. So why not drink my blood and leave the decaying body for my mom to find? Okay? Hello?"

"Ah ha!" He pulled his head out of the bag and held up a syringe, filled with a red liquid with green sparkles floating in it.

"Yeah, about that. My blood's clean. No AIDS. No hepatitis. Only good ole blood. So have at it. I'd prefer it better than the shot you want to give me. Because your meds are one deranged looking Christmas shot. Wicked sparkles, there. Make it into Jell-O shots and you could make millions. But I'm gonna pass. Pee on me again and off with my head."

Santa walked across the room and sat next to me. He sighed. "You have so much to learn. Don't worry. I'll teach you. I can tell you're going to be a tough customer. But you'll add a nice dimension to the crew. They'll love your sense of humor." He held his stomach and let out a big "Ho! Ho! Ho!"

"You don't have to do this on my account. Use me for food; I'm good with being chow."

Santa shook his head. "I enjoy you too much. Life can get mundane and repetitious. Only so many ways to kill, you know? Or change the castle or whatever. Occasionally I need an elf to provide a challenge. You, for example. Now, don't take it too far because you could hurt yourself. You, not me. Still, this will be the action of a cowboy choosing the most wild of horses to tame."

Fuck. Just my luck. I hook a guy, but he's straight. And a murderer to boot. Plus, he thinks I'm a horse. Wish I were hung like one.

I started to formulate a better protest when he leaned over, took one arm and grabbed me into a bear hug. I squirmed to no avail. Santa may appear fat and flabby, but dude has jugs for arms. With his free hand, Santa slammed the needle right into my skull.

"FUUCCKKK!!"

I experienced the most excruciating pain of my entire life, nothing I could describe in words. Imagine the feeling of getting a splinter in your finger, magnify it by twenty and quadruple the size, as in, take the wooden shaft, enlarge it to the size of a stick, and hammer it into your head.

Santa let go of me, so I dropped to the floor and writhed around in pain. Sticking to the Christmas theme, I wished for a cheery song and sugar plums dancing in my head. The liquid in the shot had looked so cool, after all.

Instead I hoped for death. No dancing reindeer here, merely agony where the needle penetrated my noggin. Worse, a burning sensation spread through my entire brain, down my neck, and into my heart. Fuck. That shit took over my circulatory system.

It felt like someone grabbed a torch and started blasting away at my innards. Mother fuck, I wanted to die. I convulsed around on my apartment floor, screaming in agony while Santa sat down and picked up my *DNA Magazine*, arrived the day before, to peruse.

Strange, how dumb ideas blast through your mind when you're in too much pain. Maybe to divert my attention as I rolled around in anguish. I cussed I never even got to jack off to this latest issue before Santa forced me to become a Christmas ornament, or something.

Or something is right. Because as the pain subsided and I caught my breath, the transformation began.

Envision a person placing your arm in a vice and cranking it a little bit at a time. Except, when the pain gets unbearable and your bone would snap in half, keep the pain intensifying. No break, only a squeezing agony on your arm.

Got it?

Well, now move the throbbing to the rest of your body. Every muscle. Every bone. All pressed together, wanting to break, compressing in a torturous way. I squinted my eyes shut and gritted my teeth, still hoping for death.

I have no idea how long it took. It seemed like hours, but in reality nothing more than a couple minutes. Santa does not have the patience for anything that takes longer. My body relaxed, the pain disappeared, and I opened my eyes and screamed bloody murder.

"Holy fucking mother of God Dammit shit all to hell! What the fuck did you do to me? What is this?"

I jumped to my feet and motioned up and down my body. I stood no more than three feet tall.

"You look marvelous." Santa tossed *DNA* onto the table and tilted his head as he glanced over my body.

"You're undressing me with your eyes. Stop it."

Santa laughed. "I don't need to undress you, you're naked."

Ah, fuck. My skivvies had dropped to the floor, too big for this little body. My hands shot down to cover my privates.

"Besides, I thought we established I don't go gay." Santa reached over for his bag, again rummaging around in it.

I thought I had my chance to run away, but for the first time experienced his new control over me. A burning sensation coursed through my whole body and summoned me back to him as I got to the front door.

"I don't often use such power, except in emergencies or more extreme cases. But I thought you should experience it since you're new to this. Your edge might need controlling more than the others."

I trotted back to Santa, my muscles working against my will and for Santa.

Santa held clothes in his hand but failed to give them to me. Instead, he pointed at me. "You know, I should pay more attention to body type when I pick elves in the future. Look at you."

I glanced down at my body again, noticing it looked and felt as it had before the transformation, but three and a half feet shorter. Still muscular and pretty lean, if I do say so myself.

My face turned red. For an inexplicable reason, I got hard.

Santa leaned over and flicked my dick with his finger.

"Ouch! What the fuck?"

"Put it away. It's disgusting."

"You're the one who brought attention to my body."

Bam! Santa slapped me upside the head and sent me sprawling across the floor. But at least he tossed the clothes at me. I put them on but decided to let him know how I felt about green tights and little red pantaloons.

"I don't go for this kind of get up. Not my scene at all. I've never worn tights. And I won't put a dumb hat on my head. No way am I wearing a green ditty with the powder puff red ball at the top. Fuck, no."

I stood up and smoothed out my green coat that matched the tights. I tightened the red belt around it when Santa smashed the hat onto my head. It hurt. A lot.

"You're a violent guy."

Santa glared at me. "You have no idea. You're not being funny right now, so watch it. Let's go."

Either the shit coursing through my veins kicked in and forced me to follow him, or I resigned myself to this strange fate and went along. Truth be told, I think a bit of both possessed me.

I already experienced his ability to summon me against my will. No reason to think some of his mojo didn't kick in as he walked toward the front door of my condo and opened it.

Yet I went a little too willingly. Sure, he could hocus pocus me and I'd materialize before him if I ran away. But I could resist. I did, from time to time. Except on this first occasion, I fell in line and sauntered along, no big deal. As if I wore my new business suit, itchy green tights and the whole thing, and marched off to another day at work. As if I stood tall and proud, not short and enslaved. Curiosity got the better of me because I wanted to check out the rest of what Santa had to offer.

I mean, I suppose you could chalk it all up to a lack of options. So I conformed. Made me understand even better how the Nazis took over.

Add the feeling of relief I somehow, someway still lived. Strange, how the will to survive kicks in. You'd think I walked along wishing he'd offed me when he had the chance. Suck my blood and leave me naked on the couch for a stranger to find at a later date. They'd dismiss it as a kinky sex rendezvous gone bad and leave it there. No pain for me. Just death. No degradation as a slave, assuming I went to heaven and not hell.

Whatever the reasons, I picked up my pace behind Santa, a little too chipper to be alive.

At the elevators, Santa pried open the door and stuck his head into the shaft. He looked up, reached down and grabbed me by the neck.

"Fuck!" I yelled as we shot straight up to the top floor. Clutching me between his bicep and side, he held to the elevator cable with one hand while opening these doors with his other hand. He leaped over and into the hallway, where he dropped me like a limp doll onto the ground.

I got a little dizzy from the trip but steadied myself and hurried along behind Santa as he took the stairs and went onto the high-rise roof. Not ten feet from the door stood Rudolph and the gang. I lurched to a stop.

"No fucking way!" I shouted. "They fucking exist? Reindeer fly your ass around?" I held up both arms and motioned toward the reindeer with my mouth wide open.

"Zip it and get in, okay?" Rudolph glared at me. Strange, high voice. A little prissy sounding.

But shit. He talked. Another sign about all the fucked-up stuff I would encounter in my new life.

Santa, however, chuckled. "Yeah. Get in. You don't want to piss off Rudolph."

I hopped into the sleigh and glanced around. Similar to the movie images of Santa. Red. Full of brown sacks of goodies in the back, gold seat. And nine reindeer pawing at the roof in anticipation of flying away. No elves on this visit.

I wonder now why Santa came to see me alone but never found out. I could ask, but I already know the sneer he'd give me and the complete silence that would follow.

Back to my first night as an elf. Santa lifted his fat butt in next to me. Then he leaned over and aimed a raunchy fart right in my direction. I gagged and almost lost my cookies. It smelled like he'd shoved my whole head up his butthole.

"What the fuck?" I swallowed a bit of vomit.

"To remind you who's in charge of your life now."

"You should have your problem looked into. It can't be right. There might be something dead living up in there, sucking on the blood you need for yourself. Ouch."

Santa popped me upside the head, and without any warning, we lurched away into the sky high above the city.

At first I experienced major vertigo and intense fear. I realized nothing kept us locked into the sleigh, and those reindeer hauled ass through the night.

"You're turning green. Drink this." Santa reached down at his feet and handed me a little cooler, full of Santa beer.

At the time, I had no idea he brewed his own stuff up at the North Pole. So when he took out a bottle, twisted off the cap, and handed it to me, I refused at first.

"I'm good." Almost threw up again before I even finished saying it.

"Drink." He shoved the bottle at me.

"No offense, but I've had enough liquids enter my body from you for a while."

Santa reached over and grabbed my head with his free hand. "It's beer, to calm you down." He took the bottle and rammed it into my mouth.

Within a couple of seconds, Santa let go because I grabbed hold of the beer and sucked it down. "This is good shit. Where do you get it?" I reached down and grabbed another one, again duped into forgetting my new circumstances. Because part of me thought I hit the jackpot. Santa gave me free beer to calm my nerves! And instead of it making me dizzier or inducing projectile vomit all over the last reindeer, it worked. No more queasiness. I felt good with a slight buzz and silly thoughts running through my head.

That's when Santa explained the brewery to me, and the other stuff they made at the North Pole. Once again I came close to forgetting I sat next to a blood-thirsty vampire who enslaved me after turning me into an elf. I started dreaming of paradise, where the beer flowed like water, or milk and honey, whatever. You get the analogy. Utopia.

As if. Santa knocked my dream out of me soon enough.

We got to the North Pole through the magical curtain concealing his digs, and soon enough I had a nice, out-of-control drunken stupor going.

When Santa banked hard to the left, lining up to make his usual landing, my head jerked over the side, and I ralphed on the nearest turret.

Santa reached over and slapped me upside the head. "Don't defile my home. And yours now too."

I grabbed another beer and popped it open. I belched and took a swig and held the bottle up toward Santa for a mock toast. "Whatever you say, big fella. But it's your beer that made me puke."

Santa reached over and pinched my ear until I screamed in pain. He let go after we landed, and I fell into the footwell, still crying out in agony.

Santa got out right away, and I heard a scurry of activity outside the sleigh. I stayed there, enjoying the drunk feeling and not sure what to otherwise do, not sure I wanted to see where I'd ended up. This is when I first met Trixy, as she hopped onto the seat and peered down at me, grinning.

"Fresh blood. Just what we needed."

"Fuck!" I scrambled to get up. "You're going to drink from me? I thought only Santa sucked blood?"

"Calm down, there, tiger. Santa and the missus enjoy blood. I meant it more as a figure of speech. It's been a while since we had a newbie come our way."

"What the fuck's that mean?" I slurred.

"Listen, I gotta get you out of the sleigh." Trixy yanked on my arm, getting me to my feet. "Then we can chat however much you want. You're a feisty one. I like 'em feisty."

Trixy gave me the grand palace tour, which I still remember, despite my inebriation. I sobered a little, but she sensed the moment I might become too sober and got us to a refrigerator full of Santa beer and kept the buzz going.

As they say, the rest is history. She made me laugh hard, despite it sinking in I had become a permanent elf and slave to boot. She introduced me to Hedgehog. Being a fag with two dykes up in ole Santaland helped us bond too. Still does.

But I digress from telling you about my first experiences once I hit the North Pole.

I passed out pretty fast, on a little bed of blankets Trixy made next to her bed. I didn't get my own room until a couple days later.

I woke rested, and in the state of confusion you get after sleeping in a hotel room or foreign place. You look around for your stuff, wonder where the hell you are, because most of the time you have to take a piss and the bathroom's not in the right place. I shivered, figured out I remained an enslaved elf, and got out of bed. Trixy stirred too.

And thus did I experience my next lesson in elfdom. We could retire to bed whenever we wanted after the work day, but Santa can wake us up at the same time and call us to duty the next morning, no matter how tired or hungover you feel.

"Fucking hate the early wake-up calls." Trixy rubbed her eyes and stretched. "Come on. He assigned you to work with me for now, until you get acquainted with everything and will get individual assignments. Or until he figures out your area of expertise."

Made me giggle. "I'm in accounting."

Trixy barked a laugh. "Funny. Not much call for that up here."

Too soon, however, Trixy moved us along, and me onto my next lesson in elfdom. Once again, the myth of Santaland blends with a not so good reality. Do elves slave away making stuff up at the North Pole, as the little kiddies believe? Indeed, they do.

But not toys and candy. Or anything good for anyone, except a demented vampiric Santa.

Trixy set me up next to her in the workshop my first day on the job. No more accounting for me, I became a laborer. Santa possesses all sorts of magical potions, spells, weapons, and other maniacal things we elves construct on a daily basis.

My first project involved a meticulous process, started by Hedgehog, handled by a couple elves, and given to Trixy, and at last, me. We constructed syringes of medicine to inject in small children. The serum lays dormant for several years until it begins leaking into their system.

First it inspires them to kill small animals, next a cat or dog. Yeah—you figured it out. Santa invented a potion to create serial killers.

As far as I can tell, since the first time, he takes these shots with him but seldom Copy Editisters them, maybe once or twice every year or so. Seems arbitrary, as far as I can tell.

"Shit!" I shouted the first day when Trixy whispered the reason for Hedgehog and her to manipulate the elements for Santa. I put a cap on the end of the syringe and placed it in a nice protective box. The other elves did assembly like this too. "Why the fuck do you two help him with this?" I yelled.

"Shh. Shut the fuck up." Trixy glanced around, but no sign of Santa, "Because he makes us. Listen, you'll figure it out. We either do it, or he takes control of our minds and bodies, and it happens anyway. Much less painless this way. Plus, the time we did refuse, he paid us back by injecting fifteen people in one night. Get it? We're slaves. No choice. But life's better when we cooperate."

So I did my work the first day, until heading off to bed. Same thing the next day. I picked my turret home the same night, with the help of an elf I never see, who Santa put in charge of elf space up here at the pole. He complained about wanting a committee to help him out with the elf-space issues, which seems ludicrous to me now, but at the time I listened to him bitch without commenting.

The rest, as they say, is history. See? Another one of those stupid ancient sayings flew out of my mouth. Why? Because I finished telling you my transformation to elfdom story and had no other way to transition out of it. Remember, Simon the Accountant turned Elf is telling you this story, not Simon the Famous Author, or even good writer toiling away in obscurity. Simon who plays with numbers to make money chats you up here. So while Tolstoy or Woolf or Rice or a renowned writer would transition from making serial killer potions to the next thing with an eloquent segue, I spew forth with "the rest is history."

Meaning, I've been Simon the Elf ever since, either accompanying Santa on his little sojourns around the world, or as part of the assembly line here at the ole Pole, making Santa's sadistic stuff.

Today we invent an intensified version of demented people who want to see other people suffer. This one in particular pisses Trixy off.

There we sit, singing my favorite Cher tunes to lift our spirits as we work the machinery making the syringes, when in pops Santa.

"Ho! Ho! Ho!" he laughs and farts.

Trixy and Hedgehog nod, while the other two elves cast their head down and refuse to look at him.

Someone has to say something. "Ho! Ho! Ho! Back at you, Fatty."

The slap upside my head hurt this time, even more than usual. He hates his weight. Santa had a weight problem in real life before becoming a vampire, or at least that's the rumor among the elves. Transforming into the undead did nothing to change his body type, and once again I puzzle at the fact he never figured out how to manipulate this magic to make himself skinny. Maybe because being fit would ruin the persona at this point. Skinny Santa would suck, no matter how you feel about the American obesity epidemic.

"Simon's a dumb-ass masochist." Hedgehog points to me while she addresses Santa.

"I'm well aware of his problems. But we all keep him in line, as best as possible." Santa meanders around the room, inspecting our work. We can get in trouble if he thinks we fucked up. Not today.

"Good job. Here's the new formula."

Santa hands it to Trixy and Hedgehog and disappears. While they go over the new potion, I organize so we could get our assembly line going. Santa always gives us a certain number of the shots to fill, then we get to go play for the day. So gruesome or not, I like to keep things moving so we get as much free time as possible.

"I don't want to be at the start of the line again." Of course, Bobby has to bitch. He works somewhere else but had to fill in for a couple days. "I have so much trouble getting the rubber on right."

I howl with laughter. "Can't imagine you needing a rubber. You'd have to have a sex partner to need one."

"Fuck you, Simon."

"Nope. Not interested. No need for a rubber with me."

"You're such a prick—" Bobby never finishes his brilliant thought because Trixy roars in anger.

"Sometimes I can't take it," she shouts. "The killing. Fucking with the people. As if they don't do a good enough job of fucking up their world without his help. Lots of war. Lots of killing. Violence galore, especially in the United States. But no. Santa has to make it worse. What the fuck is wrong with him?" Trixy points out the door, where Santa departed.

Hedgehog moves over and puts her arm around Trixy. "I know it's hard, sweetie. We don't have a choice."

Trixy starts crying, so I move over and hug her too.

"Did you see what this one will do?" Trixy asks Hedgehog, who nods. "Why? He gets to kill people all the time. Why bring down so many other innocent people?"

"Because he can." I shrug. "Nothing more to it. You said it—he's a sadistic fuck on purpose. What's special about this one?"

Trixy wipes the tears from her face and gets us back to work. "Nothing. More fucked up shit. This will generate more of those mass shooters. You know, the ones who go to movies, malls, and schools, and start mowing people down. That's what we get to make today."

Unlike our usual banter or singing to make things seem better, we work in complete silence. Too much destruction in our fingers this time, and Trixy brought us back to reality for the afternoon.

We work even faster than usual. Trixy, Hedgehog, and I retire to watch football on TV while drinking more Santa beer, which snaps us out of the melancholy.

"Did you see the guy's package?" I ask after one large specimen runs by on the screen.

"Um, not a place my eyes drift to," Hedgehog answers.

"Yeah, right. But this was hard not to notice. As in, *huge*."

"Still, not something to worry us, chief." Trixy pops open three more brewskies and gives us each one. "Didn't know you were a package guy."

"I'm not. Tells you how big this thing was. More of an ass man, myself."

"Do any elves have big packages?" Hedgehog asks.

"See, I never noticed before. Not my thing either." I start laughing, hard.

"What's so funny?" Trixy starts giggling, too, without knowing why.

"Sometimes I just think funny things." I love quoting the movie *Arthur*. Old movie, I realize, but hilarious.

"Spill it."

"No. I can't. I get in enough trouble around here."

Now Hedgehog joins the laughter, but I know they'll force it out of me at this point. I also know I'll get busted.

Not good. "What's so funny? We'll torture you ourselves if you don't tell us."

"Speaking of packages. First, it's funny to talk with lesbians about packages. Ironic, you know? Funny. We next drift to packages at the North Pole, and I don't notice them, since the other elves are straight, and I don't have a chance. But North Pole packages make me think of Santa, and Santa's package makes me laugh even more."

Oops. Beer snorted out my nose when I got my packages idea out. We laugh until Trixy lurches upright and shushes us.

I glance over to see the Jolly Ole Man himself, glaring at me from the doorway.

"Simon, come with me."

I obey. Well, I obey after downing the rest of my beer. I concentrate on stifling any more laughter, which will make it worse, but screw up when I glance at Trixy, who has the look of wanting to burst into laughter but is holding it back.

I start laughing again, even as I march toward my doom.

Again, I can't help myself. As we walk down the ice hallway, turn the corner, and head toward the one place this particular hall ends, my mouth opens. "You know, I'd never have seen your pecker if you hadn't pissed on me. You're always degrading me with bodily functions, which whips it right out for all the world to see. So I have to look, right?"

"Why don't you quit while you're ahead?"

"I don't see that I'm ahead of the game."

"You'll stay in the ice dungeon for one night. Unless anything else comes out of your mouth between now and me kicking you down the chute."

I manage to follow him without a noise until he opens the metal door and forces me to stand in front of the ice slide to send me down to the dungeon.

"One more thing?" I ask him.

Santa arches a brow but nods for me to continue.

"Why is it always bright pink?"

I laugh, even as he kicks me hard in the ass and sends me flying down the slide, then shouts, "You earned two days."

Of course, nothing funny once I reach the bottom. At first, you'd never know you landed in Santa's worst torture chamber. The slide slams you into a four-by-four cell of four ice walls. No windows. No door. Only way out, I learned the first time, was for Santa to use his magic to retrieve you by pulling you back up the slide.

So claustrophobia would suck down here, but otherwise, it appears benign.

Until the hallucinations begin. See, Santa places you in this dungeon and tortures you with mind manipulation. Everything gets icy cold, because unlike the rest of the palace, nothing regulates the temperature down here.

Now the fun begins. Whatever fear lurks in your mind becomes a reality. You experience it, or it feels so real you believe you experience it, and nothing could ever be worse.

First come the snakes, slithering out of the walls and flicking their tongues at me. They slide right over and wiggle into my pant legs, despite my kicking and thrashing and screaming. The sharp little bites send tendrils of pain through my entire body. Poison, they're poisonous. And slimy as hell.

As I decide to let myself die from the horror and fear, they disappear.

But the ice dungeon gives you no break. No sooner does the last snake vanish than a door appears in the wall and in walks a tall figure, clad in black leather, including a mask covering his face. His cock hangs out for all the world to see.

An enormous, veiny and curved thing comes to life and bounces as he stalks toward me.

Again I squirm away, but the back wall stops my flight. One by one he clamps my hands into cuffs he attaches to the wall with magic. My legs get stretched and hung in the air, spreading my anus wide open. He reaches over and rips off my clothes, tossing them aside.

"Santa says you're a good little fag and want a big dick up your ass."

I shake my head. "No, not this again."

"Should've thought about this before you went on and on with penis size reflections, I guess." He chuckles, in a bad movie maniacal way.

I can scream in agony as he rams into me, no lube, no warning, and has his way with me for what feels like hours. The blood rushes down my leg and I swear I suffered a rectal prolapse.

Again I pray to pass out but no such luck. The chains and my rapist disappear, but they took my clothes with them.

The room transforms before my eyes into a high school classroom. What the fuck? How is this horrific? I realize my classmates sit there laughing and pointing at me. I'm naked in front of them. No clothes, and nowhere to go. I feel my face flush as one of the hottest guys from the football team walks up and flicks at my flaccid dick, then sticks his finger in my mouth.

I think the physical torture is better to endure than these mental games. Until the classroom dissipates and I stand on the edge of a gigantic cliff.

I spin around to get away from it, to find a lion in my way. He lunges at me, planting his enormous fangs right in my neck as we plunge over the side. I feel the intense pain of his eating me, even as I dread hitting the bottom, and watch as the ground comes nearer and nearer.

Before I would hit the rocks below, I lurch to a standing position, right back on the edge of the cliff, and again turn around to see a hungry lion glaring at me.

Over and over and over he bites me, we fall and end up at the top again.

When my fear of heights and beasts almost does me in, it gets worse.

I land in a cesspool of shit and piss, swimming against a harsh current and screaming for help as it pulls me under. I shut my eyes and hold my breath. Immersed in poop, I resist the urge to throw up. But I can only hold my breath for so long. My mouth opens to draw in a deep breath, allowing the sewage to run down my throat.

A force pushes me back to the surface, so I barf out the nasty stuff in my mouth and thrash about, trying to stay above, until once again the current shoves me down below.

This time my feet get caught in seaweed and I take in the vile excrement until it cuts off my very life. I float, almost thinking I died for real this time, except I can see the brown guck and rot floating by my face and taste the foul sewage in my mouth, throat, and stomach.

The torturous scene lasts until I reach my breaking point, until I sit back in the ice dungeon, all four walls nothing more than solid ice, only the chute above me giving any break to the monotonous scene.

I look down my body and see my clothes, still there, covering me.

I never enjoy the tingling and pain of being summoned to Santa more than after a stint in the ice dungeon. It flows through my body, so I scream in agony, but the mental relief of moving up the slide and toward Santa and the ice hall relieves me.

I land at his feet, Santa smiling down at my prone body. "Better now?" he asks with a chuckle.

I have to get a better feel for what to say, when to say it, and when to keep my mouth shut. Well, it's a no-brainer now. Still, it's difficult for me. Witness what happens next.

I brush myself off as I get to my feet, standing in front of him. "I should keep my mouth shut, you know?"

"Well, sounds like a good elf. Not Simon the Naughty Elf."

"Right. I mean, I gotta start guessing when you'll flip. You know? All that because you're a size queen? Damn." Well, I still have a lot to do in terms of silencing myself. His fat ass and nasty self makes me say those stupid things.

Santa pats me on the back and laughs, "Follow me, I want to show you something."

I doubt we head for another view of his little pink one-eyed snake.

Chapter Three: A Little Santa History

SO I GOTTA tell you the truth regarding this episode with Santa, so you get his history right. Or at least the story as he tells it. Scratch the legends and shit, Santa the Sadistic Vampire tells a different tale, one I'm inclined to believe. Partially because it sounds so fucked up, no one could invent it. And because of his conviction in telling it. Also, as you'll see, I caught him in one lie we got corrected. So by the end, this adds up pretty much.

Why he drops this news on my lap, I still struggle to understand. Makes no sense he chooses to unleash his story on me, of all the elves and beings at the North Pole. At least it gives me the opportunity to write it down after so you can learn his story too.

I got out of hock seconds ago, with an itchy feeling of snakes and excrement still covering my body, and my mouth drops a pecker joke on him. I flinched at first, thinking he'd send me right back down the chute.

Instead we meander through the North Pole, two mates going off to drink a beer together. I stifle a giggle when we pass Trixy, polishing a statue of Santa he stole from Marshall Field's in Chicago a few decades ago.

"What the fuck?" she mouths at me, her brow scrunched together.

I shrug my shoulders and grin. "No clue," I mouth back and keep going.

We round a corner, into a short hallway with no doors, windows, or anything. A dead end. Until Santa keeps walking, right through the wall.

I figure I better follow, so I do the same. Bam! I think I break my nose, smashing into the ice.

"You fucking prick." I rub my nose and stagger to my feet.

Santa's hand and arm reach through the wall, grab me by the collar, and pull me through to join him. He sits down on a throne-looking chair, laughing like a lunatic.

I glance around at the rest of the place. "Never been here before. Nice digs."

In addition to Santa's red throne, red velvet tapestries of various Santa scenes line the walls, with a few cabinets displaying other Santa-legend history.

"I get it. A little Santa museum. A shrine, right?" I run my finger along a row of books, each one about Santa. "A little narcissistic. But cool."

"This is a privilege I'm allowing you. I'd watch your tongue."

"Not one of my strong suits, but I get your meaning. I'll do what I can. So, why me?"

"Because my past makes you so curious. No one else seems interested. You want to know my story. So, ask me anything. I want you to know my history. All of it."

My bullshit meter shoots off the charts. Something is amiss here. Santa, deciding to grant Simon a wish and spill the beans? Right. And monkeys will soon spew forth from my ass.

Oops, better keep monkey dread to myself, lest it happen next time in the ice dungeon.

I decide to play along. "Okay, you're a funny guy. Let's go with the truth now. Why am I here?"

Santa nods. "You ask too many questions. You'll learn why I wanted to tell you this, but when I'm ready to explain it. For now, am I incorrect, or do you desire to know my entire past?"

I scratch my forehead, wondering if I want to take this bait. Always ulterior motives else going on with him. But why not? What the hell else am I going to do? "Okay. Shoot."

"What do you want to know?" he asks.

"If you're offering? Everything. Every damn thing. Are you the Bishop of Myra from the fourth century, around Turkey? Is that you?"

Santa laughs.

"Why the fuck is this funny?"

"For a number of reasons. Not the least of which is I never pegged you for knowing such history, any history, let alone legend of Santa history."

I smile because he has a point. "My brother loved history, especially how the holidays evolved and crap. He went around spewing forth about it a lot. I got in trouble if I teased him, so instead, I endured it, and, I might add, some of it stuck in my brain against my wishes."

"So allow me to answer your question. No. I wasn't born until 1796 in America. So the history of the legend is accurate to there. At least, it's a truer tale of the monk whose identity I stole and how the myths grew up around him."

I sigh. "I'm disappointed."

"Are you being an asshole again? How could that disappoint you? You detest me but come with preconceived expectations? And you accuse me of being complicated."

"Well, okay. I understand. But still. I always thought you were the fucking bishop! I wanted to get a major scoop here. Instead, I find out this dude existed in real life, doing nice things so people began celebrating him, and he became a saint. My brother's going on and on about him was accurate."

Santa twirls his finger in the air and rolls his eyes. "Blah, blah, blah. Yes. True enough. He helped little children and sailors and gave a dowry to poor girls so they wouldn't have to become prostitutes. No one ever stops to wonder if his help led to a better life. They still had to put out at the behest of their husbands. It wasn't unheard of for prostitutes to enjoy their profession. But we'll go with the happy smiley-face version for you. The wonderful Bishop of Myra, how delightful. And yes, in 1087, the citizens of Bari in Italy raided his hometown and stole his artifacts, thus solidifying his reputation. All leading toward sainthood. Don't you get it? I needed the perfect foil, and the stories, the truths if you will, of his life provided the perfect ruse."

I take my hat off and scratch my head. "Now who's being the boring historian? Sounds like I'm back home with my bro."

"Except for the obvious reason I bothered to know the history because I built my own legacy upon it."

"Okay. I gotcha. So back to what I remember. He becomes the most popular saint by the Renaissance, also true?"

Santa shrugs, looking more and more annoyed. "Yes. Obviously. Even some Protestants held onto him after the Reformation, when they cast out the other saints from their belief system. Those fools in Holland overdid it." Santa points to one of the tapestries, of a bishop-looking Santa wearing red. "And by then we have the stupid idea he bring nuts and berries and sweets to good little boys and girls. Now, we get fallacy. It was stupid parents doing it. But that was the legend. Lined up for me to perfection." Santa takes his hands and taps them on his chest, yet his voice grew edgier and edgier as he detailed the history.

"You don't appreciate talking unless you're the focus, huh?"

Santa squints his eyes at me. "What are you implying?"

"Um, you were hot to trot in telling me your history, so I start where I figure the legend of Santa begins. Which it does, but not with you. And in clarifying how the original St. Nicholas was a good man, you go apeshit, even question whether he did any good. So we pull it through history, you're still not alive, so you get angrier and angrier. A psychiatrist would say, in the least, you've got issues." I hold my hands up. "Not me. I'm sayin' what the experts might think."

"You're inching onto very thin ice." Santa's voice goes flat.

I hold up my hands again in mock surrender. "I'm merely reporting."

"What else do you want to report?"

"Well, let's finish up this bit on, on—" Not sure how to say it without provoking him.

"On what?"

"On the rest of the mundane and ridiculous history of Santa up until 1796 or so." See, I can placate him from time to time, without a smart-ass comment thrown in.

"Of course. What else would you like to learn?"

"So the Dutch are credited with bringing him to America. New York? Washington Irving included this fact in his brief history of New York."

"How did you know? More lessons from your brother?"

I smile and point to one of the cabinets. "You've got it right there. I read it."

"Okay, wise one. The answer proves more complicated. Let's say, it's possible. It seems the Dutch brought their myths and legends. Others think their Santa legend came more from a study of Dutch culture, a celebration of their perceived past, as opposed to actual practices. And to finish this nonsense with you, it's also true elements of the German god Odin crept into the myth. The long white beard, for example." Santa tugs at his own beard for emphasis. "He brought gifts, too, and was leader of the wild hunt. Have we had enough of this already? It's not pertinent."

"We sure delved into rather heavy-duty history. Which was not my best topic, I'll have you know. Brother or not, I struggled with it. Bored me to tears most of the time. Who gives a fuck about the Civil War? I know, I get its importance. But on and on with the Lincoln chatter. Whew. Too much. And those re-enactors freak me out, too, maybe more than you do. Dudes in old uniforms pretending to fight battles already done. And those fuckers in the Confederate uniforms. What the fuck? Nice modern racism. And other history too. World War II. Yikes, I'm done with it. Sure, remembering the Holocaust, we gotta do it. But enough already. So yeah, let's shove this forward. I got excited you let me in here to your inner sanctum but would prefer the fucking dungeon to this history."

I lied on the last part. I'm thinking that planting a fear of history in his head might lead to a lecture as torture next time in the ice dungeon. Instead of getting butt raped.

"What else do we need to know before we get on with it? You're sure you're done?" Santa's eyes flicker from blue to black and back to blue. Uh oh.

I frown. "But you must have co-opted this legend we chatted about. Built upon it. It must have relevance?"

"A little, yes. Enough of it now."

I laugh. "You don't like he was a good person. You're a vicious murdering vampire shithead. And it bothers you he helped people. And society continued the legend as positive, a good force in the world."

Without knowing how it happened, I find myself pinned against the wall, four feet off the ground, with Santa's hand gripped around my throat. Those jovial blue eyes disappear and those horrific black pits replace them. "And you'd do well to remember I'm a vicious murdering vampire shithead."

Santa drops me unceremoniously to the ground. I stand up, brush myself off, and readjust my clothes. "Got it. Note to Simon: Santa's a dick."

"Why don't you proceed before I send you back to the ice dungeon, or worse. I don't believe for a second you prefer it over history."

I nod. "But it's your story, not mine. I'm not in charge here. Which you point out a lot."

"You were doing the questioning."

"Okay. Cool. So Clement Moore? Do we get to you yet?"

"Why, yes. But we need to back up first. Let me tell you my human history, and how I became a vampire. Clement Moore enters our tale soon afterward."

I slap my hands to the side. "You know, you told me to lead this fucking thing, and now you take over."

"Because I remembered you're a stupid elf and need my leadership. How can I explain my history as Santa if you don't know where I came from? You carried on with Saint Nicholas's life, don't you think this is at least as important?"

"May I?" I ask, and walk toward the little fridge. He nods. I grab two Santa beers and crack them open. One for each hand. I go over and settle onto a gigantic red pillow with Santa's face sewn onto it. I take a swig of my beer and fart right on the face.

"I heard your flatulence." Santa settles back onto his throne. "But this part is too important to tell, and we mustn't get distracted by your antics."

I already finish a beer and toss the empty bottle to the side. "Well, fire away. It does kinda intrigue me, you ever being human." Then I fire away with another juicy fart.

Santa sighs. "I have a peculiar relationship with you. I find you amusing and yet often want to kill you. But your role here in learning my story is vital."

"Whatever. My role. Fuck it. Anyway—" I scratch my head. "—the feeling of confusion is mutual. Not that you ever amuse me. Far from it. But I acknowledge our peculiar relationship. Must be because you got excited when you saw me naked the night you kidnapped me. I still have a good ass."

Santa ignores me and launches into his story while I get yet another beer. "I was born in 1796 to a poor farmer. Nothing remarkable about my childhood. Solid parents. A couple brothers and a sister. I tortured small animals—"

"Whoa, whoa, whoa!" I hold up a hand to stop him. I didn't even catch the few words he said after "small animals" because I was a little stunned. "You were going to be a serial killer? I mean, you say you tortured small animals like it's a normal thing. It's a sign of serial killers. Jeffrey Dahmer. Ted Bundy. John Wayne Gacy. Hannibal Lecter. So he's not real, but still. They're your buddies, huh?"

"I don't see any reason to dwell on it. And I hardly consider them buddies. Or anyone, for that matter."

I grin, knowing my answer will annoy him. "We could be buddies." I spit beer out laughing.

"No, we couldn't. Can we dispense with the serial killer conversation?"

"You brought it up. Could have skipped the small creatures part, if you wanted."

Santa clears his throat. "I was quite young when I ran away and joined the military. Which again adds little to my story, other than the complete boredom I suffered most of the time. I did manage to kill a couple humans by this point. Never got caught, but it ended any pleasure from assassinating animals. I needed the bigger kill. Thank God the War of 1812 started."

I laugh. "Right. Most people think—yes! Killing!—when we go to war. Yes! Lots of dead people!"

Santa smiles with glee. Sadistic fuck.

"So nothing more so far?" I ask. "Little kid in a normal family has his wiring wrong, kills for fun, hides in the army, and comes to his own because of a war?"

"That will do."

"So, serial killing is a good business, for a soldier in a war, I mean?"

"Combat provides ample opportunity and good cover. I killed with relish. I drenched myself in blood more than anything. I could lick at it, bathe in it, without anyone becoming the wiser. All was blissful warmongering, especially when I joined General Jackson's ranks and ended up at the Battle of New Orleans."

"Figures you'd end up under him. Pretty nasty fellow, in a lot of ways."

Santa roars at me. "Do not denigrate such a great American!"

I sip my beer and point the neck of it toward him. "You got a lotta issues. I keep telling you so it might sink in one day. Maybe your next elf changeling should be that psychiatrist I mentioned. I mean, talking to me will only get us so far. You can't process this without help."

"I often wonder why I put up with you."

"Hello! I ask myself the same thing, constantly! Trixy and Hedgehog think I'm a lunatic, and you're going to off me any day!"

"Well, you have a purpose."

I tilt my head, surprised. "I do?"

"Yes. And you'll learn it in time. But don't do anything to change my mind."

"Mysterious. I like your flare for mystery. So, you and Ole Hickory fighting away in New Orleans. Go on." I don't want to dwell on this conversation about whether or not he wants me to stick around.

"I didn't get to participate in much of the fighting in New Orleans. I fought for one day before I was transformed by one of the most grotesque creatures I've ever seen."

"An alligator?" I chuckle and get beer caught in my throat, then choke it right out of my nose.

"I know you think me frightening." Santa leans back in his throne, as if a philosopher deep in thought and not a vampire telling why he masquerades as a Jolly Ole Elf. Sometimes it hits me harder than others, this whole fucked-up thing with a fucked-up guy.

"Um, yeah, you're a little scary. I thought you meant to be petrifying."

"Right. I commented on your fear of me by way of comparison. Because so many disbelieve now, no one thinks vampires exist, and still fewer understand vampires create themselves."

I hold up my hand. "For the record, before we get into this creating vampires thing, I believe in vampires. Totally."

"This will take a century to tell you if you keep interrupting me with your ridiculous comments. Now, let me explain. The transformation to a blood-drinking creature happens against our will, but once converted, we can assume any personification we so desire. As our human selves. As a different person. As a demon, angel, whatever a vampire envisions, he becomes. Yet so many vampires revel in the cruel and vicious aspects of their lives they get stuck appearing as pure evil. But many today become rather trite and go with the modern sexy vampire look."

Santa becomes Satan sitting on a throne, with the pointy ears, red hooked tail, and clubbed foot. I scoot back toward the wall as he rises, laughing. Just as fast, Edward Pattinson stands before me with his glittering skin and longing face. Next Santa transforms into a bird-like creature with human legs but a terrifying bald eagle head and beak, but with teeth. Anthony Hopkins as Hannibal Lecter sneers at me a second later. He kind of snarls, "Is this what you meant, about my buddies?"

I want to throw up. "Okay, I get it," I whisper.

Whoa. Santa became a hot little number, my type, with tight muscles and cute little red cheeks. He sashays toward me and winks. "Or seduction works for some. It's just not very exciting. No threat, so no fear generated." Santa runs his soft little finger along my cheek, and I get aroused despite knowing the merciless vampire fuck toys with me.

Santa straightens himself up and returns to his red Santa outfit, long white beard, and black leather boots. "Now do you understand?"

"Is this still related to alligators?"

"No," Santa shouts. "It's my transformation description. You try me. Never mind. Let me continue with my history. I was patrolling in New Orleans, near an alligator-infested swamp, speaking of alligators, when he grabbed me from behind and dragged me into the swamp with the snakes and muck. I struggled against him to no avail. When we got to a small island, he threw me against a tree and stalked toward me. For the first time in my life, I was terrified. Do you understand? Nothing frightened me because I commanded the world to my bidding. I never played the role of prey and always hunted. This reversal of fortune almost unnerved me."

Santa turns around and manifests as the creature that attacked him so long ago. He has the build of an average-sized man but stands naked before me with green and black scales covering his entire body. A forked tongue flickers out of his mouth as his oblong, glowing gold eyes take me in. I pee my pants.

Santa turns back into Santa. He hurries over, rips my pants and underwear off, and smears them in my face before throwing them out the window.

"I might need those." I point at the window.

"Now you understand my fear."

I get up and walk my de-panted self back to the fridge for another beer. "I'm thinkin' I need to get blitzkrieged to get through this."

As I return to my pillow, Santa tosses me a little red skirt. "Put this on. I can't stare at your Johnson all night."

Regaining a little of my composure as I put the skirt on and twirl around, I smile. "See. There's something to what I said earlier about our relationship. You always jump at the opportunity to get me naked." I settle back down. "Okay. Nasty. Not my being naked or even your smearing my piss in my face. The lizard thing you showed me. You must've pissed yourself, like me. So a creature snatches you out of the swamp and you're screwed, right?"

"I thought so at the time. Never envisioned the beauty of what he gave me. You see, he let me know he watched me for several days. Said he wanted to drink from me until he spied me making a kill. Made him want to convert me instead. So he knelt down, shoved my head to the side, and drank my blood until my human self died. He pried open my limp mouth, ripped at his wrist with his teeth, and forced his blood down my throat.

"Before I knew what happened, he disappeared. I had become a vampire. No training. No way of knowing what to do, other than instinct, and on my own."

"Quick question. I hate to interrupt, again. Still, how did you look in life? Santa but human without the demon eyes? You never described yourself."

"I was young, idiot. How could I grow a long white beard? Or run around in the army with this weight? Are you so dense? I explained the vampire powers of transformation to teach you how I created this persona."

"Got it!" As I nod my head, the room wiggles around because the alcohol takes control. Feels good. "Right. So you looked like, what?"

"A guy. Nothing special."

I almost let out my next question, but by a stroke of luck choke on it instead. No reason to ask if he had a small pecker as a human too. "Okay. Go on." Good Simon, sometimes I do learn my lesson.

Santa grows silent. Thinking? Hope he can't read my mind with the last thought.

I finish my beer but decide against grabbing another one, for now. "Okay. You've got my attention. Serial killer soldier for General Jackson gets taken by a lizard vampire. Creepy. High on the creep factor. Now, before we continue, I do want to point out that just because you affect a softer, gentler appearance, it doesn't make your killing any nicer. Right? I mean, you enslave elves. You murder the innocent. And I know for a fact you relish scaring the shit out of people. So, wait! I had a thought. How did you learn the magic? Did that come with being a vampire?"

"You're getting ahead of yourself. Let me tell this story."

"This skirt is drafty. Tickles my balls."

"How did we go from your being terrified and peeing all over the place to worried about your cool balls?"

Makes me laugh. "Just the way it is, Nick. It's existence as an elf. No one else would believe it. One minute we run in fear, the next accept life as the slave to a vampire. It's either that, or go drown yourself in the ice moat. No thank you, on the freezing riverfront. So, tell me. What did you decide to appear as? Santa right away?"

Santa shakes his head. "No. This version of Santa didn't even exist yet. I sat on the island for the night, appearing as me. Hungry but lost. Until the sun started to rise, and I dug into the ground to bury myself for the day. Instinct kept me alive those first days and months. I woke the next night and clawed my way back to the surface, half expecting to find my maker there.

"Nothing greeted me but unquenchable thirst. So I swam off the island, back to land, and grabbed the dumb woman walking down the road and drained her. I moved on until another victim crossed my path. I drank him too. This routine went on for at least two days, until lizard man showed up again."

"Did you piss yourself the second time?"

"I never said I did the first time. You did. Now, be quiet and let me finish this part. He attacked me, could have killed me if he wanted, but instead, warned me to leave his territory. So I headed away, not even paying attention to what direction. I—"

"Whoa again!" I lean forward. "You always skip shit. Interesting shit, if I'm going to know your story. So he never trained you, never said how to survive, and kicked you to the curb. This, despite his apparent intrigue in turning you into a vampire and not simply feeding off you. Didn't you ask why he converted you? Or want him to explain how to survive as a vampire? Teach you tricks, like turning into a lizard? You just left? Why not fight back? Nothing intimidates you."

Santa rubs his beard, as if contemplating my questions for the first time. "It never occurred to me to consider any of such notion. I had become a perfect killing machine and cared little about how or why or what I needed to learn. I understood I'd never make it if I stayed around him in New Orleans. I always detested companionship. Never even had comrades in the army. Why concern myself with others, once he made me a vampire? As for fighting him, I wasn't ready. Today, I could tear his limbs apart. I fear no one."

"So he's still alive?"

Santa scrunched his brow. "I've no idea."

"Huh. How'd you even know you were Nosferatu? Undead? Eternal life? Whatever? How the fuck did you know to drink blood and hide from the humans? Or shelter yourself during the day?"

"I knew by instinct. Same as you know to breathe and eat and drink. Maybe not all the beer you consume, but water and such for survival. My body hid itself from the sun. I ate to survive. The problem being I kept running into problems that made me flee. A couple more vampires. A lot of witches and warlocks. A roadblock always got in my way and threatened me. It did not intimidate me, mind you, but I wondered if I could beat them. So I continued to move on, until one day in a little town called Mebane, North Carolina, when an old woman took an interest in me when I arrived at her house to eat her."

"Cannibalism? Or do you mean to drink her blood? Because 'eat' gives me an image of you stringing her up like a pig over the fire and roasting her, followed by sitting at a table with knife and fork, civilized, and munching away."

Santa frowns. "Drink her blood. Don't be disgusting."

"Right." I laugh. "You describe a human life of killing creatures and eventually people, for fun. Become a vampire and enjoy killing humans and sucking up their blood, but I cross the line at cannibalism. Again, your shrink's going to have a field day with this."

"There's no need for a shrink. You're the one sitting in a dress."

"A little homophobia coming out there, Santa. No pun intended. Or transgender prejudice. Transsexual. Nothing wrong with a guy in a skirt. Tell me about this old doll who got your panties in a bunch."

Santa gets up and grabs a daguerreotype. He shows an image of an average-looking older woman, similar to lots of pictures in a history book. Regal. Composed. Stern.

"I wandered into Mebane, with no particular plan or reason, to find her sitting on a porch, as if she expected my arrival. No one else but a few naughty slaves ran around in the complete blackness of a Southern night. I decided to kill her, because she appeared so arrogant. I walked right onto her porch, my fangs already descended, yet still she made no move to protect herself or scream for help.

"'Before you drain my veins, I want to make a bargain with you,' she said to me.

"You can imagine my fascination. No one ever bargained with me, they only pled for their lives until I killed them. I smiled and told her she had my attention.

"'I know about your kind. And everything else supernatural out there. Look at my body. Times almost up, no matter how you slice it. However, I can offer you immense power. More than your undead self could imagine. I hale from a family of witches. My magic could destroy this town with a sweep of my hand. And if you attempt to feed off me, we'd have quite a battle.' She but twitched her index finger and a bolt of lightning shot across the porch and right into my chest. Before I realized what hit me, I slammed into the railing. Not to give her an advantage, I returned to my feet, brushed myself off, and walked back over.

"'Do I have your attention?' I nodded to her. 'Good. Allow me to explain myself. You give me eternal life, and I will give you this magic.'

"'Have you been waiting here, all these years, for a vampire to wander by?' I asked her. She chuckled. 'Not exactly. The spirits foretold it. Do we have a deal?'

"Well, you can imagine, how could I pass it up?"

This sent me into peals of laughter. Santa forgets how absurd this sounds to us outsiders. Sure, I believe in vampires and witches and magic, ever since he transformed me against my will and enslaved me up here at the North Pole, where he commands that night always reign over his castle. But at times I recall life back at the ranch, where none of this exists. Add his warped mind, and it tickles me. Only a serial-killer-come-vampire would get his jollies off at the thought of adding sorcery to the mix.

"I know I chose you for this tale in part because of your sense of humor. However, you need to remember I'm telling you a serious story."

I get control of myself, at least a little, except I still grin. "I know. Serious stuff, this. Because I get this leads to your figuring out how to transform us into elves and enslave us. Still, there's humor here. Because you think like a demented lunatic. Not a normal person, even though you kind of treat yourself as an average Joe. You think it's so obvious and self-evident to grab for the magic, so you never consider the ironic horror of it. But do tell. Did you make her a vampire?"

Santa shakes his head. "No. As clever as she seemed, and despite portending of the future, she proved naïve. Or perhaps too eager. I assented but demanded she give me the magic first. She attempted to negotiate, but I walked away. She envisioned either a fight to the death between us or an agreement. She never figured I could merely leave her. Her magic failed to force me back, so she called for me to return. I did. 'Here. You win. I give you the magic, and you uphold your part of the bargain. I don't think I have much time.'

"Speaking of that part of the story, I believe we've explained it. She was dying. As if desperate, she reached out and grabbed me with both hands around the neck, but instead of strangling me, a warm tingling sensation passed through my body. Much like my transformation to vampirism, I became a warlock."

"You became The Wicked Witch of the West with a twitch of your nose? Forgive me, seems implausible. I mean, you made her out to be so cunning. She waits for years because of this vision of the future, and the dumb ole bat lets you get one up on her with such ease? Give me a break."

"I became a warlock, not a witch."

"There you go again with your gender prejudice. Afraid of the emasculation of the feminine reference. Must be a penis-size thing." Crap. How did a penis comment slip out?

Santa glares at me, then with his mojo reaches across the room and magically grabs my nuts and squeezes hard as hell. "Next time, I rip them off."

"Sorry," I squeak out. "Go on."

"However, you do have a point." He continues as I gasp for breath and massage my balls. "I suppose the truth will play better. I fudged the story a bit when I told you."

"Liar, liar, pants on fire! I knew it! Plus, your story went way too smooth for the truth. So out with it. What, did you fuck her brains out? Back up, and give me the truth this time. How did you get her to share the magic?"

Santa clears his throat but, as usual, ignores my comments. "I did walk away from her, and she did grovel for me to return. When I demanded she give up the magic, first, she refused. She knew. So instead, she offered to exchange our gifts at the same time. I would drain her blood while she transferred the magical knowledge to me. So I agreed, figuring she'd give me the power, but I could suck her life out before giving her the blood. She thought of my ploy, too, because as I sucked her life into my mouth and as the magic coursed through my veins, I sensed its incomplete nature and knew I must deliver on my end of the promise in order to gain the power. So I did."

I groan. "That's it? You pretend to trick her in the first version, but in reality, you went through with the exchange? Boring. And it makes you into the dumb ass."

"Did I say I was finished?"

"No. But this does not seem exciting. At the movie theatre, I'd toss popcorn at the screen right now and boo. Booo!"

"Hold tight. Yes, I made her into a vampire, and she gave me her magic. Because she placed a spell to force me to transform her or lose the magic I had gained. I never dreamt, even as she offered it, what power her magic gave me. Nothing like before. I sensed it. I first thought of how no one stood in my way now. No vampire I ever met who chased me out of their territory could defeat me. You see? The combination of magic and vampire blood molded me into the perfect and omnipotent being. Of course I transformed her in order to keep my new power."

"I see. I mean, I guessed before we started this whole history thing, right? You figure out how to create the North Pole, fly around with reindeer, enslave us, kill, maim, and hide as Santa. Something gave you this power. And since we never run into any trouble with other vampires or witches, you command the situation. Got it. Except for her, am I right? Because she has the same voodoo."

"Had. Had the same voodoo. I overcame her."

"Is this another lie?"

"No."

"So you killed her?"

Santa shakes his head.

"What, then? Why all the mystery, other than it's what you do."

Santa's eyes light up, a cartoon person with his finger stuck in a socket, shocked. "I tell you what. Since this is my story, we don't want to bog ourselves down with her existence. Let's do this. I left that night. Two powerful entities on equal footing with a mutual respect yet disdain for each other. But I returned to finish our feud. We'll let her tell you this part of the story later. She can explain everything."

I get it, a slap upside the head get it: Mrs. Claus. He never killed her. It explains how she lives forever, yet somehow she never leaves here. "The missus, am I right? Is she trapped? And a vampire?"

"We'll let you chat with her later. Let's get back to my story."

Wow, did he have my attention. See, he has an ability to captivate me. Weird, I know. A killing machine, vicious as hell, yet I want to hear this shit. I yearn to learn his story, and now hers too. So I roll with it, hoping my stupid mouth stays shut long enough for me to get to the end of it.

"Okay. What year are we in now, by the way?"

Santa knit his brow. "Not sure. I lost track of time because it meant nothing to me. I know the next date in the sequence, because Moore publishes the story in 1822. So between the Battle of New Orleans in 1814 and 1822."

"Oh, yeah. I almost forgot Moore. So you promise I can learn the missus Claus history later?"

"Yes."

"Cool. So where are we in your story?"

"I left her in Mebane and spent a few years learning how my power worked and making sure no one could ever defeat me. Which brings me to the point of wanting a better gimmick. I tired of the stale vampire running around with complete power. As my magic developed and I gained total control over it, I longed for something different. Something better. With more of an impact, more of a statement to the rest of the supernatural world, and even humanity, to proclaim how I reigned supreme."

While he pauses for a second, I think about it. That grand scheme leads to Santa Claus? The beer spurs me on again, because I find this funnier than anything so far. So funny, I roll over and hold my side from laughing way too hard. When I sit back up, red in the face, Santa watches me.

"Sorry." I cough a little and stifle another fit. "It's—you know. To come up with Santa out of all this chaos. It's kind of funny. Right? No evil plot to rule the world or become supreme leader. Nothing grand in any of it. Just good ole St. Nick."

Santa folds his hands across his lap, neither joining my amusement nor getting angry. "It's brilliant."

"Right. My bad." I roll my eyes.

"Okay, I acknowledge a bit of truth to your reaction. I tried to keep my designs rather simple. Ruling held no allure."

"So you're not like Lex Luther? Or Hitler?"

"How could you put Lex Luther and Hitler in the same question? A comic book villain and the most notorious dictator in history. Unbelievable." Santa frowns.

"What, you're going to go bananas because of what Hitler did? That's why I don't get you. You enslaved us against our will. You fucking murder people left and right. Yet you've got a Hitler moral qualm? Can we get back to your invention of a Santa fetish?"

Santa pounds his fists on the arms of his chair. "It isn't a fetish. It's brilliant, as I said."

"I keep forgetting. So weave your magic and explain the brilliance. Why not wander around as a badass vampire with magical powers?"

"I explained this to you. Because vampires meander around. It's too dull. And it led me into their territories. I had the choice of combating a vampire and taking his territory or roaming from place to place and taking their territories, except it feels like a mundane conquest. A game dull humans play."

"I do agree playing the board game *Risk* is as dull as it gets. Ever try *Risk*? Boring as hell."

"No one understands your ruminations half the time. I wanted to mark my dominance over them as a vampire and my control over anything I desire, which also gave me a challenge. Do you understand? Instead of total control, I got the best of both worlds. I can kill and dominate at my whim. And no other vampire dares challenge me. But keeping up the Santa Claus myth in the midst of it provides the challenge. It keeps me fresh and on my toes."

"That's it? Again, wow." Seriously biting my tongue now on all the things I want to say about the insanity spewing from his mouth. "I keep expecting a grandiose tale and instead get more weird from you. You must have another reason for the flying reindeer and red outfit. I keep going back to a fetish to explain it."

"No!" Santa bellows. "I don't even appreciate sex."

"Not even masturbation? Nothing compares to blowing a load. But let's not get into jacking off together, okay? So, what? Why the Santa charade? Enough with the secrets. Or I'll find out when I chat with Mrs. Claus."

Santa almost continues but pauses and leans back in his chair. "Okay. The truth. Despite my magical advantage, I don't know I could take on the whole vampire world. And we need to conceal ourselves from humans. Who knows what might occur if an all-out war ensued? In so many ways, this modern age conceals us better than ever before because so few believe anything is possible of a supernatural nature. So there you have it too. I desire status as the ultimate vampire, with my undead powers combined with the witchcraft. But if I confront too many vampires, it risks a war against them. Or it might encourage them to figure out how to employ magic themselves. I also monitor so humans never come after me. So why Santa, you ask? Because I dominate my realm with little risk."

I scratch my chin. I know this time, even before I say it, I should keep my mouth shut. Still, when it's funny, sometimes you have to let it fly no matter the consequences. Especially if it comes with the drunk giggles. "So Santa's a pussy?"

Santa lunges forward and slaps me upside the head. Even as it stings and I flop to the ground, I laugh hard.

"Who's using pejorative language for women now?"

I rub my head and sit up. "You got me there. Sorry. Don't tell Trixy or Hedgehog, because I'll never hear the end of it. My bad. Okay, so did you kill Moore? Or what? Let's get back to the story here."

"Obviously not. Otherwise how would he write his poem? Though I first arrived at his place with that very intention. I had contemplated, for a while, the idea of a new personification, but nothing appealed to me, so I kept killing and wandering around. I know this date because of the now-famous history of what people think Moore wrote. It was 1822 in New York. I got to his house—"

"Whoa! Set the scene! You're going too fast. Remember how much beer you made me drink?"

Santa sighs. "You exasperate me. Here." Santa gets up and grabs two beers. He opens them, takes a swig of one himself, and hands me the other one. "I'm tired of telling you the story like this. Let's use magic to help out. You better not barf all over. Because what I'm about to do makes people sick, even sober people. It messes with your head a little."

"Which head?" I giggle.

"I thought we weren't going there together? Stop it."

I laugh again. "What's going to make me blow chunks?"

"I'm spinning you into a mystical realm, so you can see my interactions with Moore and experience them. So I don't have to keep telling you this story."

Santa raises his hand in the air and snaps his fingers. The room swirls with a rainbow of colors swishing before my eyes. Good thing he warned me because I focus on a couple of colors to keep from projectile vomiting.

Either he sent me to the past or recreated the scene before my eyes, but I sit in an office with a fire burning and a gentleman writing at a table. I can see his back, but the coat, candlelight, and general décor tell me I landed in the nineteenth century. I glance around, but no Santa in sight.

"Whoa! What the fuck happened? Who are you?"

Nothing. He keeps writing away, as if I never spoke. I stagger over and tap him on the hip. Still nothing. I lean my head between his thigh and arm to see his face. Yep. Nineteenth century, with a black scarf kind of tie thing wrapped around his neck. Makes me gag to think about putting one on. Ties and turtlenecks around my neck make me throw up.

I get it all at once. The beer slows my brain function, but over a couple seconds it fires up the pistons. This must be Moore. Santa's showing me how they met. Wish I had popcorn. I stumble back to my chair, sit, and wait for the show to begin.

Santa appears, walking right through the office door, his eyes black as pits, fangs descended. Remember, he wears the same kind of digs as Moore, not the jolly red suit or anything yet. Santa from the past here, not the enslaver of my life. When he gets close enough, Moore flinches, lurches away, and slams to the ground still in his chair.

"Please, I have children! I'm a man of God! Spare me. I beg of you."

I chuckle, knowing such entreaties do nothing to stop the onslaught. Still, Santa pauses before he launches at him. Santa reads the paper on the desk over which Moore labored, and I see something click in Santa's feeble brain. The black eyes turn to blue, the fangs retract, and he stands before Moore as a typical human, minus the fact he played the demon a second before.

"Perhaps I *will* spare you. Will you make a bargain with me?"

Moore pauses. Must be a moral quandary, I'd guess. Man of God, confronted by the devil but wants to save his own hide.

"I'm a pastor. A professor of biblical languages at the Episcopal Theological Seminary. I can't bargain with the devil."

Santa chuckles. "I'm not so grandiose. One of his minions, nothing more. And your credentials don't matter in our affairs together. It's your choice. Either we work together, or you die. Your status may do good in this. Would you at least hear my bargain?"

Moore nods his head.

"Get up. You look ridiculous sprawled on the floor."

Moore rolls over and gets to his feet. He sets the chair upright and again returns to it with great caution. Santa pulls over a larger lounge chair and sits next to Moore, both facing toward the desk. Santa taps the sheet of paper.

"This poem. I want you to publish it. We need to refine it a bit. But it would help me out. If you work with me on it, I'll spare your life. Easy enough."

Moore squints at Santa. "Nothing more? But it's a nonsensical lyric I'm writing for my children. Nothing of import or for others' eyes."

Santa shrugs. "Up to you. You help me; I spare you. Easy as that."

I next watch the two over a series of nights together as they craft this poem. Moore always a bit hesitant and trembling, Santa acting as if people write with a demon assistant on a regular basis.

"No," Santa shakes his head. "Make him happier."

"A right jolly old elf?"

"Yes!" Santa points at Moore in triumph. "And keep the portly thing. I like a happy fat man."

Next a different night, with a harsh rain crashing against the window. "Who will believe a being could nod his head and go up and down a chimney?" Moore slaps his quill on the table.

"People already think nonsense about Santa. We toy with a legend already in existence. Besides, watch this."

Santa nods his head and swooshes through the room, right up the chimney despite the burning fire. A second later he returns the same way.

Moore coughs in embarrassment. "I forget."

"Don't."

Moore raises his finger in the air again. "Not to mention, in other books it tells of Europeans long believing Santa entered through the chimney, but not how. Or Odin entering through chimneys—in the old Norse. So it will work fine."

"Precisely."

"Okay, so he nods his head and goes up and down the chimney. What else? Can we keep the part when he brings gifts to the children? My girls love the presents."

"Sure. Keep the stockings over the fireplace too. But what transports him in this little sleigh? We could pull it with deer. Not horses, that has nothing magical because people see them everywhere."

"Even if we make them fly?"

"Not horses. Deer?"

Moore scratches his head. "They're not strong enough. Let me think." Moore crosses the room and fingers a number of books before pulling one from the shelf. He pages through it and points. "I knew I'd read this before. The Saami people in northern Scandinavia use reindeer to pull their sleighs. They're far sturdier than our deer, and a might bit stronger with thicker coats and flat hooves for the snow." Moore reads the last part from the book.

Whoa. Even in this other realm, with me peaking in, this dude sounds the part of a boring professor. Who would know this reindeer shit?

"I like it." Santa smiles. "Reindeer, fine. Shall we name them?"

"Name the animals?"

Santa nods.

"Why not? Dasher, Dancer." Moore writes and pauses before holding his pen in the air. "Prancer, Vixen, and Comet. What else?"

"How about Cupid?" Santa offers.

"Yes, Cupid. Dunder and Blixem."

"What on earth are Dunder and Blixem? I understand the other names."

"Old Dutch for thunder and lightning."

"Ah, German. Donner and Blitzen."

"Yes, but I prefer the Dutch."

While neither comments on the transformation, Santa begins looking more and more the man of their poem with each passing night. I mean the actual person turns into the man they invent. First the beard, followed by the boots, and over time he costumes himself into the spitting image of Moore's creation. Or, their joint creation.

I laugh, pretty hard, because again it makes Santa look like such a doofus. He was a normal dude a few months ago, minus the vampire thing, then transforms into this ridiculous legend. Even knowing his reason, it seems silly. Reminds me even in this magical realm how Santa has serious mental problems.

I wish I could ask him more questions but know the limits now. He refuses to answer in any detail. I mean, why not go around as Satan? More fitting. Or a Greek god? Even lizard man who transformed Santa makes more sense to me. Or use his special power to change his appearance from time to time, from human to creature to the unusual. Santa doesn't fit. That's it. Deranged, how he latched onto this persona from a glance at a poem.

Still laughing, I almost tumble over when the earth shifts under me. Oops. My humor pisses Santa off. He snaps me right back to the present. "Moore never found my visits humorous."

I shake my head. "No. Because you threatened to kill him. Not much funny in that, I imagine. I already dodged the kill bullet, at least for now. But Moore? He struggled with the morality, don't you think? Making a deal with the devil to save his own life?"

Santa sputters. "I forced him to publish a poem. Which he did, in the *Troy Sentinel* on December 23, 1823. Remember December 23rd as important in my history. At Christmas time. Even at that, he insisted upon being anonymous. Chicken."

"Right. But a Santa poem never fit with him being a professor and all. Can I ask you something else?"

"You will, whether I give permission or not."

"What clicked in your noggin when you read his poem? You went there for dinner and came away as a coauthor. What gives?"

"At last, a serious and pertinent question from you. As I mentioned, I struggled for a while with what to do with myself and my unique combination of magic and vampirism. I contemplated using lots of myths, of course, from a Roman god to a werewolf. Anything to make me distinct. It was Christmas, so I saw the stories about Santa and people talking up his legend. He was in my mind, and it appears in Moore's as he wrote for his daughters. A spark lit when I read but a portion of his story. He hit upon what I searched for. And he knew the words to make it happen."

"Because creative writing never struck me as one of your talents."

Santa's eyes got black. "I detest intellectual snobbery."

I flash a cheesy, fake grin. "Never know what's going to push your buttons. We come with different strengths and weaknesses. I couldn't write my way out of a box either. It surprises me you and Moore had such a thing going, because he seemed pretty brainy. So nothing else? Now you became St. Nicholas with your sleigh, reindeer, and a brand new legend?"

"Almost, but not so simple."

"Ah!" I take a big drink of beer. "Right. Way too complex to happen with the snap of a finger, with no disrespect to the chimney trick. More a fine wine, this takes time."

"Indeed." Santa sounds very serious. Interesting, sometimes he bashes my head in, other times my sarcasm goes flying over his head, a jumbo jet in flight.

He continues without noticing my giggling, or at least he ignores it. "It took a few decades to fashion the outfit, enhance the enchantment on the reindeer, and create the North Pole in which you now sit. In the meantime, American culture developed much of it without me having to do a thing. It was brilliant. Gift giving, selling goods, the desire of Christmas; it happened of its own accord. They advertised even in the newspapers for Christmas gifts by the 1840s, hinting at my existence and importance the whole time. But I needed more help to move my master plan further along, to a new and grander level."

"Yeah, wait. Quick question. Did you leave Moore alone, per your promise?"

Santa twirls his finger in the air. "Yes, yes. Quite alone. He published the poem and went about his dull life without my interference. Unlike poor Thomas Nast, who I bothered for several decades before killing."

"Who's Thomas Nast?"

"You're a poor student of history, I must say. For all your callous and snotty disregard for my brilliance. Your brother must have been embarrassed at your stupidity."

"Fair enough. I sucked at history, as I admitted from the beginning. This Nast fellow never hit my brother's radar."

"That's not all you sucked at."

Beer shoots out of my mouth and across the room. "Touché! But there we go again talking penises together. Not cool. Who's Thomas Nast?"

"Thomas Nast was a famous political cartoonist for *Harper's Weekly*."

"Oh! Stupid me! What an idiot for not having Nast on the tip of my tongue."

"He was quite famous in his day. And I needed to push my image forward and thought pictures would do a better job than another story. So I visited him, first in the 1860s. As with Moore, I propositioned him with either death or assisting with my legacy. He possessed none of the moral qualms of Moore and agreed without the drama. So I employed his services over time to solidify my image. First in 1863, and in 1881, his masterpiece."

"So he made a career of drawing pictures of you? Did you pay him?"

"Quit being so dense! No. He covered the Civil War and politics. He's famous for taking on the New York political machine in the late nineteenth century." Santa stands up and shouts. "I can't take your foolishness! You're so trite."

I shrink down a little at this outburst. "You're the one in the red outfit here."

"And you're still wearing a skirt."

"There you go again with your homophobia. If you're going to make gay elves, you gotta work on your phobia."

"You noticed none came before you? Or since?"

"Yeah, lucky me. Simon the Only Gay Elf."

"You should ask Rudolph." Santa grins.

"Figures a prissy-pants reindeer with his high-pitched voice is involved. He's an asshole, you know. Finish with Nast. I get it—famous political cartoonist you co-opted. What next?"

"He did my bidding well enough, but not to my liking until he got it right after much effort. In 1881, he captured what I sought. I was rotund, cheerful with my beard, carried a sack of toys, and wore a big smile. He depicted my red suit and white fur trim as I hoped. He even got the North Pole into the story. Well, he and a poet did it first in the 1870s, but you get the idea. Brilliant!"

"So his depiction helped solidify your legend. But you said you killed him?"

"Yes. With a touch of regret."

"You're remorseful about a kill?" I raise both eyebrows, unconvinced. "Like you hate Adolf Hitler?"

"Kind of. He had helped without complaint. But his career took a downturn by the end of the century, which embittered him. When I returned in 1902 to brush up on our work together, he refused. So I drank from him. End of story."

"That's the thanks he gets after his help? What will you do to me?"

Santa glares, but chuckles. Freak. "Maybe the same thing, but I enjoy you. And I torture you in other ways, yes? Besides, as an elf, you have no connection to the human world to help me."

"Got it. The whole slave thing. So Moore and Nast did all this?"

"From dense to a complete simpleton. Don't forget I orchestrated the whole thing. They helped a lot, but not alone. A little boy in Colorado assisted me in order to save his family when I visited them. He wrote a children's story in 1874 that again mentioned the North Pole. The Salvation Army, and this time I had nothing to do with it, started dressing people up to look like my image in the 1890s to collect money from idiots on the street. And so on and so forth. You see why I love this! I roll a tiny snowball down a mountain, and the fools I feed off keep rolling it along into a gigantic boulder!"

"You are a scene from a bad movie, with a supervillain getting his crazy on."

Santa stands in front of me by this time, raising his arms to the ceiling. He drops them to the side. "Why can't you appreciate this? I took this legend from a little-known tale, a small part of Christmas, and crafted it into an important and relevant tradition, a major part of Christmas. And you get the irony? The most vital part! They hail and worship me during their celebration of a pure and wonderful story, while I lurk as a vampire sucking out their lifeblood!"

"I've always thought the dichotomy was the most charming part. And of course I get the irony. I got it long before you spun this little story for me. Can I drink more?"

Santa snatches my empty bottle out of my hand. "No. You're getting to the point where you won't remember."

"There's more to tell?" I almost pop off with the fact this begins to bore me but think better of it. Besides, he could have more bizarre tidbits to throw at me.

"A little. I'll hurry, before you pass out. Let's pull this into the twentieth century, shall we? I assume, given your proclivities, you know about L. Frank Baum?"

"What the fuck are proclivities? I am too drunk to keep up with you. Oh! You mean my being gay? How does fagdom lead to Baum?"

"Trace it forward, stupid. Baum wrote the *Wizard of Oz*, which becomes a movie starring Judy Garland, who blossoms into a diva."

"Ah. Got it. Right. Not my scene, but I get your meaning. A little older gay reference there compared to me, gay generation wise, to dwell on the whole Oz thing. But sure, I know the story. Though I much prefer the musical, *Wicked*, and Elphaba. Gregory Maguire's novel rocks. Or James Franco as Oz in the new movie gets me going, in a lot of ways. And I love the Flying Monkeys, in every one of their manifestations. We need them up here at the Pole, don't you think?"

"Only as your imprisoners."

"Oh. On second thought, no thanks. You do that well enough on your own."

"Would you like to flashback again to see what Baum did?"

I consider the offer. "I did almost upchuck. But seeing it as a vision way entertained me." I almost add more than listening to him drone on but bit my tongue. See, I can filter when needed. "So sure, take me to the past."

Without so much as a word or motion, I step into the past. I steady myself, gulp back a bit of bile, and glance around the room. Another author's den, another period figure writing at his desk. This time with a Teddy Roosevelt kind of appearance. Big waxed mustache, slicked-back hair parted in the middle, with round wire glasses.

I should give Baum a big smooch on behalf of the gay community for what he set in motion. I remember this drag queen as she sang "Somewhere Over the Rainbow," farted in my face, and grabbed my balls hard. Embarrassing and disgusting. Never went to another drag bar again. Fuck him. I mean, Baum the drag queen. But not literally.

Baum stares out a small window while tapping a pencil against the side of his desk. Lost in thought, he jumps when Santa stands next to him. Mind you, unlike Moore seeing a typical human-come-vampire, Baum looks at Santa Claus. "Excuse me?"

"My good man, you're a wonderful writer, and I need your assistance."

Baum launches out of his chair and straightens his jacket as he speaks. "I don't know who you are, or how you got into my home, but I expect you to leave at once."

Santa sighs. "And here I thought this might be easy. Let me put it another way. I hate always resorting to these tactics, but you leave me little choice." Santa transforms from the storybook vision to the vampire, still in his costume, but with cesspool eyes, a scowl, and those fangs sticking out. "You'll either help me or die."

Baum seems more comfortable with the abnormal than the others. He defers to Santa by sitting back down and again straightening his jacket. He fidgets a bit but continues the conversation in an even voice. "You have the leverage here. What can I do for you? And how do I know you won't kill me, regardless?"

"No one ever asked me that before. Good question, but you may find the answer rather inadequate. You have my word. I need your help, which makes you more valuable alive than dead. Otherwise, I have no way to guarantee it."

Baum coughs. "Fair enough. What do you need?"

"Your writing skills. To write a new history of me."

"I'm sorry. I don't understand. Of you? A vampire?"

Santa shakes his head. "Of me, Santa Claus."

Baum's jaw drops open in disbelief. "You're real?"

"Yes, in many ways. Not with the visits on Christmas Eve to children and such. But otherwise I exist as Santa Claus. Will you do this for me?"

"I'm very interested in a new series of children's books. They tell the tale of a mystical land of Oz. I don't know if I can pull myself away. I may need more time."

"You'd rather die than work on this project?"

Baum picks up his pencil and taps it on the table again. "Are the stories true you'd die if I stuck a stake in your heart or wore garlic?"

Santa laughs so much his stomach jiggles. "Your spunk is wonderful. But no. Two options lie before you. Death. Or writing."

"Give me the parameters and I'll see what I can do."

"I'd need a refresher, a story for children, which is why I came to you. Make up my childhood too. Invent a reason I became Santa Claus."

"Wait." Baum holds up his hand. "Give me an example. Do you mean like a baby found in a forest and raised by a lioness or a wood nymph?"

"Yes, yes. Anything. Make me educated by immortals in the forest. Then work in the typical stuff, how he invents toys for children. Keep with reindeer who assist me. Blah, blah blah. It's almost been a century since Moore crafted his story about me. I need an update. Maybe I'm mortal and almost dying when the wooded creatures grant me immortality, so I live forever bringing gifts to children."

Baum scratches notes onto a pad the entire time Santa talks. They part with an awkward handshake and Bam! Simon the Elf returns to Santa and the North Pole.

"So you wrote *The Life and Adventures of Santa Claus*?" I point at the book sitting on a nearby shelf. "Not Baum? I also notice you offed Nast the same year you went to Baum. Not a coincidence, is it?"

"Oh, you've turned into Astute Simon all of a sudden. Correct. With Nast out of the picture, I sought new assistance. But after the initial meeting you witnessed, I returned to find the entire book complete. Baum published it and never saw me again. He behaved, unlike certain naughty elves. Or Nast, for that matter."

"Well, in fairness at least to this elf, he obtained freedom through his obedience. I avoid a slap aside the head if I obey. Otherwise nothing but slavery and death in my future. Any other history we need to cover. And, uh, I'm sobering up."

Santa jerks his head toward the fridge, so I grab another beer. I deal with him better with a slight buzz. Or blasted off my rocker.

"The brilliance of modern advertising and capitalism come into play now, with almost no assistance from me. Consumerism takes over the story. In truth, I last intervened in building my legend with Baum. I almost visited Norman Rockwell to give me a spruce up, but he beat me to the punch and took me on as a subject from time to time without any prodding. The same with the White Rock Beverages Company and Coca-Cola. They needed a marketing ploy during the holidays and fashioned more likenesses of me. A few historians credit Coke with my red outfit, since it matched their cans. Again, this happened without interference from me. My legend established itself enough to keep itself updated and me front and center throughout the twentieth century without my doing a thing."

"Oh! Wait! What about Rudolph? He came around later, didn't he? Wasn't he a marketing ploy too? Did you invent it?"

"It's actually the truth. But he can tell his own story, as Mrs. Claus will reveal hers. I had nothing to do with Rudolph. Well, not at first."

"So you didn't make him into a bitchy prima donna?"

Santa laughs. "No. You'll see."

I scrunch up my forehead again, deep in thought. "So the department store Santas, cartoons, TV shows, movies, this modern image just happened. You don't do a thing to help it along?"

"That's why I'm so brilliant. I set it in motion and benefit from it without lifting a finger. I became master vampire, hid from the humans, and still get to tweak them. Kill them. Do my bidding, whenever and wherever I choose. The world acts as a model train set for me to play with. Still, it does get a bit dull, even for me. This fact helps to explain why I want you to know this history."

"Right. Too much Santa when he trots out in September now. Over the top, I say. What about the dudes in department stores?"

"The volunteers who get Christmas lists from children?"

"Yeah. Did you invent the whole fucking thing? Oops, I don't mean fucking as in molestation, only an adjective for thing. To get kids, right from the start, to trust Santa and therefore hide your real identity?"

"No, again, that happened naturally. Did you know you curse more when you drink?"

"I love cursing, a lot. Doesn't surprise me it flies a little more when the inhibitions get loosened up. Naughty words make the world more colorful. More interesting. Back to you. So, no on the department store mall guys?"

Santa shakes his head.

"Have you ever been the real dude in the Macy's Parade? That would be hilarious."

Santa chuckles. "No. The parade takes place in the daylight, if you'll recall."

"Anything else? We're winding down."

"I detest the asinine Santa songs."

"*Up on the housetop,*" I sing this one at the top of my lungs, especially "*O! O! O! Who wouldn't go?*"

"Stop it."

"Let's go with 'Grandma Got Run Over by a Reindeer'? A good newer one, I'd say."

Santa clamps a green-mittened hand over my mouth. "Enough. We need to finish this before I change my mind and do kill you."

I nod, and he removes his glove from my face. I spit out a little fiber. "Tempting to launch into 'Santa Claus is Coming to Town' right now. The modern, rock version."

"Don't. Besides, you're correct. We're finished. You may return to the lesbians and regale them with your stupid stories."

"But not this one, right?"

Santa squints at me. "This was our little secret."

I hold up my hands in surrender. "Cool. Just checking. But, the wall is in my way. Remember, I run into it if I try on my own."

Santa waves to dismiss my concern. "Go. It won't stop you this time. I made it stop you last time to amuse myself."

"Ha, ha, ha. Funny guy, you." I get to the ice wall and hesitate, afraid to hurt myself. A question pops into my mind, so I whip around.

"Yes?"

"The hunters. We dodge them every now and then. For example, the other night when you made Dasher poop fire on them. You mention them in passing, call them the Secret Hunters, but always refuse to talk about them. They weren't in your story either. What gives? Are they special hunters after you? Or generic vampire hunters, like Van Helsing? Humans, or vampires?"

"Van Helsing isn't real. You always mix up your truth and fiction."

"I'm trying to make a point, not write a history book. And you avoided the subject again."

"It bores me. But I'll answer in the spirit of our openness. Both of your scenarios are accurate."

Maybe I did drink too much. "Huh?"

"A very small and old-school group of people hunt vampires. A vestige of the past, most of them Romanian. I must watch for them, but truth be told, they focus on the more traditional vampires and have no notion of my existence. They don't worry me. You, on the other hand, have seen those from the vampire world who search for me. They detest my power. My dominion over the earth frightens them since I defy their territorial nature. Similar to humans, most vampires now don't believe Santa Claus exists. But a few do and attempt from time to time to come after me. Secret Hunters, they call themselves. Vampires who seek to rule all vampires, but feel they can't until they conquer me. In time, I will take care of them. I might let you help."

My mind races with the possibilities. Would they free us? Probably not. Just eat us. "Well, thanks."

Santa nods and again waves for me to leave. He seems tired, or sick of me. I start to go again but stop. "Can I have pants back?"

"You don't like your skirt?"

"It's not me. Nothing else. Could be it's internalized homophobia or a sexist thing. And I don't want anyone on the ground looking up at my pecker."

Santa snaps his fingers, and with that, I wear my pants again and stand in the elf recreation room, transported against my will.

Trixy sees me and tilts her head. "What the fuck? Where'd you come from? You and your pal Santa have a good time?"

I rush over to her and Hedgehog, struggling to contain a huge outburst of laughter. "You won't fucking believe what happened to me. No fucking way. We need more beer."

I grab each by a hand and drag them toward the Santa beer taps. "Get two. Trust me."

We each get our drinks and I lead them through the palace, the entire way up to my little room in the turret.

"It's fucking cold up here. I'm nipping out." Trixy pokes her tits to make the point.

Hedgehog reaches over and gives them a twist.

"Um, please no lesbo porn. And yeah, well, the cold shrivels me right up. But we need the privacy. 'Cause you won't believe what I learned."

I retell the entire Santa history to them, despite his orders to the contrary, and after they depart, I pull out my little diary and commit it to paper too. I'm so glad I stole this journal from one of Santa's victims. I ripped out their pages and took this over as my own. I want to expose him with this blog. Like I wrote at the beginning, if you read this, I'm probably dead because I figured out how to get this from the North Pole to the rest of the world. But everyone needs to know this story, so I'll martyr myself. Simon the Fucking Elf Martyr. No, Simon the Astute Fucking Gay Elf Martyr. List me as the author with those titles. And tomorrow I plan to follow up on his promise to let me hear Mrs. Claus and Rudolph tell their stories too. Add them to the mix, in particular prissy Rudolph. No way he gets off the hook.

Chapter Four: The Missus

I RIDE, WITHOUT chatting, for a couple minutes in the sleigh, only Santa and me, fuming and with the stench of reindeer poop still in my nostrils. Got shit on my shoe. Literal shit.

"And I thought we were pals now!" I scream at Santa as we fly through the air, back toward the North Pole. Sitting right next to him, I wonder if I should keep my lips sealed since he could reach over, grab me, and toss me overboard with little effort. Nah, too fucking pissed.

"You and I both know that was never the case. Nor will it *ever* be the case." Santa makes no move against me; he keeps pushing the reindeer toward home.

I slam my fists onto my legs. "Right. I know. Still, we had a deal. I listen to your stories; you have to give me something in return. Instead, my first mission out afterward and you assign me to follow around and pick up reindeer shit. Who cares? We never worry about their poop. Half the time not even at the North Pole." I hold up my shoe and put it under his nose. "Reindeer poop."

He twists my ankle until I scream in pain and shoves it back down.

"There is no deal." Santa continues to speak in a monotone. "You invent a lot of things in your feeble mind."

It dawns on me. When does he make me clean out the reindeer stalls? When I deserve a punishment, at least in his eyes. So he forced me to clean up after the putrid reindeer on this mission to teach me a lesson. Usually I know why. No clue this time.

"Why reprimand me? What did I do?"

"You needed to be reminded of your status, though your idea you earned special recognition tells me I failed in my attempt to communicate this lesson. I'm afraid telling you my history might go to your head. You require discipline. So you and I will go alone from time to time, while you assist me and otherwise experience the same dull and humiliating life of an elf, to keep you grounded while you enjoy the privilege of extra knowledge."

I take a deep breath. Privilege? What an egomaniac, to believe learning his lurid history serves as a special treat for me. How far should I go? Fuck it. "Listen, I like the tidbits. But nothing goes to my head. I have no visions of becoming King of the Elves or Santa's Special Helper. Whatever the reason you lay this on me, I appreciate it, in a sick and twisted sort of way. But that ends it for me. Nothing else to worry over. If it's all the same to you, I'll continue being Simon the Elf unless you want to unburden yourself to me. We'll let twinkle toes Rudolph continue as your special agent."

"You're an imbecile."

I scrunch my brow and frown at him. "You don't have anything else?"

"No, it's all you could understand."

I scratch my head. "So you made me gather the shit in a bag—again, I'm talking literal manure—to remind me this life fucking sucks? Are you kidding me? Listen, I enjoy the background information. Don't get me wrong. Found it quite insightful and interesting. But, I wonder if you further considered the idea of seeing a psychiatrist? It sounds like most vampires have a lot of issues, I suppose. But yours seem rather deep and disturbing. We can otherwise continue business as usual, because the mundane everyday existence of an elf sucks too. No reason for special Simon treatment. Oh, by the way, the elf vet better examine Dasher, because the stuff flying out of her ass is not right. At all. Makes my worst diarrhea explosion seem mild in comparison."

"Enough with the scatological talk."

"You're the one commanding me to play in the muck."

"Stop it. You do as I command, when I command it. Besides, you get your next little treat when we return."

"What?" I glance at him. "Clean out your toilet? Squeeze out the reindeer anal glands?"

"One more comment and it becomes a reality."

The North Pole comes into view. We crash right through the invisible force field that conceals it from the rest of the world and suddenly a grand palace looms before us.

"Okay, I'll bite. What's next?"

"Another special treat for Simon."

I so want to ask if this has any excrement involved in it but keep it to myself. His last warning about making it come true sounded authentic to me. "When do I get to find out? This isn't a sick joke, is it? And you're going to throw me a dog biscuit?"

"No. And you'll find out soon enough."

Santa commands the reindeer to bank hard left, tossing me to the side and sending us too close to a turret. Before I even sit up again, we slam into the ground, feeling like the sleigh might blast right through the ice platform and into the depths of hell.

Santa hops out, issues a few orders to waiting elves, and picks me up by the collar and sets me on the ground. "Ready?" he asks.

"For what?" I scrape my foot along the ground to work out the nasty stuff. "You never finished telling me."

"I never started. Here. Allow me." Santa lifts me in the air again and steals both my shoes, throwing them into the trash. "All better."

"Except for my toes freezing off. Conjure me up replacement boots. Stylish with a fancy buckle and zipper up the side."

"As if I obey orders from you. I was concerned you would track shit through my palace. Your toes don't concern me. Come."

He begins walking away, so I rush to follow. "Seriously, no shoes? Frostbite is real. Did you forget you made your palace out of ice?"

I bang into the back of Santa's leg when he halts. "Shut up, got it? Do you want to find out Mrs. Claus's story, or not?"

I shut my mouth and nod.

"So quit worrying about your footwear and follow me. She keeps her place rather warm. No need for clothes, even."

"Still, I don't feel comfortable being naked around your wife."

"She's not my wife. That's part of the pretense. In reality, we detest each other."

"No shock there. Since she fancies herself a powerful witch but you trapped her up here. So what will compel her to spill the beans?"

Santa glares at me. "She has no choice but to do my bidding. She already knows of your approach and will cooperate."

Santa begins an odd chuckle as we turn down a couple halls and stop before a huge wooden door.

"Something funny?" I ask.

"The combination of her imprisonment and having to deal with you amuses me. And it comes with the added bonus of you having to deal with her."

Before my next witty retort, Santa motions with his hand and the door flies inward. He shoves me through, and it slams behind me.

I stare down a blackened stone hallway, lined with torches affixed to the wall on both sides every ten feet for illumination. I see nothing but a dark tunnel all the way to the other end.

"Hello?" My voice echoes down the hall, but no one answers. I clear my throat. "Anyone there?" Still nothing.

I take one nervous step forward, and my hands begin shaking. I think to turn around and bang on the door or see if it opens, but even this frightened I can think clearly. Santa pushed me in here and locked it behind me for a reason. No way he feels compassion and releases me.

Another couple steps, to the second set of torches, before my fear halts me again. "Yo? Mrs. Claus?" Oops. She may hate the moniker. Better watch myself. At least I can gauge Santa's mood and wrath with our bit of rapport. Who knows where this tunnel leads, or about her demeanor?

I take a deep breath and march forward with hesitant steps. My toes at least begin to warm up, as he promised.

It hits me. I feel like Sigourney Weaver in those fucked up *Alien* movies. I found it. The courage will come from Sigourney. Picture myself in a hot black-and-tight outfit with a wicked laser gun space thing to blast this witch-come-Christmas-icon out of the sky. Yet I hope she looks nicer than the alien creature.

Okay, more than worrying, this rambling monologue in my mind musters the courage to keep moving. I turn around and no longer see the door, nor is anything up ahead but dark hallway and torches. I must have traveled halfway around the world at this point.

Fuck. I should have grabbed a couple Santa beers for the journey. What the hell? Santa wants me to face this sober? Maybe she keeps her own stock. If I ever get there. If this exists and isn't a ploy by Santa to further punish me.

I halt. Getting pissed. "FUCK!" My scream reverberates up and down the chamber.

This awful cackle fills the room around me. The Wicked Witch of the West happens upon me and wants to replace stupid Dorothy with my stupid self, I'm convinced. I even glance down to see if I wear ruby slippers all of a sudden. Nope. Only socks.

The blackness vanishes, the torches disappear, and I'm standing in the middle of a very large chamber. Still the same stone as the tunnel, but gray, not blackened from smoke, well-lit but without the need for fire or even lights to my view of things. More magic powering this place.

I also have little red boots on my feet now. Whew. No barefoot visitors to Mrs. Claus. I would prefer green, because red makes my feet look bigger. And it almost smacks of ruby slippers, but no glitter or sparkles here, plain red with no frills. Still, better red than nothing.

I spin around, taking it in. Nothing too incredible stands out. Appears as I imagine a castle in Europe, with fine furnishings, a comfortable atmosphere, and very, very warm. Santa warned me. No sign in here of an ice brick or anything else cold you can find throughout the North Pole palace. Unlike the rest of his ice palace and its frigid nature to keep you nipping out above and shriveled up below, Mrs. Claus keeps it toasty warm. Like next to a cozy fire. Or Hades? Guess I'll find out soon enough.

I almost get comfortable when I make my final turn and see her sitting in a rocker next to a little fire, still laughing away. Loud. No, not laughing. Cackling.

No matter how long I live up here, and no matter how many crazy, fucked-up things I witness, I still get startled at times by what confronts me. So I know I entered a witch's chamber. A witch turned vampire turned captured beast. Still, it strikes me as I stare right into the kind and gentle face of Mrs. Claus, right out of a storybook.

Same gray hair, tied up in a bun behind her head. Same kind blue eyes behind the round wire-rim glasses. Same red dress with white apron, even a gingerbread man sticking out of her pocket.

Well, the cookie brings me back to reality. A gingerbread man with no head, nothing but teeth marks around the neck. And the old woman staring back at me continues with her heinous laugh.

Facing her, I stop and tilt my head. "So he imprisons you, no different from the rest of us? And it drove you to insanity?"

The laugh stops at once. Her face becomes angry, the lines seem to indent farther into her skin, and dark circles appear around her eyes.

"If only I had the pleasure of such a thing as insanity. Oh, no. I maintain full control of my faculties, my power, my lust for blood, my control over the magic. Except for the spell to keep me here, at his behest. And except for the enchantment to lock me in this prison. Don't be fooled by the comfortable surroundings I created. I'm trapped here."

I kick at the ground, scan the room, and twiddle my fingers, not sure how to respond or where to begin. "So, uh, you—probably not—don't get a lot of visitors?"

She leans back in her chair and rocks back and forth.

"Almost never. I could have more in, mind you. He offers to let elves visit or do my bidding in here whenever I so choose. Or the reindeer. Whoever lives up here can come to my place if I call them forth. But I prefer it alone. Unless I escape this jail, I detest interacting. So I content myself with the elf who brings my food when I require it."

I clear my throat. "Food? As in, human victims?"

"A vampire requires blood. But Santa likes to torture me by disallowing the kill. Instead, he sends me cups of blood. I've no idea where he gets the juice."

Well, that makes my presence downright awkward. Hope my being here doesn't provoke the desire for a ripe snack. "Yeah, about no one visiting you." I decide to stay away from the feeding thing. "I had no choice in coming this way. See? So, I, uh, hope you won't take it out on me."

Why the fuck did she make me so nervous? Odd. I spout off at Santa endlessly, despite the fact he could flick his finger to inflict injury upon me, or with a mere thought assassinate me. Dead Simon. But in those situations, I let loose with anything and everything in my mind. Not here, where in a matter of minutes Mrs. Claus has me uptight and afraid. Worried to say the wrong thing.

This all when I know Santa commanded me to come here, when he claims to have ordered her to spill the beans. I have to get a grip.

"I know why you're here." Mrs. Claus pushes the glasses up from the end of her nose. "And, despite what he may have indicated to you or tried to order from me, even he can't make me talk."

"Ah, well. Perhaps I should go." I scan the room but see no doorway. Spinning around after I first arrived, I failed to pay attention to the entrance. Maybe it vanishes, too, like the hall.

"I said he can't make me, not I don't want to. He came upon an amusing scheme this time. First time since he trapped me up here."

I tilt my head in confusion. "Scheme? I don't get it?"

Mrs. Claus puts a hand over her mouth and mocks surprise. "Oh, I forgot. He doesn't want me telling you this secret. I best stop before he steals you away."

Great. She is as cryptic as him. "What the fuck does that mean?"

"I don't appreciate your cussing."

"Neither does Santa. But I'm a slave, no power over myself, so cussing gives me an emotional release. I can't stop it. It's a form of expression to add weight to my ideas. And you were fucking going to fucking tell me about a fucking scheme?"

She laughs. "Nice. He told me you had moxie. Or is it fucking moxie?" Her chair creaks as she leans back. "I'm not daft enough to spill any more of the beans. I hear you have a taste for the spirits. I brew my own moonshine, if you want some."

"Now you're talking. We're moving in the right direction!"

Mrs. Claus gets up and walks across the room. Fooled again, I expected her to move like an older person and need a cane. Nope, she pushes out of the chair, same as a twenty-year-old and goes over to a copper contraption in the corner.

"Not into Santa beer?" I ask.

"Oh, no. This works much faster and requires less urination. Before I came here, I took an area of Romania as my vampire territory."

"Stereotypical, to go to Romania and be a vampire. Transylvania, Vlad and all."

Mrs. Claus stops and turns to me. "In some ways, yes. But because of those stereotypes, not many actual vampires take up in Romania. The peasants there still believe and hunt for us, perhaps more than anywhere else in the world. The gypsies in particular. It makes it more dangerous. But, as a new vampire in need of a home, and wanting to get as far away from him as possible"—she points at the wall, indicating Santa—"I took the chance and set up shop there."

"Ah, cool. So you lived Vlad the Impaler style."

"I suppose. A few of the gypsies brought tribute to me in return for protecting them."

"That's more Dracula in the novel than real life. But cool. What kind of tribute? Human?"

"What else?" she says without inflection or irony.

I stare hard at the floor. "What else, indeed."

"I lived there a short time before he came to get me. Back to this moonshine. The gypsies make it, as well as the Romanian commoners." She takes two shot glasses and fills them with a clear-looking liquid from the copper contraption. She hands me one.

I sniff and swear it caught my nose hair on fire. "Wow. Strong stuff."

She wiggles her eyebrows. "And you haven't even tried it yet. You'll have to trust me here. Don't think about it. Don't sip it. Throw it back. Remember, they still make this there and drink it. Not because it tastes good. Two reasons. They can make it cheap because they're poor, and it gets them drunk fast. You must do as they do, which is what I instructed."

"A shot?"

She nods. "A shot. Cheers." She holds up her glass, and we clink them together. "To our time together."

She throws hers back, and I follow suit.

Holy mother of God, shit, fuck, damn. First, it smells like liquid fire, as if it contains nothing but pure alcohol. You toss it in your mouth, and it has this odd gritty taste. I throw it back, trying to decipher the taste, but one second later, I feel it burning down my throat. I must have dropped a match down there and lit my innards on fire. I cough, take a deep break, and my stomach ignites.

"Shit," I manage to mutter. I walk in a circle, thinking motion will help. I cough. Take a deep breath, still feeling on fire deep within my belly. "They drink this stuff all the time?"

Mrs. Claus returns to her wicked witch cackle as she watches me. "Indeed."

I drop to the floor. "Whoa." It hits me. At least I found a description for it. "Tastes like dirt. I mean, if you could transform dirt into a liquid and make it into alcohol, it your moonshine would be the taste in my mouth."

"Not a bad description. But wait another minute." Mrs. Claus closes her eyes, savoring the taste or the moment.

I try to survive it.

We sit in silence for a while when another revelation comes to me. I get why they drink it. I mean, from what she said, it starts with poverty. In America if you drink Old Milwaukee or Busch beer, or grab a Colt 45, it's a lot of times because of being poor. Or drink the crap out of a plastic bottle, which my mother does. The Romanians produce this moonshine on the down low and inexpensive. So I get the cost factor from her brief description.

I do, however, tingle with a wonderful sensation of inebriation. Drunk. Or at least already very, very buzzed. Only shot's worth, and I achieve this blissful state. Makes the dirt taste and burning of every organ in my body worth it. It would take a six pack of Santa beer to reach this state of nirvana, this fast.

"Nice, isn't it?"

I nod. I almost think I may appreciate her, but I remember she's a witch and a vampire. So best be careful. Still, she hates Santa as much as I do. And she can't be all bad, if she shared this wicked firewater with me.

Mrs. Claus grabs my shot glass, refills both, and hands it back to me. "This will make the story go down better. At least for me. Might as well join me in inebriation."

"To getting fucked up," I toast.

We each toss back another round of the Romanian firewater.

"Stop cussing."

Since the alcohol starts to take hold, I get a little bolder with her too. Her good spirit relaxes me from the terror I started with in here. "You know, it's hard to keep up with you Christmas vampires. Do you have any idea what we elves put up with? Slavery, sure. That's the worst. But I mean, given our condition in life, you'd think we could rely on a few things. But no. You two throw wrinkles at us at every turn."

Mrs. Claus returns to her rocker and motions for me to sit in a lounge chair across from her, which I do. "Do not lump me in with him. What are you talking about?"

"Your issue with my potty mouth. I own it, by the way. I cuss up a storm, like a drunken sailor, my grandma used to say. It relieves the tension around here. It's who I am. And it baffles me a blood-sucking witch would take issue with it. See what I mean? The other day, I'm chatting away and Santa goes apeshit because I mention Adolf Hitler. He's offended by the dude. Hates him. Don't get me wrong, so do I. He killed my people too. Tried genocide, which is not cool. But my point is Santa goes around killing the innocent too. With no moral qualms. It's exhausting. That's what I'm saying here. One minute he's offing people, the next minute he reprimands me for referencing a bloody dictator. Now, I don't mean to compare you to Santa or genocide or a dictator. But you're a witch, he told me so. And you became a vampire. So you feed off human blood. How could I predict cussing would offend you?" I take a huge breath and settle back in the chair. I almost ask for another shot, but more burning alcohol would make me catatonic. Better wait.

Mrs. Claus smooths her dress in front of her. The corners of her mouth almost curl into a smile. "He warned me you could exasperate anyone. Even him. Yet he also said you have a certain charm. I see what he means. You forget yourself, often, given your precarious existence. Still, I'm drawn to you in the oddest way." She smiles.

It unnerves me a bit, because she glances over, a hunting cougar glaring at her prey. Not the animal either. "Um, yeah. You know I don't go that way, right? No offense or anything. Just a preference. Though I never liked calling it a preference because it implied a choice on my part. Orientation, however, sounds clinical."

"Stop." Mrs. Claus holds up her hand. "I didn't mean anything of the sort. I detest sex and always have."

"Quite a relief." I wipe sweat from my brow. Interesting, she shuns it Santa style. I wonder if the vampire transformation de-sexes them, if such a word exists.

"I meant nothing more than to indicate my appreciation for why he chose you for this task. And I think you and I will get along."

I still wonder about the cougar thing but keep it to myself. "You wouldn't want to let me in on the meaning, would you? The task thing? Because as far as he informed me, I get to learn this shit—I mean stuff, for no real reason."

"I wish I could tell you more. I can't. But I will offer you one piece of advice."

"Cool. What?"

"While you may fool Santa, I know what goes on here. He thinks he commands everything. He forgets he leaves. And when he leaves, I have free reign to move throughout the North Pole. I know you're transcribing his story to expose him. I won't tell him, on one condition."

She makes me sweat again. Even Trixy and Hedgehog don't know the secret journal exists. "What?"

"You tell my story too. Without embellishment. Exactly as I impart it to you. Understand? I may be a beast like him, but you and I share imprisonment. If you get this manuscript out to the public, they will know my story. Try to give it a little empathy, if you will. It's not always easy to be a woman on this planet."

"If I can simplify—because you launched pretty big words at me there—you won't rat me out with my secret history of Santa and everything going on up here, as long as I include your story. The truth, and make you look good?"

She almost nods but shakes her head. "I don't need you to doctor it on my account. The truth will do."

"Right. But there's different versions of the truth, you know? Depending on who writes it and how?"

"I suppose."

"So you want bra-burning feminism in there too?"

Mrs. Claus rolls her eyes and looks away from me. It takes a minute or two before she engages me again. "You prove my point. Be fair to me and women. You'll understand better after you hear my past. Dispense with the misogyny. I'd never sit down with Rush Limbaugh to explain this, so don't impersonate him."

See? Complicated. She knows I'm a sarcastic fuck and accepts most of it. Except the cussing, and the nasty feminism comments. "Well, to set the record straight, again I'm not sure straight is a word I should use and no pun intended— I'm on board with the women's rights movement. Always have been. Sorry, the bra comment was out of line. I was goofing around. Back to those conditions: I agree to them. You want to see the part about you before I finish?"

She smiles. "I'll see it with or without your permission. You may assume as much, if you get to the point of releasing this little project, I sanctioned it."

"Ah, you're like a spy up here at the ole Pole."

"Of a sort."

"Cool. Um, before we begin, can I get another shot of your shit?"

"Not yet. I'll keep you nice and lubricated, trust me. But carefully so, to avoid your getting sick or losing focus. And again, please stop cussing."

I scratch my brow, more as a stall tactic than because of any itch. "I don't know if I can promise to turn it off. The F-bombs and shit fly out against my will. See! It just happened. I'm constructing a sentence to talk about the cussing without cussing, but right in the middle of it, shit lands against my will. See! There it is again! Shit all over! I was concentrating on not saying fuck, when shit slipped in without my knowing it."

Mrs. Claus laughs. Good. Maybe I broke her down a little. "I come from a Southern, gentile background. Your colorful language offends my sensibilities, regardless of my current state of being. But you do amuse me, Simon. I'll admit you humor me. I can overlook a bit of your language if you'll at least attempt a bit of decorum otherwise."

I hop out of the chair, straighten my little jacket, and give her the best impersonation of a nineteenth-century bow I can muster. I must look ridiculous, stumbling from the moonshine making it even worse.

Mrs. Claus claps her hands and laughs. "Very well. Shall we begin?"

Feeling a little embarrassed at my display, which had more to do with the demon rum than anything else, I climb back into the chair and sit back. "Yeah. Fire away."

"I don't wish to dwell on my early days, or much of my human life."

I expect her to continue, but she falls dead silent. Challenging me to ask questions? Done already? I don't know her well enough to read the situation, which leaves me speechless too. I squirm in my seat. These vampires and their issues. Hard to keep up with them.

The silence drags on for months. I can't stand it. "You and Santa, interesting."

She arches a brow.

"He did the same fucking thing to me." I cough. "Sorry. The same thing to me. Got hot and bothered to tell me his story, then wants to launch ahead of the stuff that preceded his vampire life. As if it didn't matter. Still, when he spilled it at last, it mattered a lot. A shit load a lot. Oops. A lot, more than a lot. Do you know he was a serial killer? Hannibal Lecter with the fava beans and Chianti? *Before* he even got to the vampirism."

Mrs. Claus nods. Still not giving me a very clear signal. She gets out of her chair and moves toward the distillery. She pours a shot, throws it back, and fills two more glasses. She brings one to me, and this time we toast as we drink up.

"Whoa!" I yell as the burn runs down my throat. I swear it chars a line right to my anus. "Whew. Well, thanks for that."

She jerks her head in acknowledgment and sits back down.

She pauses a moment but looks right into my eyes. "I understand your point. Yet I don't agree with the comparison to him one bit. Our stories have almost nothing in common. He tried to conceal his because of its morbidity and depravity. He spent two centuries concocting this asinine Santa image and crafting himself into the perfect vampire with the perfect ruse. The stuff of legend! The awe of modern society. But if they discover his past as nothing more than a two-bit serial killer getting lucky with eternal life, it diminishes the aura, don't you think?"

"Indeed. I guessed all along such an explanation as to why he tried to keep mum. So I take it you never did any killing. Before the vampire thing?"

"Not directly."

"Suspicious. And dodgy." I smile when she grins.

"If I agree to give you the cliff notes version of my human life, will you promise to leave it at there? I'll be as thorough as I wish, but not a lot of details. Otherwise we skip right over it to the night he created me."

"Sounds like a Biblical thing, him creating you. Wouldn't it be better if you say you tricked him into it?"

She claps her hands together. "See! Your style suits me. Do we have an agreement?"

"You don't leave me much of a choice. But here's the thing. I assume you've gathered that keeping my mouth shut and going by the rules never was my thing. So, if I blurt out a question or two, tell me you won't answer. Don't get pissy about it, like he does. I'll try to understand your desire for privacy, if you can accept my stupidity and mouth problems."

Again she smiles. I may break her down. "Agreed. For the record, as I begin, it has nothing to do with privacy, except I suppose we Southerners always did value such a thing. It has more to do with the pain of the situation and not wanting to remember."

This time I let the silence hang because it seems the right thing to do. Her admission takes a moment to sink in, at least for me. Goes back to being a Southern woman, I'd gather. Even if she was a witch.

"Here's what I'll tell you. I was born in North Carolina to a very aristocratic family. In Mebane, as you may recall from what I hear he told you. We lived a life of luxury. Or, should I say, that's the public image and what the family wanted everyone to believe. And the tale was true for my father and brothers. It was true for almost every aristocratic Southern gentlemen.

"For women, life proved much harsher. We lived at the behest of men. Fathers. Brothers. Husbands, if we married. And then sons. We had none of the freedom. The luxury imprisoned us in decorum and proper behavior. In clothing to bind us. Unless one of those men who controlled you chose to unbind it, with or without your consent."

She has me worrying here. This sounds more human, more deep, than anything I hear from Santa. I sit without making a sound again while her mind drifts away. She returns to the moment, though I swear the trickle of a tear forms in her eye.

"In terms of my unbinding, my father saw to it to teach me the ways of the world. And my two brothers after him. Ruined, I had nothing to look forward to but the life of a spinster. And spinster I became, even with moving to my own house, with my own slaves, and interacted with those men only as expected."

A lump hangs in my throat. Deeper even than I anticipated. And fucking depressing. What the fuck does one say after hearing miserable, shitty tragedy? I mean, like she said, no need to prolong this miserable story. No wonder she refuses to relive it in the telling. Worse, I imagine oodles of women suffering a similar fate, over and over and over. Almost makes Santa slavery into a better deal. Except all the killing we get to help facilitate and witness, of course.

"I get why you kept that one to yourself. Sorry I pried so hard."

She tilts her head, and a slight smile forms again. "I appreciate your words. So we covered my human self. Are you satisfied?"

I almost agree, but one thing sticks in my mind. Maybe two. It takes me a second to ponder whether to go there or not. I don't want to push it. Or pick at this, because it depresses the hell out of me. Still, she left a couple key gaps.

As if reading my mind, she kind of presses her lips together and looks at me with sympathy. "Go ahead."

"Thanks." I twiddle my thumbs a couple minutes before continuing. "Two things. Okay?"

"Fine."

"The witchcraft, and the earlier reference to 'not directly' killing as a human. Seems important to our story."

"The witchcraft comes first. The killing second."

"Makes sense, because I bet they relate."

"And you don't have to worry. This story won't send you into the doldrums. I'm rather fond of the ending. The killing proves rather charming. Nothing like the serial-killer-come-Santa, I assure you."

I kick back farther into my chair. Strange as it seems, Mrs. Claus starts to grow on me. I think I may even appreciate her. Not Trixy or Hedgehog fondness. But she has an interesting way and doesn't seem as demonic as Santa. "I'm all ears. Were you from a family of witches? A deep, dark past I get to learn about? Perhaps Shakespeare's witches, hiding in a cave?"

She laughs this time. "No proper Southern family would harbor witches in its midst. The power came my way after I left the homestead and set up my own situation. You see, I had a great aunt, who also lived as a spinster. I've no idea why, but she was the one family member who understood me. We cared for each other. This is pure speculation, but I suspect she suffered from the same abuse. And so when she died, she infuriated my father by leaving her entire estate to me. I used the money to leave home and even had enough to combat the legal challenges my father and the rest of the family waged against me owning property.

"Once I had my own place, I almost never socialized with them, except where expected, of course. But one day, a distant niece appeared at my doorstep."

"Distant, as in from Mars? Someone you knew, or had never met? How did this person show up out of nowhere?"

Mrs. Claus holds up her hand, as if to slow me down. "You get ahead of yourself. Patience, dear boy. It's not as if we have anywhere else to be. In fact, so long as he knows we do his bidding in here, we have a reprieve from Santa's interference. Maybe I should ration out the plum brandy with more care."

Makes me giggle. "You turn it into a delicious sounding beverage, not acid running through my intestines. Anyway, sorry to go too fast. Just curious. You're right about Fat Boy leaving us alone for the time being."

Mrs. Claus nods. "I never met her before. Remember, now, even a gentile Southern family kept skeletons locked deep in the closet. In fact, the higher up the aristocracy one climbed, the more skeletons lurking in the closet. With all these philandering men running around, mistakes cropped up from time to time. It was inevitable. But remember, they possessed the power to clamp down on any embarrassments and make them disappear. It's simply that, after too many gaffes over so many years, those dark secrets will pop out of the ground when you least expect it."

"Can't be good." I smile.

Mrs. Claus, too, grins. "Indeed. Would you like to see the interaction with my niece, instead of listening to me? Santa indicated he sped things up by allowing you to witness the past. Of course, he's stupid to think you transport back to it, while any real witch understands you get to see what took place. Now, I realize he gave you no choice, and it made you a bit queasy. Still, you may enjoy meeting her. I did. Even if we only had twenty minutes together."

"That's it?" I shout. "Twenty minutes, and you learned to be a witch from an unknown niece? No fucking way."

"I assure you no intercourse took place." Mrs. Claus presses her lips together in disapproval. Oops. Didn't mean to drop the f-bomb. "However, I spoke the truth. We met for no more than twenty minutes. Thirty minutes at most. Now, do you want to see it?"

I pause. It makes it lots more interesting to witness the actual event. Then again, I almost threw up from the Santa beer. Who knows how this Romanian stuff will travel? "I'm nervous I'll blow chunks."

"Here. Take this."

Mrs. Claus hands me a little bottle she grabs off a nearby shelf. What the hell, I take it without asking any questions. If she wants to poison me, she could have done the deed already. It tastes kind of like chocolate milk. Once I get it down, nothing happens.

I hold my hands up to my side and shrug my shoulders. "Nothing."

"Good. That's how it should work."

Without any warning, Mrs. Claus snaps her fingers and transports me back in time, back to the porch where I saw Santa come upon her as a witch and transform her into a vampire, back to the Antebellum South.

SHE SITS ROCKING on the porch on a sunny afternoon, while a slave stands beside fanning her.

Makes me wonder, this slavery business. It came natural to the family and all, but I have to be careful about liking her, what with this loitering in her past. I get everyone did it back in the day. She grew up around it. Blah, blah, blah. Still, better keep my eyes open around her.

Then it hits me, a ton of bricks smack me in the face. I sit right in the corner of her porch, watching the past, with no hint of queasiness. No bile. No swallowing vomit. The chocolate concoction did the job. See, that's the Mrs. Claus contradiction I need to figure out. Slave owner, but nice to me with the magic stuff to let me witness the past without vertigo. Cool.

She rocks back and forth when a woman in an exquisite hoop skirt comes strolling down the lane with a parasol shielding her from the sun. She pauses outside the house and looks up.

"Aunt Runnel?" she asks.

I never learned her name. I knew her as Mrs. Claus, even though I know that's made-up bullshit.

Runnel leans forward and tilts her head. "I'm Runnel. But I don't know you as a relative."

"Well, you wouldn't because your brother kept a secret. May I join you for a refreshment on the porch? I would love to share my story with you."

Runnel creaks back in her chair. "I never refuse to be hospitable. What's your name, by the way?"

"Margaret."

"Well, Margaret, please join me."

Margaret climbs the steps and closes her umbrella before sitting in a chair opposite her aunt.

"Cynthia, will you get us two mint juleps, please?"

As Cynthia puts her fan down and goes inside, Margaret claps her hands together and laughs. "My mother told me I could trust you. My observations deduced it as well. But offering me a good stiff drink instead of vile tea, I adore you already."

Runnel gives a slight grin. "I keep my own house, so I figure the delights of the male folk are mine to choose when I wish, what with no man to drink it or give orders."

The women wait until Cynthia returns with a tray of two glasses and pitcher of alcohol. They sip before Margaret begins.

"I hate to cut this short. And I realize it violates decorum awful since we met a minute ago. However, if a person of any import saw us together, it would end our conversation. I'm afraid there is urgency here."

Runnel sets her glass down, half empty already. "Of course, dear. Perhaps you should explain yourself."

"Your brother, who I know raped you, also raped my mother."

"May I ask how you know so much? How can you already trust me with such information? How did you learn so much? You observed me?"

"In time." Margaret takes the second sip of her drink. "Let me give the background, first?"

Runnel nods without comment.

"Do you remember poor Agatha?"

"The invalid down the road? Poor dear, had no hope for a future. But a kind soul."

"And my mother." Margaret pauses to allow the news to settle.

"My brother raped her? I wish I could say it surprises me."

"After my birth, he and his concubine raised me in the city. His concubine did it. Until later in life, I knew her as my mother. She told me the truth when I came of age. Despite his keeping her safe and well off, she despised him and plotted her revenge through me."

"You mean Agatha, or his concubine?"

"I never met my birth mother. Agatha means nothing to me, other than another poor creature victimized by the fiend and the vessel who brought me into being."

Runnel nods understanding. "Please, continue."

"My mother waited until my sixteenth birthday and revealed it to me, about my birth mother and her condition. His bringing me as a newborn to her, ordering her to raise me as her own. His forcing himself upon her and occasionally bringing others to join. She also knew you and the entire family. She liked you, having studied you from afar."

Runnel refills her glass. "You have now made two allusions to spying upon me, as if you possess the eye of God. I must insist you explain."

Margaret smiles. "My mother knew witchcraft." Again she gives a dramatic pause.

Runnel plays it, almost without reacting. "Rumors always had it the slaves practice such things. I assume this woman who raised you was a former slave? Or at least a free black?"

"Free, yes. A mixed-race person."

"I see."

"My father knew the witchcraft was practiced and hired a voodoo priest to counter anything she attempted against him or his family. She bided her time, and after revealing the truth to me, took me to her mentor, and she taught me everything and more. I became an even more powerful witch than my mother, despite my naïve father never suspecting a thing."

Runnel's eyes lit with recognition. "My brother didn't die from falling off a horse during a hunting chase, did he?"

Margaret shakes her head. "I tortured him, making him see demons. Snakes coiled around him. He never suspected I might come for him. He feared my mother but became careless because his voodoo priest incapacitated her against him. He never imagined she could teach me on the sly. So when he arrived one night, I unleashed the full fury of my power. He fled from our home, terrified of the beasts hunting for him. He raced away on his horse until he saw a dreadful winged lion rear up and roar in his face. He lurched back and flew off the horse. I often wonder if he died of fright before bashing his head against a rock."

Hoping Mrs. Claus won't take offense, I have to laugh a bit at this scene. Margaret described this haunting, this bewitching, in the most casual voice imaginable. They could sit there chatting mundane reflections on the weather, in terms of the tone and inflection. Must be a Southern thing.

Runnel smiles again. "A most charming end to him. I must say, I rather enjoyed the news of his demise. Did you come to tell me this story? That alone makes our acquaintance worth the wait."

"No. There's more. I want the entire family ruined. Except for you. As I mentioned, I observed all of you with my power. I only like you. And, well, your aunt who left you this estate. I almost proceeded with killing my uncle and grandfather when I thought, perhaps, it more proper for me to offer you the task?"

Runnel sets her glass down, hiding well whether the offer surprises her in any way. She contemplates for a minute. "What if we did it together? Right now?"

Margaret beams at her aunt. "Delightful."

Something transpires between them well above my pay grade. As in, I have no clue how to explain it. Because they sit there, sipping those drinks, Runnel rocking back and forth, without speaking a word. Again it appears as a charming Antebellum scene, with no hint of the power charging through the air.

I know they accomplished their task through magic when they finish, because Runnel has a different presence about her. Again, if you saunter by and tilt your hat her way, she looks as always. A Southern woman on her porch. Glance more closely, and you see the alteration. The gleam in her eye. The fierce expression behind the soft smile.

"What shall we do?" Margaret asks.

"I imagine castration, followed by bleeding to death."

Margaret laughs. "Marvelous! Do you want to do the honors?"

"I insist we do it together."

I watch a scene from any corny witch movie you could imagine. They lean forward, and between them, a bubble appears. Two men sit chatting in a sitting room. With no warning, a force lifts them in the air, strips off their pants, and hacks off their testicles. Makes me reach down to grab my own, to ensure no one snips them off too. The two men float, suspended in the air, until they die. I should add it looks a lot more gruesome than my words depict, with the blood oozing down their legs and pooling on the floor. Their bodies turn blue. Yuck. The witches drop them to the floor, and the bubble vanishes.

And the past vision too.

MRS. CLAUS SITS before me, back in her North Pole prison, rocking, as centuries ago she greeted her niece on the porch.

"She left afterward. I never saw her again. I hear tell she ended up in Boston with a wealthy husband and two happy children."

I smile despite myself. Maybe hanging with Santa the vampire jades me too much. Because nothing repulses me in this tale. Or worries me. Or anything. I enjoyed it. Her revenge in particular.

"Cool," I say. "Can we toast to it?"

"I'd love to." Mrs. Claus gets up and readies two more shots, then brings one over to me. We clink the glasses together and swallow more clear-brandy-come-acid.

"Shit!" I yell and claw at my throat. The burn tingles through my body and feels real good. "So, uh, I like your story. Good stuff. Better than Santa's junk. Thanks for sharing. But your labeling of the killing as indirect seems off."

"I wasn't even in the room."

That makes me laugh. "A technicality, I suppose. Still, they don't die without your sorcery."

"My niece planned to kill them either way. I see your point. But I insist without my presence in the room, the crime remains indirect. Even modern criminal investigating techniques would find nothing to tie me to the crime."

"Right you are. We'll agree to disagree regarding the indirect thing. But, uh, thanks again for telling me."

"Remember our deal."

"Yeah. No problem. Listen, I don't think I even need to doctor the story to achieve the goal. People will eat it up. It's good for up until Santa comes. Well, except how you saw him coming. How does that play into all this?"

Mrs. Santa laughs. "My premonition was much ado about nothing. I played it up to him after he arrived to try to gain leverage or scare him a bit. Going against a vampire presents insurmountable odds. Even with my witchcraft, how could one know in advance if it worked against a vampire? I wanted any and every advantage against him I could muster and figured I could win with intellect."

"You mean you didn't see him coming before he got there?"

She shakes her head. "No, I did. But not with the force or power I alluded to him. I was toying with him."

Her comment makes me laugh harder. Not the snobbery, but the truth of it. Mrs. Claus can dance circles around Santa, who uses more brute strength and intimidation than cunning.

"So I let him know from the beginning I had powers he couldn't imagine. And it was true, despite my embellishments. You saw what we did to my father. But if he attacked me from the first, I doubt I could have warded him off.

"However, I did see him coming long before he got there. It's the witch's eye. I could portend the future but on rare occasions, and with the vaguest of senses in terms of what may come my way. The window into what will come controls itself. In other words, a witch cannot manipulate it or demand to see what she wants, when she wants. Oh, no. It chooses the times and places to offer it to you. I had a vision, soon after my niece granted my power, of an eternal life-form visiting me. Mind you, this rather ambiguous phrasing explains what I knew, which wasn't much. It could have been an angel. An object. A ghost. Or, as it turns out, a vampire. I also foretold how it could either destroy me or grant its power to me."

"Wait!" I lean forward, fascinated by this part of the story. "That's power, to see the future. You still got it?"

Mrs. Claus shakes her head. "I lost a few abilities in the conversion. Thankfully, he doesn't have it either."

"Did you use a crystal ball?"

"No." Mrs. Claus frowns. "And there weren't any flying monkeys either."

I snort. "Funny. Got ya. But I didn't reference Dorothy and the gang. You're not green. Or ugly. I can't speak for the mean part, but I suppose you aren't too worried about it. So how did you see the future?"

"In visions. I could sit there, glancing at the sunset one minute, and the world would go dark, and shadows and ideas swept through my mind to give me these ideas. Or they came to me in dreams. This one, with the eternal creature, came to me multiple times, and in multiple forms. This kind of attention meant it possessed monumental consequences."

I almost lose focus on her story, because the Romanian fire water hits me. I relax. Slump even more into the comfortable chair. Feels real good. Still, I best remember a vampire sits in front of me, even if we become pals of sorts. "You lived a few years as a witch, controlling your own destiny, managing your own house. Beating your own slaves."

"I never beat them," she interrupts with a stern voice.

"I tested you. You passed." Not really, because she still owned them. But better to appease her than risk pissing her off right when we hit it off so well.

"I suggest you dispense with the testing. You mentioned the mean aspects of the Wicked Witch and how it may or may not relate to me. I doubt you want to learn. Remember, I killed those who crossed me in life, even if it was indirect, and became a vampire with no qualms about my feeding habits. You and I have established a nice repartee. I would hate to damage it."

"Sorry. At least I didn't cuss this time, right?" I got her to smile again. "Back at it. Where were we? I think we got to the point where Santa saunters down the street one day. Right?"

"Precisely. I had no idea the time of the vision had arrived until I saw him. His shadowy figure lurked along the sidewalk, moving in a funny way. I believe he already told you the story of my making."

I giggle again. "Yeah. Lied at first, to try to hide how you got one up on him. But his story didn't add up, so I called him on it and he told me the truth. Pretty clever. Wish I could get him like that."

"Maybe someday."

I almost follow-up on her mysterious comment but decide better of it. Her expression stifles any comment. As a teacher warns a student not to say one more thing, or a mom giving the final warning glance before a major time-out in the corner. Or, if we flash back to my childhood, a firm swat on the rear. Serves as a good reminder, too, to think hard before getting too close to her.

"So, Santa makes you a vampire at the same moment you make him a witch. Did you leave Mebane right away?"

"Yes. Another vampire already lived in the area. I had no choice."

"Off you went, a witch vampire to explore the world, huh?"

"Yep."

"Oh, wait!" I almost fall out of my chair with excitement. "Can I ask more questions about his version of the exchange? To clarify?"

Mrs. Claus nods.

"He said you begged to become a vampire because you were old and dying. True?"

Mrs. Claus rolls her eyes. "A total exaggeration. I was older, but not infirm or near death. Who knows how many years remained? But nothing portended an imminent demise. When I sensed his vampire nature, well, who wouldn't want eternal life?"

"It might give people pause to think they'll drink human blood the rest of their lives. You know, anyone with a moral compass. I mean, come on with the Anne Rice vampire shit and killing the deserving or drinking animals. You're all cold-blooded murderers. Even if you off evil peeps, that's still controlling the death penalty and killing."

"I meant it more as a rhetorical question than to get you going again."

"Got it. My lips are shut." I motion to zip them closed, but they open again. "So, you weren't desperate and dying?"

"No. But I was desirous of avoiding my eventual demise. What other nonsense did he tell you?"

"It freaked him out when you mentioned destroying the entire town with the sweep of a hand. I think you warned him with it, or at least wanted him to understand what you could offer in return. You downplayed your ability when you explained it to me, but if you could wipe out the town, you're a fucking powerful witch."

She stares daggers at me.

"I ask to strike the fucking from the record." I grin, hoping my retraction pleases her.

"Better."

I smile again. "I'm trying."

"Regarding the destruction of the town, that holds truth, and an exaggeration. If I marshaled my power and concentrated, I might conjure up a storm or flood to decimate the town. Certain methods could make a bold attempt at it. It would take more than the wave of my hand." She waves it to demonstrate, and I duck, which makes her cackle. "I gave him a half-truth on in order to intimidate him."

"What about the lightning bolt you shot at him?"

Mrs. Claus laughs hard this time. It takes her a few seconds to regain her composure as she wipes at a tear in her eye. "I forgot. Why, yes, I did incapacitate him with a slight electrical charge. Serves him right, preying on innocent Southern women and trying to trick them. Coming after my declaration of power over a small town, it might have scared him a tad."

"His version of the episode comes pretty close to the truth. I mean, once he admitted the real version. You went your separate ways afterward, but not forever, huh?"

Any joviality evaporates in a nanosecond. "Too true. I went to Europe for a time, as I mentioned earlier."

"To find your space."

"Limited options remained by the time he converted me. Ironic, as I mentioned earlier, that by the 1800s it became much easier to reside in parts of the world where the scientific revolution vanquished belief in us. In Romania, they still believed. You tested your luck there against people who still hunted for you. However, with so much of the globe already controlled, I set out for Romania when a kinder vampire than most suggested I could find space there after I wandered into her territory in Mexico."

"Huh. Fascinating. Did you meet Vlad the Impaler?"

"He's dead. And not a real vampire."

"Too bad, because it makes one badass story."

"Well, his human life makes a bad enough story. Note how one can say the same thing without the use of a derogatory term for human body parts."

"Even 'ass' offends you?"

"Offend seems too strong. I prefer a gentler discussion."

"Got it. Anything else I need to know about your time in Romania? Or did you creep around the countryside, drink dirt water, and kill people?"

"I drank from humans when needed but wanted to avoid any cause for alarm. I think I spent more time tapping their distilleries and figuring out how to manufacture plumb brandy than murdering the peasants. I enjoyed my time as a free vampire with a territory. The power. The thought of eternal life. It was a charming region of the world."

"Plus the witchcraft helped too? I mean, you must have made one bad a-" I choke on my own spit in order to swallow the two s's. "One bad vampire."

"I warded off any vampire competition with little trouble. The sorcery assisted my concealment from the people too. It gave certain advantages over the mere power and nocturnal habits of a typical vampire. I amused myself with magic to alleviate the loneliness."

"Never thought of that. I mean, you get to live forever but by yourself. Lonely existence, could suck."

"It's not for everyone. Many vampires extinguish themselves because of it. I doubt despair would've happened to me. I rather enjoy being alone. A solitary life would trump imprisonment in this ice palace. And, as I said, Romania is one of the most beautiful countries imaginable. I loved being lost in such an old world."

Sounds like a Hallmark moment, except she downplays the death. I decide to keep this thought to myself. No need to provoke her when we have a good thing going. "Then Santa returned, right? Fucked the whole thing up?"

"If only my witchcraft gave me a warning. He took me by surprise."

"Was he Jolly Ole Saint Nick? Or still John Wayne Gacy of the nineteenth century?"

"I never saw him until they took me high atop a mountain and strapped me in his sleigh. By then, he looked all Santa Claus again. I realized his true person after he spoke. I recognized his voice. It made sense at that moment. Oh, those idiots."

I scratch my head. "I think I missed something. Could be the alcohol. I lost track of your story. What idiots?"

"Forgive my reminiscing. It was my fault this time. Let's go back, but first, we need another shot." Mrs. Claus serves up two more rounds, looking a little tipsy herself now, and settles back into her rocker. "Better. Takes the edge off."

I wonder if vampire magic and Santa elf doctors can recreate my intestines, because this stuff burned them away. I doubt my innards remain. But if I must die this way, it provides a great buzz, even better than downing a bunch of Santa beer. However, I must concentrate a little harder to hear her. Well, not hear her so much as follow her logic. Not because she doesn't make sense, but because I'm getting fucked in the head.

"I'll back up and explain. I walked down the road, enjoying a beautiful fall evening, when I fell flat on my face without warning, incapacitated. Like I had a stroke or heart attack. One minute, everything was fine, the next, I lost complete control over myself. Seconds later, a coven of witches emerged from the forest. At least twenty of them, maybe more. Their combined power overcame my own, even with the vampire strength mixed in. My head whirled in a million directions, trying to figure out how they found me and what they wanted. I didn't even know any of them.

"When they began chanting, I panicked and screamed out, but nothing came from my mouth. I knew their spell, given their collective forces, would enslave me to them. Or, in this case, to another witch. Still, witches so seldom did this to one another. It took too much energy. And what are the chances of so many witches and warlocks coming together against one of their own, for no reason? It made no sense to me. I had nothing to do but ponder this until they dragged me up the mountain and threw me into his sleigh.

"They struggled to sit me up so I could see. I sat right there, in the passenger seat, so to speak, bewildered and angry but powerless. I glanced out the corner of my eye and saw Santa. I knew of the Santa legend, but he did not come with the same acclaim in this rural part of the world and during this century. His commercialization had begun in America at the time, nowhere else. But his strange appearance and costume made my capture more frightening. Even before I knew who captured me, I could tell something bizarre and awful was unfolding. As I said, when he spoke it all came to me."

Mrs. Claus pauses. She seems to struggle here.

"I should have known. I should have kept my defenses up. I thought he would accept our exchange of power. But no. Of course not."

"He convinced a bunch of witches to kidnap you? How?"

"Oh, we're back to the idiots. He showed them his vampire power and promised to deliver it to them. In fact, that's why I heard his voice. I thought I recognized it, but couldn't place it right away. They surrounded the sleigh, and one demanded their payment. Said they agreed to deliver me in exchange for his converting them into vampires." She rolls her eyes. "He did his stupid 'Ho! Ho! Ho!' laugh, got out of the sleigh, and asked them to line up. Oh, but he had learned since he confronted me. Too fast for them to realize it, he raced down the line of them and snapped their necks. He pretended to drink from the first few and claimed they fell to the ground limp as they converted and would awaken. He moved fast, and by the end, when the last two attempted escape, he drank from them and dropped their bodies to the ground. Dupes, all of them. Unscrupulous dupes. If they had an ounce of sense or had taken any precautions, their collective energy could have at least done what I did to him and forced the exchange. Or they could have put my enslavement under their control until he changed them. He hoodwinked the entire lot of them."

When she goes silent, I decide to clarify. "A bunch of witches wanted to become vampires, right? So he sells them on using their ability to get you, then betrays them? Just like that?"

"Just like that."

"Wow. Plays into my theory on humanity. A bunch of stupid dumb fucks." Dammit. People. Why not say people? Except they were dumb fucks, not mere people. But now I lobbed another fuck at her by mistake. "Sorry."

"I think this time I may agree with your use of the word."

"Cool." I smile. "You said you knew it was him when he spoke, not before when he killed them? I thought he talked to them first."

"He did, and the voice sounded familiar, but it had been a while and I didn't recognize it." She shakes her head. "No.

I confronted another vampire. But his ridiculous suit disguised him. With the dead strewn about, he climbed back in the sleigh, whipped at the reindeer to go, and we flew into the air. Scared me to death."

"Yeah," I laugh. "Still scares the, uh, poop, out of me." Whew. Avoided cussing.

"Once we got well above Earth, he released me from the paralysis. I moved my head, looked around, and wiggled my toes and fingers. But when I tried to use magic against him, nothing worked. He laughed at me. I even attempted to jump out of the sleigh. I could get up, lean over, but the minute I pushed to jump away, a force snapped me back into my seat. He grinned, glanced at me, and said, 'Hello, Runnel.'"

A totally sucky part of this story. I think even worse than my enslavement. Whoa. Poor thing. I mean, she was a blood-sucking vampire witch. I know. Still, nasty moment for her.

"I think I blacked out because he had me, and I knew it. He tricked them into enacting the magic, the idiots handed me and control over to him and thought he would live up to his end of the bargain. Instead, they died and left everything to him. I awoke in this chamber, and in this outfit."

Despite myself, I laugh. She looked nothing like Mrs. Claus in life, or as a vampire. He kidnaps her and she wakes up here with a new appearance. Funny. Even she smiles and laughs a little. I figure I get a little pass on the humor, given my transformation to being an elf sucked bigger balls.

"I did not laugh at the time. However, I do understand the humor."

"Yeah, and in fairness, at least you remain your original size in life. Not pint size."

"Very true."

"Did he explain anything once you got here? What did he say?"

Mrs. Claus sighs. "He told me everything. First, he went into a long, drawn-out tale about his brilliance in co-opting the Santa legend for himself and building upon it. I did laugh at him in his ridiculous uniform until I realized I wore the same thing against my will. Then he got to the point. I was a threat to him so long as I remained free. Another vampire with the same powerful sorcery existed who could challenge him. So he imprisoned me."

"Do you think he was still pissed because you became a vampire? I mean, yeah, he wanted to be king of the vampires. True. But don't you think he also had a hard-on because of how you tricked him?"

"Please, stop with the colorful language. That's an image I don't need in my head."

It pops into my mind and out my mouth without a choice. Part of my brain screams to shut the fuck up. This will not go well. The other part has to know. She brought it up. Mine was a euphemism; she makes it literal. So I say it and brace for the anger. "Speaking of Santa's hard-on, since you two have the illusion of marriage and all, did you consummate anything?"

Wham! Without Mrs. Claus moving so much as a finger, I fly across the room, slam into the wall, and drop to the floor, a limp rag doll unceremoniously deposited there. I regain my senses and crawl back to my chair. It takes a minute to shake off the pain and climb back in, the alcohol coursing through my veins making it worse. "Sorry," I whisper.

"Apology accepted. And, no."

"Good. I worried about, you know, rape or an awful occurrence. A flashback to your early life, not good."

"It was a distinct possibility. Except he seems asexual. Aroused more by the killing than anything, don't you think?"

Her ire disappears. Flung me across the room, now back to normal conversation, even commenting on what pissed her off in the first place. She's as complex as Santa.

"Yeah. Makes sense. No sex for Santa. Thankfully, for all of us."

"Indeed. Now, I believe he will soon retrieve you. Is there anything else for us to cover? Do you have any more questions?"

I glance at the ceiling, wondering if I need more information. "I assume you don't play into the Santa nonsense? I mean, he forced you into the dress and white hair and bun. But, you don't go around playing as Mrs. Claus like him, do you?"

"No. Ridiculous."

"So no baking cookies and stuff?"

"Do you ever see me wandering around with a tray of cookies for the good little elves?"

"You come out when he leaves."

"I do need stimulation but detest being anywhere near him. Since he brought me to the North Pole, he leaves me alone in my quarters to do as I please."

"I see what you mean." I point to the headless gingerbread man in her pocket.

She giggles and put her fingers over her lips to suppress it. "I do enjoy my gingerbread, even though I need blood and nothing more for sustenance. However, I beheaded this one and placed him there as a prop, in case you tested me too much. I had no idea what to expect, what with Santa's description of you."

"Funny. Scare me with a headless cookie. It worked. I mean, I was kinda alarmed by it at first."

"Well, it gets boring up here, with no obligations and nowhere to go."

Her comment prompts another question. What the hell does she do every day, locked in here? I sat with her for quite a while, listening to her story, but never wonder what she does daily until now. At least we elves, as good slaves, perform tasks and other assignments as instructed. So I ask. "What do you do all day?" Note, I manage to keep from even adding "the hell" when I voice the question. I can learn.

"Not much." She smiles, at what I have no idea. "Unlike you elves and how busy he keeps you. Even the poor reindeer work. I have no duties. No assignments. He keeps me here to protect his supremacy as the ultimate vampire. I can watch television, any station in the world. I've become quite an aficionado of American professional sports; football is my favorite. I record every game and watch them in their entirety."

"Even the total blowouts don't get boring?"

"No. At times it quite amuses me to see the utter humiliation."

She let on to her sadistic side again. Better change the subject. "The lesbians would love you." Dykes would party with Mrs. Claus. Not so much with the gay boys.

"I'm sure they would. Which reminds me I have several WNBA games to catch up on. I also interact with the elves from time to time when Santa leaves. And I have an assortment of other hobbies. Reading. I adore reading many types of literature. Otherwise, not much. I keep from getting bored, because I would rather survive and enjoy my imprisonment as much as possible to spite him."

I hesitate for a second, worrying my next question will set her off. But what the hell. "Ever try to release yourself from the spell? Try to get away?"

Her eyes light with excitement. "You discovered another one of my hobbies!" The smile disappears. "But to no avail. Still, I keep trying."

She lets her statement linger, done telling about her life. I stifle the urge to ask her to take me with her, if she ever gets away. Seems intrusive. Or maybe too hopeful.

We sit in silence for a few minutes with nothing else to say. I ran out of questions or stupid things to let fly. I feel badly for her. In many ways, she's one of us. When a little red light illuminates near the fireplace, she gets up.

"I appreciated our time together. Thank you for listening."

Without a chance to reply, I find myself back in the long, black hallway, the torches relit, and I move toward the door against my will.

Santa opens it and ushers me out. "Enjoy your time with the bitch?"

"You're an asshole."

"Brilliant, Simon. Did you just figure that out? Now come, I have an appearance tonight and need Rudolph with me, but he's insisting on your presence beforehand." He points at my feet. "I see you found boots."

Chapter Five: Rudolph

AFTER COMMENTING ON my new and nasty glow-in-the-dark boots, Santa spins around and hurries down the hall, so I scramble to keep up with him.

"About the boots," I say a little out of breath. "Red makes my feet look big. Can I go back to the green? Suits me better."

Santa turns a corner. When I lurch around it, I see him way down the hall. He halts with his back to me. I run so fast to catch up I skid on the ice floor and slam right into the back of his leg. I do duck my head to avoid my nose diving into Santa ass. Close call.

"Keep up, please. Didn't I say we're pressed for time? Rudolph gave us this short window of opportunity for you to learn his story or he'll refuse to talk."

We get moving again, Santa slowing at least a little so I can keep pace. "Don't forget the short fucking legs you gave me." I point to them for emphasis. "They can go only so fast. And, um, who the hell made Rudolph king? I mean, you don't take shit from anyone, but a red-nose fucker has the power to decree what he wants, when he wants? Doesn't fit Santaland protocol, if you ask me."

We arrive in the chamber where the sleigh lands and hurry across toward Rudolph's door.

"I allow him certain considerations. He presents a special case."

I snort. "Yeah, special as in deranged or crazy. Or maybe needy. A prima donna. Still doesn't explain why you allow it."

"It's complicated. Let's say he possesses a special place in my heart." Santa stops in front of the door to Rudolph's place.

"Bestiality? Santa, that's gross. Are you two an item? Hiding the old pole in a reindeer ass, are you? Not my scene; for sure. What's it called? A beast fetish?"

Santa stares at me, his blue eyes turning to black, his lips pressed together. He says nothing, so I stare at the ground and hope he lets it slide because of this urgency he keeps mentioning. I glance up and point to the door. "Something tells me this won't be as fun as Mrs. Claus."

Santa smirks, letting my Santa's butt romp with Rudolph go with the visual transformation warning.

"You reminded me." Santa reaches into his coat pocket and pulls out a pretty big flask. "She said you may need this for your next interview."

He hands it to me. No need to even sniff to know she sent along a supply of the Romanian firewater to keep me company.

"Cool!" I reach out and take it, tucking the nasty stuff into my pocket. "So I can prepare myself, this will suck, right?"

Santa sighs. "Always with the questions and demands with you. It leads me to believe you'll get along well. You're as big a prima donna as him."

I jab at the sequined nameplate on Rudolph's door. "I don't have my own fucking wing of the ice palace, or prance around as Judy Garland cracked out on drugs. He gets his way with everything. I don't think he has any friends up here. Who would want to hang with him? Which makes me think. Is he a reindeer you allowed to talk by magic and implanted a glowing nose on?"

"You can ask him yourself. Please, go."

Santa raps on the door and waits. Funny again how he defers to the snotty reindeer. Everywhere else on the North Pole, Santa barges in when and where he wants. Never considered knocking on Mrs. Claus's door before he sent me in. Here, he knocks like a Mormon missionary waiting to get bitched out by the next person annoyed with his presence.

After a long pause, we hear hooves prancing along the floor, the door being unlocked, and it swings open.

There stands Rudolph, in his glory. Red nose, dim for the moment, skinny little body, tiny antlers, even after all these years.

"Ready?" Santa asks him.

"If I must. I detest this one, okay? More than most of the other elves, even. I don't see why you put up with him, okay?"

"Yeah, well the feelings—" Santa's hand clamps over my mouth before I finish, or before I launch into my diatribe.

"Humor me." Santa addresses Rudolph while still stifling me.

Rudolph steps back, so Santa shoves me from behind and I trip over the threshold and into the red-nosed reindeer's space. I fall flat on my face, sprawled out.

"You look like an uncoordinated douchebag, okay? Get up already."

I hear the door slam shut. This almost feels worse than the dungeon. Trapped with Rudolph, Polly Prissy Pants himself, and nowhere to go until Santa or he determines he's told enough of the story and releases me. I stand up, brush myself off, and stare at him.

"I knew you were too stupid to do this. Okay? How can you record my history, when you struggle to walk?"

I breathe in deeply, trying to control my temper. Nope. Useless. "Listen, shit-licking, ugly turd of a reindeer, you can make fun of me all you want, but you're the talking animal freak around here. An opera diva strutting around the place. No one even likes you. We pray the Phantom of the Opera will come along and drop a chandelier on your deformed-looking head and bust up that glow-in-the-dark nose and detonate it, a nuclear bomb right off your face. And what the fuck's with you saying 'okay' in every sentence? Dumb ass."

Rudolph turns from me, motioning with his head for me to follow. "You amuse yourself, okay? Everyone else thinks you're a dildo."

I pause before following him and take out my present from Mrs. Claus. This time, the burn feels good, knowing the buzz to follow. I need its help and ammunition against this one.

Walking along, I calm a little while I take in my surroundings.

Rudolph enjoys pretty nice digs compared to anywhere else up here. Still with the ice walls and chill atmosphere. No way to help that at the North Pole. But it appears he shops at Room and Board or an upscale furniture store in New York. Fancy shit everywhere. Contemporary. Sleek. And I swear the paintings and prints are real. As in: Monet, Picasso, Mocek. I bet stolen. At least he steals in good taste. Wonder if Santa helps him out, or if he does it on the side.

We walk into a gigantic living room, again with high-end furniture, leather and plush. The one sign of his goofiness here hangs above the fireplace. A gigantic picture of himself. As in, huge. Maybe fifteen feet long, ten feet high. The pose, resolution, and quality almost came from a professional photographer. Rudolph stands, his head held high, his nose shining bright, a winter landscape in the background with mountains and pine trees. Good to know he's not narcissistic or anything.

As I glance around at the crystal chandelier, antique side tables, and other fine art, the full force of Mrs. Santa's moonshine hits me. Loosens my tongue, lord help us.

"Nice place. Didn't expect refinement from you." I bend over and smell roses, sitting in a glass-blown vase. "I anticipated pink frilly accents, children's toys, dolls and plush bunnies. Not elegance. Nothing about you speaks elegance. Real flowers, even. Wow."

"Fuck you, okay?"

"What's with the high voice? Ever think you should try for a deeper sound? Muscle up a little, to sound more like a big, bad reindeer? Since you fancy yourself the head reindeer around here. You sound like High-Pitched Eric on the "Howard Stern Show." Or a ten-year-old little boy. At least three or four octaves too high."

"Okay, we're done. Goodbye."

"Make that ten octaves too high."

"Santa!" he screams and stamps his front hoof on the hard floor.

Oops. Why did I provoke him? Santa will kill me. How can I fix it now? Because he appears ready to let out another scream.

"Whoa, whoa, whoa, big guy! Please, stop!" I inch toward him with my hands extended in front of me, palms forward. A smile spreads across my face.

Rudolph pauses, his mouth still open and poised to let out a big holler, eyeing me before deciding if he'll continue.

"Sorry. Sorry." I wipe a bit of sweat from my brow. "Can we talk before we get him involved? See if we can make a go of it?"

Rudolph closes his mouth and lifts his chin in the air, adopting his haughty better than thou demeanor. At least he stays silent, but by no means ready to reconcile yet. It gives me a chance to breathe and plot the next thing to fall out of my mouth.

I search for a way to make this okay, but nothing comes to me. We hate each other. "Can we talk?" I catch my tongue before I add, "Before you go insane all over me." Even I recognize my jab as a sure way to get him screaming.

Rudolph glares at me. "You're a repressed pole smoker, okay? Fudge packer. Fag."

Great. Name calling to get back at me. How do I respond to this? I smile and stifle a laugh. A prissy reindeer with a red nose throwing gay slurs at me? Contains a little humor. "Sissy. Backdoor Bandit." I add to his list. Now he grins.

"Donut Puncher. Nancy Boy. Butt Pirate."

He laughs. Maybe insulting my sexuality will give us hope. Might as well continue with him. "Poo Pusher. Queen. Fairy."

"Turd Burglar. Shit Stabber."

He gets me laughing. Never heard that one before. "Twinkle Boots."

"Twinkle Boots?" He tilts his head.

"Funny take on 'twink' I heard a guy use once. So, does this mean we can talk? Or should we come up with more insults for me? By the way, you're Mr. Butch, Manly Man. No doubt you learned most of those slurs when people threw them your way."

I cringe, wondering if I went too far this time.

"You don't need to know my sexuality, okay? I don't go around advertising it to everyone. You feel such a need, not me."

"I don't wear a sign telling everyone I'm gay."

"Please." Rudolph rolls his eyes. "You want everyone to recognize your special little status as the one fairy boy up here, okay? Except you're not so special. Others choose to live out their preferences without making it a big deal."

Did he come out to me? Just my luck, I find another gay guy at the North Pole, but he's a closeted animal. And I accused Santa of bestiality. Well, let me get this straight from the beginning. Straight not the right word here, but you get my point. I am in no way attracted to him. Nada. Nothing. Gross.

"Okay. Can we get along now? Carry on with the business Santa assigned?"

Rudolph walks over and sits down. "This doesn't mean I like you, okay? Or to think we're going to become pals. You stick with the little dyke elves for your friends. We have nothing else in common. And don't go around announcing what you learned here, okay? I keep my private life private. Got it?"

I scratch my head. "Listen, I don't need to go around rapping Rudolph stories with other people. But you realize everyone knows, right? I mean, you prance around a little too lightly to think no one has a clue."

"Whatever, okay? Zip it. If this goes well, I'll let Santa bring another gay elf aboard to keep you company. Well, I might allow it."

Which surprises me. "You prohibit any more gay elves after me?"

Rudolph nods with a smug smile.

"Why?"

"Because you annoy me, okay?"

"So it's a punishment?"

Again the nod with a smart-ass smile. What a fuckwad. I take a deep breath, squashing down the barbs I want to fling at him. I still need to make this work.

He pisses me off. Not that I need other gay peeps around me to survive. In many ways, Rudolph's snit with me kept my people safe around the world, because Santa avoids targeting them for slavery because of it. So power to the people, I say. And I have friends at the North Pole and deal with being enslaved here well enough to never contemplate a relationship. True, Trixy and Hedgehog make it work, seem happier up here together than if alone. But singlehood suits me.

I do wonder if Santa kills gay people because of this Rudolph rule? I mean, what if he found someone, thought bringing them aboard as an elf was a good idea but remembers this pact with Polly Prissy Pants over there, so decides to off them because of their sexuality? So instead of protecting them, my presence became a death sentence. Of course, I also realize Santa never thought that far ahead. Never.

And here I always watched every time Santa brought a new elf aboard, wondering if he might join my ranks. But light in the hooves over there prohibited it. It annoys me. Because the elves assume we live in straight elf land, no need to concern ourselves with sexuality. Except they acknowledge the lesbians, because a few of them wander around up here. But no gay boys. So it would be nice to gain a companion for solidarity. I guess the North Pole operates a lot like the rest of the world. Makes me miss the open and affirming life I led in Chicago.

Of course, bitching Rudolph out about it and his fraidy-cat closeted life will get me nowhere. Nothing good would come from discussing it right now.

My pause gets the best of the red-nosed reindeer, because he wiggles in his seat before speaking. "I'm done with this topic, okay?" Rudolph's nose goes back in the air. Always with the body language to signal how beneath him it is to even sit in my presence.

"Whatever. Speaking of okay, are we okay now?"

Rudolph squints at me, the corner of his mouth curled in disgust. "Santa promised me a new bedroom set if I played nice with you for the afternoon and told my story. It goes against my better judgment to even sit in the same room with you, okay? Let alone allow you into my quarters. Let alone speak with you. And let alone telling you my history, okay?"

I sigh. "I get it. We're not friends. Duly noted. So let me cut to the chase. Do you want a new bedroom set, or not?"

I shut him up for a second. "What's in it for you?"

"Good question. Wish I had an answer." He glares at me in disbelief, but I tell him the truth. Other than my secret journal, which even I see as doomed to failure, I get nothing out of this but knowledge. "That's the truth. Let me explain it this way." I point to his TV. "It's like kicking back and watching Discovery Channel for a while. You learn the mating habits of penguins or how African lions fuck each other. Useless information. But interesting at the time." A thought comes to me I have to ask. "Does watching lion sex get you hot and bothered? Animal porn?"

"Santa!" Rudolph screams.

"No, no, no!" I rush over to him again. I hold out my hands to signal for him to calm down. "Sorry. I didn't mean anything by it."

He closes his mouth and motions with his head for me to return to my seat. I walk backward to it, watching for another outburst.

"Sorry," I repeat. "Just curious. Where were we?"

"You were being a shithead, and lying to me about why you're interested in my story. I still don't understand, okay? Explain the TV analogy or whatever?"

"Well, it's complicated, I suppose." I speak to stall for time. Despite my negative attitude, I gather this information for my little diary, hoping to get it out to the rest of the world to teach them the reality of Santa and everyone. That's a secret no one knows, except now Mrs. Claus, and this self-absorbed reindeer would love nothing better than for me to give him a reason to run to blab to Santa. So I need a better cover since the truth fails to work on him. Or the half-truth. "Santa offered up a bit of his story and I listened. So for whatever reason, he wants me to learn all this. I'm a slave, so I do as I'm told."

"Bullshit, okay?"

Got me. "Yeah. Bullshit. I do it because it gets me out of shoveling reindeer dung and other fucked up elf slave tasks as assigned. It's kind of interesting too. So I do it. Not as if I have a lot of other options."

Rudolph still looks skeptical.

"Listen, believe me, or not. I don't care at this point. You either want a new bedroom or you don't. Ball's in your court."

Rudolph giggles. It takes me a second before realizing he thinks it funny I said balls. Oh, brother. Next he curls up, a cute dog in front of me, but keeps his head up and pointed in my direction. "Know what I want?"

I shake my head. "No idea."

"A big sleigh bed, okay? Right now, I have this exquisite antique bed, like Louis XIV would have slept in. Ornate and carved wood. Beautiful. As you can see." He motions around the room with a hoof. "I've gravitated toward a little more modern and simple. There's a furniture store in Chicago, Walter E. Smithe, I went to the other night. They have a cottage set with a big sleigh bed I adore. I want to transform the room."

Do you know how whacked I feel at this moment? You get used to the strange and exotic up here. Flying around. Enslaved elves. Santa as a vampire. Anything and everything takes on an ordinary aura about it. You start to forget you live in bizarro world until a small thing or experience slaps you upside the head and reminds you once again of the oddness of your life as an elf slave.

That happens at this moment, listening to a talking gay reindeer ponder the new bedroom set he wants to pilfer from his favorite furniture store in Chicago, for this penthouse suite at the North Pole. I literally pinch myself, hoping to wake up back in my condo, safe and sound.

Nope. Still here. Still a lounging reindeer with a red nose in front of me.

"Sounds grand." What the fuck else am I supposed to say?

Rudolph grows quiet, his chin still high, something very interesting on the ceiling to keep his attention. I wait, thinking he will start or at least offer his agreement to our conversation. But I lost him in fairyland. Too bad he uses his talents to assist Santa, because he would make a great interior decorator. Well, if people could get over the fact of his animal-ness. Or tolerate his voice and his constant use of okay.

I reach for my flask and take a swig. Might as well keep the buzz alive, if nothing else.

"Good idea." Rudolph hops out of his chair and crosses over to a huge wooden bar along one wall. He pushes aside a sliding door and reveals a large refrigerator with glass doors. Holy shit. A stocked wine selection.

Rudolph grabs a red wine glass, opens the fridge, and takes out a bottle.

You may wonder at this point how he manages this with hooves, right? Because I think the same damn thing right. How did he open the door when I arrived? How does he maneuver around this place, which for all appearances appears as if a human lives here, when he walks on four legs and has no opposable thumbs?

I wish I could explain, but I've got nothing for you. I sit here watching him open doors, grab things, and take out a corkscrew and uncork his wine before pouring it. He holds his glass in one hoof and walks across the room on three legs before returning to his seat. I witness this scene with my own eyes. And still have no clue. Watching him carry the glass, I can explain it looks as if he glued it to the side of his hoof. Or he has a magnet installed in the hoof, and the glass has a magnet to cling to his hoof. North Pole Santa magic at work in here I assume. I hope he will explain this rather odd reality in his story.

In fact, I almost ask him about it but hesitate because we still haven't started anything yet. I decide on a little more chitchat. "Good wine?"

Rudolph's eyes grow wide with offense. "Only the best."

"Of course." Like I'm an idiot for not assuming a talking reindeer demanded the finest wines in the world.

"What do you think I do while Santa feeds himself and does his business? I acquire things. Furniture. Art. Anything I want. Including this delightful supply of wine. I'm a connoisseur."

"We're back to the thief thing, aren't we? You steal this stuff?"

"Of course!" Rudolph shrugs. "Why not? At least no one dies from what I do. Besides, I select most of this wine from the cellars of people Santa kills. They won't be around to enjoy it, so I might as well."

Strange, how the logic makes sense to me. In a trapped at the fucked-up North Pole kind of way. So I nod and sit as my own moonshine continues to soothe my nerves.

"I won't share any of it with you, okay? It's mine."

"Good enough. I got what I need." I pat the flask, now back in my pocket.

"Do you have the moonshine Mrs. Claus makes? So unsophisticated, okay?"

"A matter of taste, Snobby." Yeah, I had to release a little jab.

"You're jealous of my refinement."

Right. How did he ever guess? "Regarding your bedroom set. Did you make any decisions yet? He said we had to hurry. You were in a time snit, remember?"

Rudolph sips his wine. Funny, how refined he makes it appear for a reindeer to drink wine. "I have plans this evening, and he wants this done soon. I told him, insisted, we must accomplish it this afternoon or I'd be unavailable for at least a month, given the duties I perform for him and my other, shall we say, things. Okay?"

"I assume at some point we'll get to how it occurred that you give Santa restrictions. Because no one else around here gets by with it. Shall we?"

"In the interest of time, yes. I do want to note for the record, from the beginning of this recounting of my tale, I do it in protest, to an extent, and for the explicit reason of obtaining the bedroom set."

"Got it." I scratch my head, confused. "Why don't you steal it, like you do everything else? Why the need for Santa's approval?"

Rudolph rolls his eyes again. "He gives me free reign unless he wants more than my usual service. He blocks my plans or thwarts my efforts. In this case, he found out about my bedroom remodeling and will allow it if I speak with you. He can put a spell on my quarters or not allow the furniture onto the sleigh."

Rudolph pouts, his lower lip sticking way out. Funny.

"Understood. So I made note of your protest, or conditions, whatever you want to call them. Now, your story?"

"I've never done this before, okay? Where do we begin?"

I almost feel sorry for him for a second. Almost. He sounds lost and uncertain, not the cocky shithead of moments ago, or of all my experiences with him. Makes me wonder, we have a talking animal, so what kind of world does this reality create for him? Do the other reindeer communicate with him? Still, his isolation does not mean he has to be an asshole at every turn. So soon enough, I shove aside any compassion for the little tart.

My silence does spur me to figure out where to start.

"Let's start with what the fuck you are. Not as in, a talking reindeer up at Santa the Vampire's North Pole. I mean, animals don't talk. They don't live in exquisite houses with elegant furniture and the best supply of wine in the world. Glasses don't cling to their hooves so they can carry them around. So, what are you?"

Rudolph straightens his posture and rubs his nose, making it shinier but still extinguished for now. "If you want to continue, bedroom set or not, I need you to change your tone."

"My tone?"

"Yes, your smug tone. A little tiny elf with drag queen red go-go boots has no place thumbing his nose at me, regardless of how I came to speak in animal form."

I wonder if he could score me a new set of boots? Nah, he'd delight in making it even worse. "Sensitive, aren't you?"

"A little." He returns to pouting, yet still with the upright carriage.

"If you're in a hurry, I don't think we can quibble every time I ask a question. As you indicated earlier, it's not like this is going to make us bosom buddies. We didn't enjoy each other before this started, won't enjoy each other once it's finished. We came together for different reasons and need to live through it. My shaping up and asking questions in a nicer way won't mean I'm not thinking the other stuff. Might as well be open and honest about everything."

"Similar to how I think you relish being a slave, and are the biggest snob up here, okay? You accuse me of being what you despise in yourself."

"Whatever your feeble brain wants to think to keep this train moving. So, what the fuck are you? Enchanted animal? Demon? Another form of freak?"

Rudolph grins. Strange, until he speaks. "You're right, okay? I'm much more comfortable with this honesty between us."

"Maybe you should try it out with your sexuality too."

"And go around scratching my Johnson like you? No thanks, okay? I do need to get through this as soon as possible. So if we could dispense with the pleasantries and get on with it."

"You're the one with the delay tactics. I asked a question to get us started, at your request. So tell me. What the fuck are you?"

"There are a lot of things you can't understand, okay? Everyone thinks they figured out the whole world, no more mysteries, science has it covered, blah, blah, blah. Not true. Plenty remains unanswered. Sometimes, no one knows unanswered things because no one asks, okay? Other times, everyone senses the unanswered, leading scientists to search for the answers. Then there are those things a few wonder, or a single individual, but they don't know how to answer it, okay?"

Damn. My head almost spins right off my neck. Either Rudolph possesses a profound philosophical bent, or his comment made no sense. What the fuck? In fact, I think I need to let it out. "What the fuck are you talking about?"

"Maybe you drank too much, okay?"

"Maybe you're a lunatic philosopher, okay?" I say this with a mock high-pitched voice.

"Fuck you."

"Nice comeback. Powerful."

Rudolph leans forward. "What I mean is I don't know if I can explain what I am, or how I came to exist in this state. And no one else could explain it, either, because we don't know. No one's asking the question but me, and now you. Oh, perhaps a few others up here, but no one with the intellect to figure it out, okay?"

"So what do you know? Anything? I knew you were a dumb fuck."

"Shut the fuck up for two seconds! You give me a headache, okay? You want me to try to figure out how to explain this, or not? Shut up. Shut up. Shut. Up."

I glance to the ceiling and start twiddling my thumbs. It may take years for his mind to gear up.

I almost shit my pants right in the chair. I lurch back and realize I have no place to go. No way to escape. Holy Buckets. And to think, Santa's black pit eyes in vampire form creep me out. They pale in comparison.

Rudolph's entire form goes limp in the chair, a dead reindeer carcass draped over the front of a Jeep in the Wisconsin backwoods, except it flops over in a plush lounge chair. And except for his ridiculous nose sitting at the end of the snout, whereas no typical hunted deer has one of those gems. If a dead animal isn't bad enough, the misty form hovering above it scares the crap out of me. Not a ghost, but an entity with a sinister feel. An aura not quite right. It has no face yet seems like it glares daggers at me, like it contemplates shoving my essence right out of my elf body and commandeering it. No way I could get myself into the reindeer if he fights for my body and wins. I'd be screwed. It appears to coil there, waiting to pounce and sneering at the world.

I take my turn to fidget in the chair.

A low rumble fills the room, right out of a horror movie, where the demon cackles at the fear it creates.

I concentrate with all my power not to piss myself, because that would send Rudolph into complete hysterics when it ruins his furniture, providing he returns to the reindeer form. I gasp for air when I realize the entity reaches across the room and takes my breath away.

It releases me, then absorbs itself back into the reindeer body and reanimates it.

Rudolph's nose lights right up, he grins and sticks the chin back high in the air. No more low rumble, back to the high-pitched voice of before. "Scared the shit out of you, didn't I?"

I gulp. "Impressive."

"Does it answer your question, okay?"

I shake my head. "No. Don't get me wrong—it's the most impressive thing you've ever done." Well, the only impressive thing he's ever done, but no need to throw that out there to see if he attacks me with his ghost self. "But I'm still confused about your origin, or what the fuck you are. And, if you can accomplish what you did, why the ridiculous high-pitched voice in an animal's body?"

Rudolph reaches over and lifts his wine glass back to his mouth. "I'll answer as best as possible, okay? Though it confuses me too. I don't know where I came from, okay? I don't even know how long I've existed. Centuries? Decades? Seconds before Santa found me? I have no idea. I remember latching onto the little baby reindeer because it was so vulnerable. It became lost in the woods, by itself and afraid. No mom around. No herd. Who knows how it happened? But young and separated, it had no defenses whatsoever, okay? So I swooped in, easy as pie, and took over the body. Because I longed for an entity to possess, to give me meaning, okay? I could think, but in animal form, I could better rationalize. I comprehended the world and could take advantage of my essence."

"So Rudolph's a corpse, possessed by a demon?" Unbelievable. I mean, it makes sense, in a fucked-up nothing is right up here at the North Pole sort of way. Still, whoever would guess such a thing? Fuck me.

Rudolph sneers. "You turn everything into a morality play, okay? Make everything so simplistic in your stupid elf view of the world. Did I possess the form? Yes. But demon? So trite. I have no idea how to explain me. I simply exist, took advantage of the opportunity, and voila! I became a talking, animated reindeer."

I laugh. "That's not normal. Or something to strive for."

Rudolph's smile disappears. "I can end this at any time. Santa would come around to giving me a bedroom set, with or without my cooperating with you."

I take another swig of the plum brandy. I need to get shit-faced. A talking reindeer who transforms into mist but despises the demon label—seriously? "Seems like you could take any body you want? Or, at least pick from a wider variety. Why a baby reindeer?" I concentrate to sound as sincere as possible, so I channel my inner Ellen DeGeneres to appease him and keep him talking. This way I can ask my smart question and demean him without his having a clue.

Rudolph shrugs and smiles. "No reason. Can't explain it. I just enjoy this, okay?"

"Is the voice your choice too?"

"Don't know, okay? The whole package came together and suits me well."

So we live through a moment of freak fest, as if I landed in the middle of a horror movie, and snap back to the odd world of prim and proper Rudolph the Talking Reindeer. Did Santa send me back down into the dungeon to torture me with impossible images and things that defy explanation? How can I wrap my mind around this lunacy?

It gives me pause about the entire journal concept. What if I record all this information, tell these stories, and sneak it out to release this information to the world? Who in their right fucking mind would believe a word of it? Stephen King's aliens sound more plausible. Or Anne Rice witches controlling a huge empire in New Orleans. Or even Clive Barker wild-animal-come-people-forms going around haunting the world.

I shake the doubt from my mind and return my full attention to Rudolph. Still, his last comment proclaimed his effeminate-reindeer-come-Christmas-icon suits him well. No wonder he and Santa became BFFs.

"So we'll go with your being a spirit, or vague entity, who latched onto the reindeer as its form. Is that what you're telling me?"

"Yep." Rudolph goes and refills his glass before returning. "No need for any more detail."

"Do you want to tell me how you and Santa came together? Could you already talk when he discovered you? Did you choose to hook up with him? Or are you trapped up here, Mrs. Claus style?"

"Both, okay?"

"No. It's not okay. What the fuck does both mean?" I calm down from the total fear of a bit ago and return to annoyed. My morning talk show host moment lasted but a few seconds.

"First, how I came to meet Santa. I'm wandering through the woods, minding my own business, eating a plant and monitoring a bird that fascinated me." Rudolph stares into space for a moment, lost in la la land. As if the bird flew into the room for a visit. "I forget why I found it so interesting. Anyway, Santa comes upon me, no warning, and puts the spell on me to entrap a reindeer. Come to find out he was down one and needed a replacement. No idea how he discovered or picked me. Next thing I know, he lashes me up with the other flying monkeys, and away we go to the North Pole. The fact I could fly startled me so much, I went along with it. I thought about resisting or pulling away, but knew it was useless. Or maybe I wanted to go on another adventure."

"So you're enslaved up here like the rest of us? Why not say that from the beginning?" Jesus, he exacerbates the fuck out of me.

"Because I'm not, okay? Can you shut the fuck up and listen, already?"

I sigh and twirl my finger in the air. "Go on."

"So we arrive at the North Pole, and Santa commands the elves to put us away, stick me in the Blitzen empty stall. I glance toward the stalls, where they store the reindeer, and decide no way I want to shack up in there. Smells to high heaven."

"Amen. And you don't have to clean it up all the time."

Rudolph snorts a laugh. "True enough, okay? But if you'd shut the fuck up around him, you'd save yourself a lot of humiliation. Almost every time he sends you there, you bring it on yourself with your stupid mouth. Even I know that."

"Yeah, but life gets so dull. I like to spice it up from time to time."

"Whatever. Unlike you, with the repeat visits to the flea infested den, I halt. Look back at Santa, and scare the living daylights out of him."

I tilt my head, surprised, because nothing ever scares Santa. "What'd you do? Your misty demon trick? Try to possess him?"

Rudolph shakes his head. "You're so dramatic, okay? You think I'm a drama queen? Please. That's you."

"So how did you scare Fat Boy?"

"I talked. Asked him for better accommodations. He guffaws when he witnesses my ability to talk, so I lay in to explain there's a lot he doesn't know. Weird, because I try to flee, but he contains me without much effort. Laughs at a talking reindeer. Tells me I'm sassy; he wants sassy." Rudolph places a hoof on his chin. "I guess we have that in common, because he wants you being sassy too. So he creates this wing here, throws me in it for the night, and says he'll return in the morning to decide my fate. Mind you, I walked in here," Rudolph motions around his flat, "to nothing but ice floor, walls, and ceiling. No furniture. None of the luxury you see now. It was no easy task to get this hardwood floor installed, and keep it level and nice since it's sitting on a bed of ice."

Kind of like with Mrs. Claus and Santa when they told me their stories, I hold up my hand to stop him for a second. It always takes a minute to process this shit they tell me. They say it normal, as if I sit at a dinner party, hearing the latest international trip a friend went on. No recognition of the strangeness. "Thanks for the pause."

"Too stupid to understand it all so fast? I understand, okay?" Now he speaks slow, no doubt to fuck with me. "How...is...this? Can...you...keep...up...okay?"

"Fuck you, dead rat carcass boy."

"I don't have to continue, you know."

"What about the bedroom set?"

"Maybe it's not worth dealing with you, okay?"

"Wait." I lean forward, a thought coming to me. "Why don't you float out of here? You could, couldn't you? He controls the reindeer body, right? Not the spirit?"

"Look at the brain on Brad!" Great, he watches movies too. Never pegged him as a "Pulp Fiction" fan. "Ding, ding, ding. Prize for Simon the Dumb Ass Elf, okay?"

"Get on with it. I thought you had to hurry to get out of here."

"I do. Secret mission. To piss on your pillow." Rudolph stretches out a leg. "When he came the next morning, okay, thinking he would call the shots and decide what to do with me, I did the same thing to him I did to you. Problem being, I loved my reindeer body. Still do. Couldn't imagine giving it up, okay? I returned to it but made my point. Explained I wanted to stick around as leader of the reindeer, accepted his terms of controlling the body, but needed certain conditions met or I would bail on him."

"So that's your leverage? What if he gets tired of it and tells you to piss off?"

Rudolph shrugs. "He could. Almost did once, in the 1930s when we had a little tiff. But we like the arrangement, each of us. And we agreed to it. I'd stick around, rule the reindeer, live in my own space, do my own thing as I saw fit, and he'd allow it so long as I toed the line on his missions and didn't create any trouble. See, I can think. Rationalize. Going with him when he takes off in the sleigh is my main function. He controls the reindeer, but they have no clue to run for the hills if someone sees them milling about on a roof or in a cemetery. He leaves the elves in charge, but can we trust you? No. So I instruct them too."

"And all you get out of the deal is the possession of a stupid body?"

"Fuck you, okay? It's cute. Simple. Easy to control. Plus, I get to live here and decorate it to my pleasure."

It hits me. "You're afraid. You aren't sure you could possess another body if you left. You may go find another host, or wander around. Or evaporate. That misty scary form, it's more show than real?"

"I said fuck you, okay? Just fuck off and keep your rude shitty thoughts to yourself. No one wants to hear a little puny elf make judgments or try to pretend he has a brain."

"I thought you said I did have a brain?"

"It was a movie quotation, for effect. Brain or not, you're dumb as hell, okay?"

I hit a nerve. So I figure out his fear on my own. No need to push him further, because he may clam up if I expose his fear to everyone. Without answering, he can only feign leaving to leverage Santa, because in reality, he stuck himself here. I file this information in the back of my mind, in case I can ever use it against him, or manipulate a favor out of Santa.

"Can we change the subject?" I grin. "I still don't grasp what Santa gets out of this. A reindeer guard? What else? He doesn't keep things around for no reason."

Rudolph seems deep in contemplation. Perhaps he never pondered this before. "Maybe a little like you, okay? Yeah, I help with the reindeer and do my special thing. But you're right—he could get on fine without me. But he appreciates me. That's what I mean, same as how he enjoys you. He could kill you too. And save himself a lot of headaches in the process, okay? Not listen to your unfunny jokes or deal with your nonsense. He adores you, simple. Or appreciates what you offer, which also explains why I stay around this way. Add to your situation how you get yourself in trouble so much, he also looks forward to getting to torture you for cause. I don't do that, okay?"

Rudolph wiggles in his chair, drains his wine glass, peers around the room, as if searching for an escape route.

"Let's keep this moving." I smile, trying once again to calm him down. "To summarize, you stick around because of the body." I motion toward him, stifling the million comments racing through my mind regarding the small little body he dons. "And he gets a willing helper, one smarter than your average reindeer. In return, you get the penthouse suite here, pretty free will in most things. Sound accurate?"

"Essentially, yes."

I can't stop myself. If I must learn this information, I need to find out. "What if he figures it out? Learns your fear? Don't you worry all this will disappear? He could call your bluff, you know. Force you to live with the rest of the reindeer, make you another commoner, no different from the rest of us. Doesn't it worry you?"

Rudolph shakes his head, an impetuous child, a three-year-old refusing to go to bed. So immature. "If it got bad enough, I would take leave of this whole situation. It's to our mutual benefit to keep it in place, okay? His too."

"Liar." Time to change the subject again. "What about ticks? Do you have them? They're common in deer, you know."

"You disgust me, okay? You're jealous because you have lice."

"Yes or no to the ticks?"

"Of course not!" he shouts at me.

We fall silent. I do intend to stop antagonizing him at this point but need to let the other smart-ass, "call him on the carpet" thoughts absorb into my mind and go away before I continue. Rudolph goes quiet because I hit too close to home. No one challenges him around here because of his status and prissy attitude. Perhaps he worries I plan to take his secret to Santa, as I contemplated a minute ago.

"I think we should end this now." Rudolph jumps out of his chair and heads for the hall.

"Hey, wait. Come back. Come on." I run after him, scurrying in front of him and pushing him to a stop. "We didn't finish. I'm sorry. Listen, I didn't mean to frighten you. Remember, I don't like him, only you do? I'll keep your secret. You know, it's your arrangement with him, between us. Don't fuck with me or threaten me anymore, and I leave you alone. *Quid quo pro.*"

"What do squid have to do with this, okay?"

Oops. Should not use Latin on a spirit-possessed creature. "Not seafood. It's a phrase. It means we reached an agreement where we both have power over each other; we share information, or whatever, and it works out. Enemies or not. An equal exchange."

"Still, we should end this. You should *not* be in my home."

My shoulders slump, because I pretend total disappointment. To an extent, it would be a bummer. More than anything, I want him to continue. Tell me the rest. And keep me from returning to the drudgery so fast.

"But I have other questions."

Rudolph takes a deep breath. He turns around and goes back to his chair, pointing for me to go back to mine.

"To get this straight, nothing we say gets back to Santa, okay? Whether he finds anything out or not, and I'm not admitting you got anything correct, by the way. I can still make your life here a total hell. Much worse than your slave existence at the moment, okay?"

"I have no doubt. That's what I mean. I keep my mouth shut, because it makes my life easier, and you leave me the fuck alone, to keep your secret, whether you want to admit my knowledge or not. Okay?" Again I say the last part in his high voice.

"At least it doesn't change the fact you're a fucker, okay?"

"Whatever."

"So what other questions? Get on with it, okay?"

"Are you a gay spirit? Or is the reindeer body gay, and you took the trait on with it?"

"Long before we got this far, I thought we established I would not engage such topics.'"

"Right." The closet thing with him again. Ugh.

"You should drink more, okay?" Rudolph gets up, runs his hoof along a row of red wine in the frig, and gets out a new bottle. Once he settles back into his chair, I see in his eyes, almost feel in the room, he calms back down, returns to the tension of our first interactions but minus the intense terror that threatened to boil over.

I take his advice and finish off the moonshine. I wince as it burns down my throat but get excited for the extreme buzz soon to follow. "We have one major thing left to learn. Your nose."

"My nose?" Rudolph sounds shocked.

"Seriously? You have a bright red nose to glow in the dark and to lead the way with the sleigh, and you think we can pass over it? Like every reindeer in the world has a color of the rainbow for a schnoz?"

Rudolph giggles. "Schnoz is funny."

"Are you stalling again? Or trying to avoid it?"

"No, no, no, okay? Nothing secret here to worry us. It's just my nose. Remember I mentioned Santa and I had a spat in the 1930s?"

Whew. Got him back on track. I realize I hold my breath, so let out a sigh. "Yeah, tell me about it."

"I got jealous. Wanted fame of my own, similar to what he created for himself as St. Nicholas. Our partnership favored him, always had. I wanted a bigger piece of the pie. I deserve more than a spot in the reindeer line up. After all, everyone still depicted it as eight reindeer, when since the early twentieth century when we hooked up, he flew with nine of us."

Funny. Santa and Rudolph in a spat over the Christmas legend and who gets more credit. "He does own a healthy ego."

"Right? I schemed it for a long time. I got the idea from him when he told me how he visits the authors and artists who helped build his reputation. So I tested it every time we visited New York. But one time when he went there and asked me to watch the reindeer for an extra-long time because he wanted to feed on at least four people, I slipped away. Went right to an advertising agency and found someone sleeping in the office. Scared the shit out of him. Woke him up, pleading for him to listen to my story. He screamed in terror. When I look back, I should have expected it. I mean, I needed a more subtle approach, because even Santa got scared the first time he heard me talk, let alone a naïve human with no knowledge of the supernatural. He screamed and screamed until I had to turn around and slam him in the head with my back hooves. Dropped him dead, right there."

"An unexpected twist. I have to say I didn't see that coming." I straighten my hat as a nervous gesture.

"Neither did I, okay? I had no other way to silence him. So my attempt to gain a little fame failed."

"Regarding your fame." I hold up a hand to stop him. "What was your goal there, I mean with him in the office?"

"To get them to start an advertising campaign to add the ninth reindeer. Kind of like Santa did with writers in the nineteenth century, okay? Only twentieth-century style."

Again, funny, this jealousy from a spirit-possessed deer. Think about it. Fucked-up and odd, and thus funny. It makes this whole elf enslavement worth it, at times. Because the odd and strange things we experience or witness, no matter how brutal and off, make you giggle because you could never predict it. Wait until I tell Trixy and Hedgehog. I mean, my pact with Rudolph does not include keeping things from them. "What happened next?"

Rudolph rolls his eyes, back to his snotty little kid routine. He's more complex than I ever imagined. At the least, a very confused spirit.

"Santa came roaring into the office, pissed as hell. Screaming and yelling, throwing stuff around, kicking stuff around, a maniac on the loose. Accusing me of trying to expose everything and being careless. I explained why I was there. He points at the body," now Rudolph adopts his high-pitched version of Santa's voice, which is pretty hilarious, "'Then explain the dead body! You fucked it up.'"

"You do a good Santa impersonation."

"Thanks. Better than you."

Good thing he reminds me he's a fucker, or I may have forgotten. "Why don't you stay on task. Keep going."

"Well, he stares me down, fuming. Without any warning, he punches his fist toward me, and a red laser thing shoots out of it and slams right into my face, okay? I lurched back, took my turn to be scared out of my mind. Because this materialized at the end of my snout." Rudolph taps his now shining nose with a hoof.

"He punished you with a red nose? Up close, it resembles a light bulb, but round."

Rudolph nods. "Not as absurd as it sounds. He told me he'd been searching for a while for a better way to see while we were flying around up there. Contemplated a lantern for the sleigh, or headlights, or a flashlight I could hold, okay? But since I demanded he teach me a lesson, those were his words at the time, he dropped this big-ass glowing nose on me to guide the way."

"Just like that, Rudolph the Red-Nosed Reindeer? Amazing. Did you have a normal black nose before?"

"Yeah. Normal reindeer nose."

"Were you pissed? I mean, you look ridiculous."

Oops. Struck the nerve again. Never know when this temperamental one will go all pissy on me. I suppose insulting their looks might tweak anyone, if I think about it.

"It does not, okay!" Rudolph pouts and stomps a back hoof on the side of the chair. "In fact, because of what happened next, everyone expects a reindeer with a red nose."

"In a cartoon."

"I think it's beautiful."

"Because you're stuck with it. As if I announced I always dreamed of living at a North Pole castle. Or that green tights were my thing."

"No, I like it. Remember, I could fly right out of here whenever I want, okay?"

"Right. Back to your charade."

"Do you want me to tell you this, or not?"

"You have more to tell? You revealed how you became Rudolph. What else?"

"It's one thing for him to create me, another for you to learn my history, okay?"

"You have my attention."

"What do you know regarding the Rudolph legend, okay?"

What's with the issues with these people, or entities, or whatever, up here, and being sensitive when it comes to their backgrounds? Never just explain their story, but drag it out and get offended if I don't express complete amazement and awe at their life, or tell them I always admired them or a story equally as dishonest. "What about it?" Snotty inflection, but I have to let loose once in a while.

"Nope. Fuck you, okay?" Rudolph motions a hoof across the front of his mouth, as if he zipped it shut. If only we could be so lucky.

"Come on. We got this far. Don't give up now. Help this little Friend of Dorothy out."

Going back to the gay slurs yanks him right out of the doldrums. "That's not a slur. Like Stick Slurper."

"I ran out of them last time. Tell me, how did we come to know the story of Rudolph the Red-Nosed Reindeer?" Back to the fake Matt Lauer voice of calm and reason. Gets him every time.

"This goes back to how tight Santa and I are."

"You mean uptight?" He left it one wide open. I had no choice.

"Fuck you, okay? I mean our mutual admiration. He saddles me with this nose and asks me what brought me to this advertising place, of all things. So I explain I tried to get the dude to tell the world how a ninth, and most important, reindeer lives. Santa promises to help, but first, we burn the building down."

Rudolph continues, but I shout at him. "Wait! What building? Why?"

"You're so slow, Simon. For the love of God, it's not complicated. We had a dead advertising guy on the floor, his head bashed in by a reindeer hoof, okay? We evacuated the place and torched it to cover the crime."

Again, they always see me as the imbecile when I ask reasonable questions. Rudolph slipped Santa when the Jolly Man went on a killing spree, no doubt leaving the bodies strewn everywhere, but he expects me to see the demand for covering up a reindeer crime in an office building? Who can keep up with these two? Not me. Especially because the killers evacuated the place of all other humans, first. What's with the conscience they can turn off and on? "Did he put you on a leash and parade you through Times Square to make the announcement?"

"I would never stoop to his leading me around like a dog."

See what I mean? Offended at the dog reference. Loves the reindeer body he stole away but freaks when I throw out a dog comparison.

"If I may?" he asks with indignation.

"I will remain silent until you finish."

"Ever heard of Robert L. May?"

I raise my eyebrows and bite my tongue hard to keep quiet. I agree to go silent, and he asks a stupid question. Who the hell ever heard of Robert L. May, except his mom and wife and kids? I take a deep breath. Keeping my comments inside, or at least half the time keeping them inside, but it gets harder and harder because I need to appease this prima donna to get his story. "No." I almost crush my teeth into oblivion as a way to push the other words and thoughts back inside.

"You haven't?" Imagine the voice inflection of a person finding out an average, twenty-plus-year-old American just learned about George Washington, or the Easter Bunny didn't exist. Wait a minute, he might. Who knows? You get my point.

The dam bursts on my annoyance. "You're fucking kidding me, right? You know one trivial fucking fact, then pretend it became universal knowledge because a space in your feeble brain reserved an area for it. You knew before you asked I never heard of the dude. No one has. Just tell the story, without the theatrics."

"Now who's the touchy one? Drama Queen."

I scratch my head to let loose pent-up energy. "Your story, please?"

"Whatever, okay? It made Santa feel bad, so he took me to the Montgomery Ward Department Store. We snuck up on the copywriter there when he worked late one night. Santa took control, said he'd do this the same way he got his story out. So he and Ward wrote a poem."

I moan. Another fucking poem? You have to be fucking kidding me! Did I learn at the heart of this drama, all these issues, lay Santa, the repressed writer? Realizing Rudolph stopped talking, I grin, fake notwithstanding, and motion for him to continue.

"They wrote a poem in 1939, pretending May wrote it to generate holiday traffic into the store. You know, competition? So Santa threatens him with death if he doesn't publicize this poem. This, by the way, explains another reason I stick around. Santa's brilliance! He changes with the ages. He understood he had to move beyond a children's story, and get into the twentieth century with advertising. Create demand. Capitalism! Desire! Consumption, okay? So they rhyme it, Moore's boring poem but tell about a young reindeer, teased by the others because of his red nose. But a foggy Christmas Eve catapults him to the top of Santa's list when they use the bright nose to see while they fly, okay? Again, with his wisdom! Embedded the truth right in the story. See, Montgomery Ward sold these coloring books every year to kids and wanted to save money by producing the store's own coloring book. After Santa manipulates May to work with us, he links it to the coloring book thing because May's boss was on him to write a coloring book, anyway. God, Santa learned this and almost shit a brick. We both almost did. Imagine! Santa swoops right in and twists it to our favor! He's so damn intelligent."

"Genius. Like Einstein."

Rudolph glares at me. "He *is* smart."

"Or demented. Could we dispense with the mutual admiration society you two operate and finish this poem, or whatever?"

"Testy, okay? I love how he has me save Christmas in the story. Shows me real respect, okay? Puts me above the others in the legend too. Right? Who thinks of Mrs. Claus before they think of Rudolph? No one. Santa. Me. Not her. All because he made amends for the nose. Most people never even consider the other stupid reindeer, other than a group of flying mutants."

"He could have fixed your nose. Turned it back to black. Could do that tomorrow, if he wanted."

"No!" Rudolph grabs his nose with both hooves, as if someone intended to steal the ugly thing. "As predicted, because of Santa's genius, the story of turning a negative into a positive, of perseverance, it won the day. People loved it. Montgomery Ward sold almost 2.5 million copies of the story the first year. 3.5 million when they reissued it in 1946. Then, the best part."

Rudolph leans forward, engrossed in the story, almost lost in it now. "In 1949, Santa teaches me how to ramp it up. We go to May's friend and brother-in-law, Johnny Marks, and write a song with him. Oh, did I tell you Santa leveraged May by threatening him with death if he failed to cooperate?"

"In so many words, but I predicted as much from other stories like this." I smirk at the predictability, but Rudolph misses it in his own absorption.

"Right. So we do the same thing, but it takes a second because May warned his friend before Santa even made the threat. Somehow, and this happened after we left, mind you, they get Gene Autry to sing it. No idea how! I'd guess they were working their butts off to get it done as well as possible, so Santa won't come back and make them dinner. Two million copies of the song, sold! Cha-ching!"

"Why are you so happy for Montgomery Ward's profit?"

"Not that, you idiot, okay? The fame! Everyone going around at Christmas, singing about me! Imagine if we sang a Simon the Elf ditty, instead?"

"Sounds dreadful."

"Jealous? It's unbecoming of you, okay?"

"Is there anything else to this tale?" I think I got the story out of him, so I hope I can leave now.

"You didn't even get to the TV show."

"Even I saw the show when I was little."

"The one with Burl Ives narrating?"

"Yes."

"See! I'm so famous! Poem to song to TV in 1964, and now everyone loves me!" Rudolph sits back in his chair, as if the thrill of the story spent him. He waves his hoof in the air to dismiss me.

"Are you telling me to go?"

"You got the whole thing, okay? The whole fucking story. See why I stick around? You think it's all out of fear. No. I love Santa. We see eye to eye."

I think Rudolph lost it a bit here. Mood swings. Thinking he owns Santa, he describes a casual relationship, and now this worship of the bloodsucker. Fuck me. Maybe he should go around and steal Zoloft instead of furniture.

"Are you so rude I have to show myself to the door? Seriously?"

He waves his hoof in the air again. "You're more hired help than a guest. Go. You give me the vapors."

I laugh again. "The vapors? What is this, the nineteenth century? Good thing you never become dramatic or anything."

"You smell human. Go. I'm done."

"Do you think we did enough to get your new bed?"

"Go!"

I hop off the chair and brush myself off, almost stumbling over. Sitting there for so long, I forget how fucked up the Mrs. Claus moonshine could get me. I steady myself. "You're still a prima donna shithead, you know? We're not friends. I don't like you. You're bonkers."

"Angry little Simon. Jealous little Simon, okay? We made our pact. Now go."

The "now go" came out in a deep demon growl, so I whip around and run to the door, pounding on it until it swings open, back into the Santa Garage.

Only a few elves toil away, touching up the paint on the sleigh.

I stagger to the fridge and grab three Santa beers. Chug one right there. Lug the other two up to my turret bedroom and hurry to record everything he told me. I pass out, waking in the morning, face down in my book, but lucky for me having recorded every last bit of detail, because when I read the Johnny Marks and song bit, I don't remember him telling me that at all. Good thing I was diligent in my writing.

I close my little book and conceal it again. Wonder what will happen next, because I think I know the whole thing now, right? No other stores lurking about Santa and his pals. Finé.

Chapter Six: Of Nutcrackers, Frosty, and Other Victims

OF COURSE, I deceive myself when I decide I have nothing left to learn because Rudolph releases me. Life goes on, after all, up here at the North Pole. What makes me believe Santa revealed everything to me? Think for a second, I came to live here a short time ago. So, lots I don't know, and the next couple of days prove it to me when I discover more and more to include in my secret revelations.

Yeah, I felt done with my journal once I recorded Rudolph's story. But I failed to get it out of here right away, not even sure how to do it yet. So I decide to keep adding to it until the right opportunity presents itself. Just pile up the evidence, so to speak.

I spend a lot of time wondering why Santa decides to reveal this entire saga to me. Why tell me his story? Strange, even if I do enjoy learning his history and trying to use the information to bring him down. I almost suspect he knows about the journal, but that makes no sense because he would beat the living daylights out of me, send me to the ice dungeon for a long time, or a fate much, much worse. Like sentence me to live with Rudolph. I have no clue why Santa went to such effort to teach me this information in the first place.

A few nights after the Rudolph visit, I sit contemplating this shit in the sleigh as we speed toward Paris. "Why Paris, bro?"

Santa peers at me out of the corner of his eye. "I'm not your bro. And we don't need to chat. Be quiet over there."

He forces me to sit up front with him a lot, even though the other two elves, a girl I barely know and fucking Bobby—Santa picks Bobby a lot because he knows how much the dude annoys me—have to ride in back with his sacks of evil magic. He knows I chat the whole way but still gets annoyed when I speak. Funny.

I glance over the side of the sleigh, thinking I see the outline of England below. "Just curious. Always seems random to me, where you choose to go. You land in America a lot. Because it's your original home?"

Santa yawns and spurs the reindeer to move faster.

"Okay. So where we go remains a big mystery. Sneaky, clever Santa. Can we go to a different subject now?"

"Do you speak for no other reason than to hear the roar of your own voice *ad nauseum*?"

Makes me laugh. "Sometimes. What else are we going to do as we fly along? You must have dragged me along for a reason. Or else I could be back with those elfin ones, bugging them instead. Bobby and I haven't had a good argument in a long time."

"What else would you like to chat about?"

Again with the Simon the Elf's special status to baffle me. He avoids addressing my sitting up here but caves all the time to the conversation. Why? If the chitchat annoys him, leave me at the North Pole to get drunk. Trixy and Hedgehog are watching WNBA games today, which is always lots of fun. Better than this adventure. Instead, he drags me along, to the point of wanting me right next to him, even as he expresses outrage at my behavior. But the minute I think he has enough, he agrees to my terms.

"Rudolph? I have more questions."

"I instructed you to cover his information with him. Why do you fail at so many things? How is it possible you succeeded at anything before you met me, with such stupidity?"

Now he reveals a savior complex. He gets more and more intriguing the longer we hang together. "Um, relax, Big Guy. He went over the whole story. This has to do with you, more than him."

"So why did you present it as a Rudolph question?"

"Holy shit!" I scream and duck way down when a huge bird almost flies right into my face. "Fuck! Hey, Rudolph!" I cup my hands over my mouth, hoping the sound carries. "Watch the fuck where you drive! I thought your ugly nose lit things up for us."

I take a moment to compose myself. Good thing no piss leaked out. "Where were we?" I ask Santa.

"Cut to the chase. What do you wish to know about Rudolph, or me, or whatever else rumbles around in the air space between your ears?"

"Oh, yeah. Why do you treat him with utter splendor? That's the question. He seems more a pain in the ass than anything. Get rid of him and find another, normal flying reindeer. You could slap the nose on all of them, if you wanted. Do you have a crush on him? A ghost fetish may explain his lofty status among us."

Santa reaches over and slaps me upside the back of my head so hard I fall into the footwell and crawl back out before he answers.

"He interests me. You think I'm shallow. Focused on the killing, the blood, the victims."

"And the power," I interrupt. "Don't forget the strongest of the vampires with special magical powers thing too."

Santa smiles and shakes his head. "I'm so much more than the simple version you concocted in your feeble head. I have depth, if you would bother to look for it. You think I live in this tiny little box." He makes a hand motion, as if a box sits on his lap. "But I'm much more complex. There are things you don't know or understand."

"It's hard sometimes, getting over the whole Count Dracula thing."

"I find Rudolph fascinating. Even with my magic and ability, I never could explain him, or it, or the entity, or whatever. It keeps things more interesting with him around. Plus, anything that annoys people amuses me. He does a fine job there."

"You'll get no argument from me there."

Santa jerks the reins to the left, banking us high above the Eifel Tower and roaring toward Notre Dame Cathedral. I think for sure he aims right at the statue of St. Michel atop it, but we land with a hard thud upon a path right along the Seine, parking the sleigh under a bridge.

"Go hide the reindeer under here," he instructs us elves as he grabs one of his bags.

I hop out, but before we get over to the line of reindeer, Rudolph rounds them up and gets them hidden as best as possible already.

"You're like a good little collie, herding these guys. Want a treat?"

I think Rudolph flips me off, because the right front leg and hoof fly in the air and jerk toward me, but without fingers who knows what the fuck he meant.

"Come." Before Rudolph and I get any more into it, Santa grabs the back of my collar and yanks me along to follow him.

I gag from the force of his holding me by the shirt, jerking my feet around until he sets me on the ground. "Keep up. We haven't much time."

"Clearly." I scurry along, almost running to match his stride. "You picked a dumb-fuck place to park the sleigh. It's Paris, for God's sake. Do you know how many people saw us dive in? Millions, no doubt. And those reindeer will be found under a bridge. They blend like a fag at a Baptist revival. Not to mention flying in with a red beacon leading the way. Either people will think the entire city of Paris went on a huge acid trip, or this will result in a serious investigation. Do the Agents of SHIELD need to be brought in? Do you read Marvel comics?"

Santa ignores my banter, which means he focuses on the task at hand. We run down the way a bit and march right up to three homeless dudes. They speak in French, but unlike up at the North Pole, where I understand what anyone says no matter the language, I have no clue what they mean. Perhaps a snide comment about a dude dressed as Santa standing in front of them with a midget little elf. Or that could just be what I would think.

Santa speaks right back at them, in their language, it appears in order to transact business. Next thing I know, they hand over their socks of all things, in return for a little packet of pills Santa hands them.

We hurry back along the sidewalk toward the sleigh.

"Times must be bad, if you resort to drug pushing. Don't you have everything you want, without the need for the nasty socks?"

"I needed them to believe it was an honest deal."

"So you took their socks?" Makes me laugh so hard I stop right in the middle of the sidewalk. Where does he come up with such stupidity?

Oops. No stopping. With a violent thrust, Santa lifts me into the air and carries me along by the scruff of the neck, a puppy in his evil grasp. "I'll keep up now. You can put me down."

"No."

"Are we dealing with the socks?"

"No."

"What?"

"We're in a hurry! I thought I told you already."

Before you could say boo, Santa has those reindeer, the sleigh, and the elves back in the air. "To Rio de Janeiro." Rudolph jerks his head in acknowledgment, and away we go.

I turn around and flip Bobby off. He sticks his tongue out at me. Fucker.

I try hard to stay quiet but so many questions run through my head. I can't stand it. "That was weird. Even by your standards."

"What was? My instructions to Rudolph?"

And he calls me the dense one. "No. The transaction. Socks for little yellow pills. Strange."

"You trivialize my creation of three new serial killers?"

I almost vomit. The banter and fun deflate, with a harsh reminder of what Santa does. Flying around and taking a victim here and there, hard as I take it every time, almost becomes a matter of routine. Until he does this shit. Random cruelty for no reason other than his ability to inflict it upon people.

But a longing inside of me fights to pull out of the depression and doldrums, because they could consume me. I struggle for a smart-ass comment and remember the socks again.

"Still, not very wicked to gather a bunch of socks."

"I almost forgot those." Santa pulls the socks out of his pocket and tosses them over the side of the sleigh. Like we do with baby Jesus from time to time, but no one will wonder about finding a random sock. I always find it curious. Walking along the road, out of nowhere you find a shoe or sock. How did it get there? I mean, people don't drive along and toss out their shoe or sock. Where did it come from? Don't even get me started on the thoughts in my mind when I pass a pair of undies or panties lying at random on the road or under a restaurant table.

"What were you doing? Sock fetish?"

"These homeless guys don't trust a random stranger offering them free drugs. They think it's a setup or a new more addictive drug. So I need to make them pay or perform a task to make them believe it's more than free drugs. I made up I had a sock fetish and needed it immediately. Told them I dressed as Santa and sucked on toes. So you got something right this time, when it comes to the sock fetish. It's a ruse, not real."

I laugh again. And such explains my fucked-up existence. Because no way I approve of his manufacturing more demented souls to torture and kill the innocent. Total downer. But Santa pops off with a reeking sock toe fetish, and it makes me giggle. A lot. A psychiatrist would chalk it up to Stockholm Syndrome. Probably is.

Thankfully, no time to get too deep with myself as we approach Rio de Janeiro.

"Whoa. One big Jesus below," I marvel as we fly by. Never saw it before. "Can we steal it?"

"Too obvious."

"Right. Kind of like flying through the middle of Paris and landing near the Seine at City Centre."

"Except we left Notre Dame there."

I glance behind us again, wishing we could snatch the sucker right off its perch and drop it into the ocean. Just to be funny. Better than the no-good I know Santa's up to right now.

This time we slide into a more conventional-looking neighborhood, instead of the heart of the historic district as in Paris. We land in a tight alley, but Santa gives no instructions about the reindeer or hiding out as he pulls me along with him, leaving Rudolph in charge of the animals and two elves. Sometimes he gives us itemized things to do; other times he leaves us wondering. I wish I could stay with them because these trips seldom turn out good. More death. More Santa the vampire tormenting people.

We move along, not so fast this time, until Santa dives into a house. I follow behind to see the husband, sprawled out dead on the floor, his head at an awkward angle suggesting Santa broke his neck. The wife struggles against Santa clutching her in his arms, to no avail, until one arm falls limp and he drops her to the ground.

Santa turns to me, black eyes at their most frightening, blood dribbling down his chin, and growls, "Come." Even for me, that gory Santa appearance silences me. I wince at the dead bodies left on the floor, no different from a chewed-up dog toy.

We hurry outside, down another street, and he lifts me into his arms as he leaps to the second floor of another home. The teenage girl fails to even scream before Santa buries his fangs deep in her neck.

He wipes the blood from his lips on his sleeve and smiles at me. Most of the crimson goo smears across his face.

I realize one motivation for the challenging way I speak to him, as if it hits me in the head like a leer jet crashing into my noggin because of the gruesome scene in front of me. I grope for a smart-ass comment or way to belittle him in order to cope with the awfulness he inflicts upon these victims and forces me to witness and even experience. It amounts to a defense mechanism to help me deal with the terror of it. "In your haste for her delicious nectar, and being a dumb fuck, you forgot to have us clean up the last kill site."

Of course, you wonder why my comment ventures into reminding him of this type of mistake, right? Why not leave the evidence there, so people will begin to believe in vampires again, maybe even hunt down the bloodsucker? Well, it's called self-preservation. I tried that once, and he got back to the North Pole, remembered, and slammed me in the ice dungeon for a day, followed by two weeks of shit cleanup for the reindeer. I must remind him for my own protection, and it swings back around to the defense mechanism because at the same time I get to point out his stupidity.

"Clean this one up and go back and do the other one. I'll come for you." Speaking of leer jets, even when I mock him it often flies right over his head unnoticed. He reacts as if I mention it as a nice reminder.

Santa dashes off with those instructions. Ugh. Always with these unpleasant tasks. At least he remembers to leave the cleanup bag before he charges off.

I take a moment to compose myself, regain my energy, forget the sad things I witness all the time, and concentrate on being Simon the smart-ass. Thankfully, with the practice at this self-therapy, I recover pretty fast. Only need to find a funny thought or stupid story to make fun of, and I snap out of it. To get busy, I grab the bag of goodies to cover up the crime scene and come across the perfect distraction.

I chuckle at the new potion he leaves. He does have a bit of Christmas flare, because I pull out a string of bubble lights. You know, the kind that heat up and produce a bubble thing inside the glass tube, and you have to straighten each one out on a different branch? Pain in the rear. My mom loved them, so we put them on the tree every year. My poor, anal retentive brother almost had an aneurysm trying to keep them upright and functioning.

I scratch my head, wondering what to do with them, but the bag contains nothing else. So I plug them in.

They heat up, bubble, and green and red snowflakes shoot out the top, coating the room. No need to witness it happen or double-check, because I know these magical flakes eliminate the evidence as they melt away. The girl's wounds heal as I glance at her, the Santa bruise marks disappear—no more fang holes—and I leave with no one the wiser.

Same thing when I return to the first house. I sit in the corner, admiring the beauty of the Christmas snow as it cleans up the living room and leaves the two dead bodies, transforming them to appear like a robbery went bad with gunshot wounds to their chests and heads.

Such is the life, as these poor people lay dead in front of me, but I ignore the lifeless bodies in favor of the snow.

"I thought you'd embrace the snowflake bling." I jump at the sound of his voice. Santa unplugs the lights and shoves them back in the bag before we head back to the sleigh.

"Yeah, pretty. Amidst your nasty-ass scene."

"I feel much better."

"Look better, too, with the blue eyes. Did you feed again after you left?"

"Yes."

"Damn. You were one hungry motherfucker."

We return to the sleigh, and everyone climbs in. I slap Bobby on the butt as he topples into the back.

"Don't ever touch my butt again!" Bobby spins around, his face crimson in anger.

"Enjoy it too much?" I settle next to Santa without getting an answer.

As we lift into the sky, Santa chuckles.

"Something funny?" I ask.

"Do you want to witness another of my creations?"

You know the idea no one wants to see the carnage of a train wreck, but you look anyway because the curiosity gets the better of you? Santa does this to me all the time. I should scream, "NO!" Because any creation of his means death and awfulness. Still, he has me intrigued.

"What creation?"

"It's a surprise. Or we go home."

"All right. Show me."

We fly along, so I hum a few Christmas tunes to pass the time. Even Santa smiles as I whistle, "Grandma Got Run Over by a Reindeer."

"Where the hell are we?" I ask.

"Over the Mediterranean Sea."

"Cool." I glance down and see boats floating below, making me wonder where they head, what cargo they carry, and what is their home nation. So many people beneath our sleigh of death, going about their business, not comprehending the minuscule nature of their worries compared to enslavement to Santa, or worse, becoming one of his random victims around the world.

We land on an island. "Where's this?"

"You need a geography lesson." Santa gets out and whispers instructions in Rudolph's ear before turning back to me.

"Well, maybe you could enroll me in school to learn instead of taking me on these crap missions. Release me from captivity, and I promise to become a geographer."

"That's not even close to creative or funny. Be careful." Santa glares at me. He turns and nods to Rudolph, who yells at the reindeer. "Let's fly, okay? Up and away!" The animals, sleigh, and the reindeer rise into the air and soar away. Bobby and the other elf peek over the side as they fade into the distance.

"Rudolph stole your transportation."

"And yours. I guess we're stuck here."

"Just you and me, together. How sweet."

Santa spins around and heads down the narrow streets, almost deserted at this late hour. Feels a bit like a hot African climate, but I think we flew over Sicily before landing here. So back to only knowing we walk in the Mediterranean.

"Do I get to know where the hell we are?"

"Shh. People will hear you."

"Who the fuck cares? You'll eat them anyway."

Santa lurches to a stop and grabs me around the neck. He lifts me off the ground and carries me along for a couple of blocks as I struggle for breath, sure he will choke me to death this time. I feel the red spread across my face as I lose oxygen.

Just as I decide to lose consciousness and slip away, we walk through a wall as if we turn invisible and descend into a dungeon.

We arrive in a darkened room, one wall hidden by a curtain depicting Santa flying in front of the moon, another wall similar to a sports bar, with tons of televisions hanging from it, but otherwise a damp, dark, and sparse rocky cave.

"Now you may learn our location." Santa sets me down. I grab my throat and struggle for a minute to catch my breath. Of course, he ignores my distress. "We landed on the island nation of Malta. It has an old history, including as a post for knights and other Christians who sought to defend Jerusalem during the crusades. It has a long history with Catholicism and the like."

"Thus you've defiled it."

Santa laughs. "You know me so well it frightens me."

I touch my hat and tip it to him. "I'm not the village idiot, you know."

"Close."

"Whatever. Don't get any kinky thoughts, on the grounds I know you so well. Fat gray guys aren't my style. Nothing wrong with it, if you're into it. It's just not me."

"Do you always think with your penis?"

I turn to him and throw my hands in the air. "I believe I was letting you know the opposite. Do you want to show me your surprise or not? Why are we in this dungeon? And where the hell are we?"

"Inside a very ancient church, deep in its bowels. People don't even know about this location."

"Very James Bond of you. So what's here?"

"Nutcrackers."

I spin on my heels and stare at him in complete disbelief. "Nutcrackers? You brought me halfway around the world to show me nutcrackers?"

"Not any random nutcrackers. Special nutcrackers."

"You don't intend for them to crack my nuts, do you? Because I'm not any more into nut busting than I would be going down on you."

"Will you please quit with the disgusting references? Let me show you."

Santa walks to one end of the room and begins pulling on ropes, which lift the curtained scene of Santa and his sleigh to reveal a row of twelve nutcrackers.

"Wow." I scratch my head. "Nutcrackers. You said it."

Well, seems like a bit of an understatement. In general, they appear as any nutcracker you may imagine. Soldiers with red uniforms, adorned with gold buttons and gold embroideries decorating their military coats. They also wear white pants with black and yellow stripes up the sides. Their rigid arms hang at their sides, and their bushy black beards sit on the lever to open up to insert a nut to crack it open. They have white faces and red hats perched atop their heads. So picture a classic-looking Christmas nutcracker. Except soldiers come alive Nutcracker Suite ballet style, these guys standing at seven feet tall. Still, I think they are made of wood. To see, I walk over and knock on one's chest. Yeah, wood.

"Indestructible, in case you're wondering." Santa joins me, running his hand over their smooth, painted surfaces. I almost crack about his caressing them, but even I know when the sexual innuendoes must cease. I have no control over how they pop into my head.

"Do I want to know what these do?" I doubt it.

"You'll learn whether you want to or not." Santa lifts one of these big suckers and carries it to the center of the room. He turns a huge key in its back round and round for a few minutes. Next he comes to the front and pushes a button on its chest.

Whoosh. The damn thing disappears from the room. "What the fuck? Where'd he go?"

Santa rushes over to the wall of TVs and turns one on. He also grabs a remote control. The screen lights up, and I see the nutcracker in barracks of human soldiers, marching down the aisle, one straight wooden leg in front of the other. All the men lay sound asleep, unaware of their Yuletide guest.

"How are we seeing this?" I poke Santa in the arm to see if I get a response to my question this time.

"Little cameras built into their hats. When they land at their destination, it pops out to fly around and beam the image back here so I can watch. I control the camera's location."

Weird. This whole thing can befuddle me. "So you can't use magic to watch them and instead need a camera? Sometimes you seem omnipotent, other times a bit limited."

"It's nothing more than the realities of my magic."

"Let me get this straight. Where the hell is he?" I point at the TV. "Because you beamed him out of here, like I landed in a *Star Trek* episode. But we need to monitor it with old-school cameras and televisions? By the way, with the *Star Trek* reference, Chris Pine is my type, to go back to our earlier conversation and what might make me think with my dick."

"It's more a combination of those things," Santa answers, ignoring my hottie Pine reference. "I need the camera, but it uses a form of magic to get the images back here, not satellites. Plus, it has no battery or power source to run out."

"Complicated."

"No, it's brilliant. Now watch what he can do and shut up." Another reminder about why he and Rudolph get along so well, what with both of them admiring their own—alleged—brilliance so often.

I comply, more out of curiosity than obedience, until I recall my unanswered questioned. "Do I get to know where he is?"

"Syria."

"That can't be good."

"Or it's perfect."

Right. Can't be good from my perspective. Perfect spot for a little Santa dementia, though.

Back on TV, the nutcracker marches right over to a cot, leans over, and falls on top of the man sleeping there. As he hits the blanket and form of the man, he disappears. "Did he vanish?" Damn, Santa does do gnarly deeds in his evil ways.

"No. The man absorbed him into his system."

When the man jerks awake, the camera moves right in front of his face but gets no reaction.

"Why can't he see the camera?"

"He can. Or, should I say, the nutcracker can."

"You possessed him with a nutcracker?" Now it starts to seem more odd than brilliant. Twisted as hell.

"I enchanted the nutcrackers to take possession of soldiers, yes. Because of what they can do without anyone suspecting me."

"Because so many people suspect you, if you don't use a nutcracker? A murder takes place and everyone thinks right away Jolly Ole St. Nicholas must have done it. You're fucked up."

"Silence!" Santa slaps me hard upside the head.

"Ouch. Where's he going?"

"You're like trying to watch a movie with a three-year-old, with the stupid questions. Just watch."

"How would you know what happens when you watch a movie with a little kid? Because of all of the children you hang out with? And how many times have you even watched a movie? Doesn't seem to be your style."

"Watch!" Santa clamps his hand over my mouth.

The soldier walks through the barracks and out into the dark night. He stops in front of a store of ammunition, taking a sort of assault rifle and tons of bullets and shit, and grabs a load of grenades. He moves in the shadows, keeping away from the night watch and sneaking into an automobile. He races away until he gets into the middle of an urban neighborhood.

The guy, or nutcracker, stalks a block or so away and hides behind a dumpster. How long we wait I have no idea, but the sun rises and people begin to fill the tiny square. At its busiest moment of the morning, with lots of people bustling around, possessed soldier boy jumps out and starts mowing down the people. He launches a grenade at the scampering and screaming crowd, goes back to his rifle, killing one after another after another. Dead. Innocent dead covering the streets.

About out of ammunition and with the sounds of sirens in the distance, he throws his last grenade and sprints back to his car, firing shots the entire way. Soon enough, he races down the road, the carnage left in his wake.

Before he returns to base or reaches whatever destination, the nutcracker jumps out of him and lands right-side-up beside the road. No one spots the Christmas soldier, because the camera slams back into his hat, and seconds later he stands in the underground room with Santa and me here in Malta.

Santa walks over and begins to put him away. "The one flaw I can't work out is how they only last so long out there, before they return and need to recharge. That's why I made so many of them."

Santa explains this to me as if he were a normal inventor searching for a cancer cure, rather than a mad, evil scientist bent on destroying the world, one innocent soul at a time.

"Was he Assad or rebellion?"

"Does it matter?"

I shrug. "Just curious if you picked a side."

"Ho! Ho! Ho!" He clutches his side, laughing. "Picked a side. Never. Why bother? This will rile things up, either way. It sets up for each side to blame the other, unless a person recognizes the soldier. But he won't have any clue what he did, or why. He came to his senses as he drove down the road, wondering how he got in the car instead of tucked in the safety of his bed. Here, let's play with another one."

"Simply for giggles, huh?"

Santa lifts another nutcracker into the center of the room and begins cranking it to life. "You want me to pick a side? I'm not saying this will display my allegiance or anything. It has more to do with the amount of chaos and friction it creates. The ripple effect, or amount of violence seeping out of it. So to Afghanistan and a remote U.S. outpost."

I gulp. No way this turns out good.

We watch this nutcracker sneak up behind a soldier out on patrol, take possession of him, and turn him around and head toward a little village. In one small house after another, the soldier machine guns down men, women, and children, in a gory bloodfest to make the Syrian version look tame.

I feel the color drain from my face, wishing I watched a video game right now instead of real events.

Soon enough, this nutcracker returns to us and Santa puts him away.

"Cool, right? I can still surprise you."

"Not sure I would describe it in those terms." I gulp back the bile. "More like disgust me. But you thrive on freaking me out, don't you?"

"Indeed. But enough of this. Let's return to the North Pole."

We walk back upstairs inside the church and out into the streets. This time we navigate as normal people, in hallways and upstairs. Still night here when we get outside. Santa moves us a street over, and a few minutes later, Rudolph and the sleigh swoop down upon us. He stops almost right in front of me.

"You didn't like the dog references, but there you go again, acting the perfect part of Santa's bitch. Come fetching his sleigh, right on command."

"Fuck off, okay? Or I'll leave you behind."

I blow Rudolph a kiss as I climb back in to settle next to Santa. We ride fast and furious through the air, landing at the North Pole with no more conversation. I first grab beer, wishing instead for Mrs. Claus's moonshine, and then go in search of Trixy and Hedgehog.

"No way you'll believe the fucked-up shit I witnessed." We settle into a private corner of the recreation room, where the elves play pool, blongo ball, and a marathon game of Monopoly.

"Let me guess," Trixy smirks. "Santa killed people."

Hedgehog snorts. "Better. He delivered the serial killer pill he ordered us to stir up the other day. The little yellow pills? Mentioned hating Parisian love and needing to put a damper on it."

So that explained a little more of the Paris story. "Yeah, part of it. But not the best part. We flew to Paris and did the weirdest transaction for the serial killer potion ever. As in, the oddest in the entire history of Santa-the-vampire-come-serial killer. Get this, he traded the serial killer potion in the guise of a drug in exchange for dirty socks. I know, right? You don't need to say anything. I see it in your faces. Dirty, disgusting socks, and then we sped off around the world, where he fed big time in Brazil."

Hedgehog holds up her hand and struggles to swallow beer she had in her mouth before starting to laugh. "Who wanted serial killer potion, and why dirty socks?" Luckily she slams back the beer before it spews all over us.

"No one! The poor homeless guys wanted drugs. Santa has an asinine theory they may suspect him if he gives it for free so they won't take a hit on the stuff. He invents a trade, but you know he's not a mental giant. So he came up with dirty socks, as if he has a fetish, so they give him the wretched things and he tosses the drugs their way. He didn't even stick around to see if they took it."

Trixy pops open another beer, hands it to me, and opens one for herself.

"But that's not the news," I continue. "We know about it."

"What else is there?" Trixy asks. "We know everything else up here too."

I shake my head. "Either he designed these suckers on his own, or a secret elf project goes on around here without our knowledge."

We glance around the room, as if the culprits might reveal themselves in our midst. Like Cold War spies lurk nearby. Not to say they did anything wrong, because even if elves designed the nutcrackers, Santa forces them to do it, no different from how he does with Trixy and Hedgehog and the chemical shit. Trixy nonetheless has an interesting point, because in general Santa keeps few secrets from us.

Hedgehog breaks the silence with a laugh. "Enough with the drama, Drama Queen. What the fuck is it?"

"Rudolph calls me Drama Queen all the time."

Hedgehog raises an eyebrow. "If the shoe fits. Tell us what you saw."

"Nutcrackers." I say nothing else, because the combination of double entendre, preposterousness of the idea, and messing with another Christmas tradition combine with the buzzing in our heads to give us the giggles.

"Too bad you couldn't put his balls in one and crush those little suckers." Trixy makes us laugh even harder.

The laughing subsides after I describe what Santa accomplished with his nutcrackers.

"Well," Hedgehog shrugs, "not the most fucked-up thing we've ever seen. Not good, mind you. Still, what did we expect?"

Perhaps the alcohol loosens my tongue too much, but keeping this secret weighs on me. "What would you think if I try to sneak out this Santa story to the world?"

Hedgehog and Trixy both grow serious in a second.

"Simon," Trixy hisses. "Watch yourself. Don't do anything stupid. It sucks up here, I know. We'd do anything to get out of it or save people. But you'll end up dead. You mean too much to me. To us."

"Yeah." Hedgehog slams her beer down. "No fucking with being sneaky. We need each other. Our little posse. No death wishes. We'll have a gay pride parade up here to cheer you up."

She makes me laugh. "The three of us parading around? Funny."

"Hey, Hey! Ho! Ho! Homophobia's got to go!" Trixy screams this out, getting stares of bewilderment from everyone else.

"From the looks on their faces, we do need one. Could we convince Rudolph to serve as Grand Marshal? But listen to me. There's something weird going on, because Santa insisted on telling me his entire story, forced me to meet Mrs. Claus, and got Rudolph to spill the beans. I recorded it."

"We know," Hedgehog whispers and scans the room, growing more uncomfortable.

I whisper back. "I wonder if I could make a difference."

Trixy reaches over and pats my knee. "We know. We wish we could. But there's no way it would leak out without him knowing."

When a good football game appears through magic on one of the walls, we divert our attention to it. I contemplate throughout my plan. I still think I could change the game by releasing this stuff, and Mrs. Claus even wants to help, I think. But Trixy has a point because Santa knows everything going on up here. Except for my journal. Or does he? Makes no sense my secret writing would slip by, when he spots so much else.

I sleep, tossing and turning, trying to figure out my next move, and greet the bell that calls us to work with pleasure, hoping for a distraction. I slip on my red boots, still pissed about the color and even madder when I see the higher heel on them, But I head down.

Right before I arrive at the lab to assist Trixy and Hedgehog in his latest plot to torment humanity, Santa saunters down the hall.

"Ho! Ho! Ho! Simon. Why, how are you?"

I stop right in the middle of the hall and roll my eyes. "You know up here we don't need the theatrics. No need to pretend with the whole Santa Claus facade. We already know you're a complete demonic turd. No need for the farce."

Santa grabs his belly and chuckles. "I'm gauging your mood this fine morning."

"What the fuck's gotten into you? Too much Rudolph dick last night?"

Santa wallops me upside the head. "Come. I have to show you this. Almost done with all you can learn, but not quite everything."

Santa leads me into another tiny ice room I never saw before, standing us in the center. I spin around, trying to figure it out, but see nothing but a circular space, maybe six feet in circumference, solid ice-block walls, with a dome ceiling of the same cold bricks. I raise an eyebrow when I glance up at him. "Another scary dungeon? I don't get it."

Santa raises one arm in the air and snaps his fingers. A television screen appears in each block. I scan them, realizing the purpose of the room. In the first one, a rapist sneaks into a bedroom window. The next shows a guy slitting another one's throat. One after the other show a gruesome scene, or an individual who looks bad, if that makes any sense.

"Um, so this doesn't surprise me." I shrug. "You've got a little room where you can monitor your creations. Until they die, I assume."

"I wanted you to see my empire." As he speaks, Santa's eyes go from piercing blue to black, the fangs pressing out of his mouth. "You see how vast? Oh, I suppose you could predict this room existed, after you witnessed the nutcracker room and how I monitor their missions. Does this give you a glimpse into the scope of my enterprises? I'm not a two-bit player without a plan. Not a random vampire, sucking blood and leaving a body or two in my wake. No, as Santa, as a vampire and warlock but with the perfect ruse, I command this enterprise and the havoc it plays on those innocent, disgusting people out there."

Santa halts his monologue, peering from screen to screen at the evil he wrought.

"You're fucked up." Another profound Simon comeback, I admit. What else to say to the demented dude? Good job? Go kill those innocent suckers? Praise his vast intelligence? Nothing to say except the obvious.

"Well, we've concluded your lessons. Back to being a rank-and-file elf again."

"Whoopee!" I yell, but with a monotone. "Can I go now?"

"That's all the thanks I get for sharing my story with you? You ingrate."

Hurt his feelings again. Complicated. Who can keep up with him? "Sorry. I'm so overwhelmed with gratitude and awe, it left me speechless."

Santa squints his eyes but opens the door without comment. We head down the hall again, back to a main lobby, like one in a normal realm to greet people. I mean, it appears as a nice greeting spot even in Santa's North Pole, but who the hell would ever end up here for a visit?

I almost trip over my own feet when I see him standing there. I come to a complete halt. No fucking way. I mean, I should stop being surprised by anything around here. But still.

Santa stops beside me, laughing. "Ho! Ho! Ho!" I look up to see he's returned to normal Santa, not vampire Santa.

I stare down the hall again. He stands next to a coat rack, unwrapping a bright-red scarf from around his neck with a top hat upon his head and a corncob pipe in his coal mouth. I reach up with one hand to close my jaw.

"Is that Frosty the Fucking Snowman?"

"There is no fucking in his name."

"You know what I mean. Who knew he existed?"

I begin walking down the hall again, wanting an up-close-and-personal look, when Santa grabs me from behind and hangs me on a hook right on the hallway wall.

"What's with this? Let me down! Isn't this part of the story?"

Santa shakes his head. "Unfortunately not. He's not under my jurisdiction. We're good friends, nothing more."

That can't be good, at least for what it means about Frosty.

Before I can say anything else, Santa walks down the hall and with a bellowing "Ho! Ho! Ho!" stretches out his arms to greet Frosty.

"Happy Birthday!" Frosty exclaims.

Did he come for a Santa birthday celebration? Or, like in the dumb-ass cartoon, did he get the holidays all scrambled in his snowy head? Whatever. They walk down a separate hall and out of my vision.

I realize my predicament. No way to get down until Santa or another elf comes along to liberate me. I turned into the damn Scarecrow in the Wizard of Oz, waiting for Dorothy to meander by. To my luck, a few minutes later, Trixy comes walking down the hall with a ladder.

"Dorothy!"

"What is wrong with you? Who's Dorothy?"

"Dorothy Gale. From Kansas. You came to save the poor Scarecrow."

Her eyes light up when she gets the reference, and she flips me off. "More like a Winged Monkey come to drag your sorry butt to the Wicked Witch's Castle. At least you got the no brain thing correct."

Trixy climbs up, unhooks me, and descends the ladder. I follow, noticing it takes my legs and feet a second to get the circulation going.

"Come on. Leave it here." Trixy waves at the ladder to dismiss it.

"How did you know to get me?"

"Santa sent word. We need your help with a problem. Well, he needs our help with a problem. Wish we could ignore it, but you know how it goes."

"What's up?" We turn the corner and head into Trixy and Hedgehog's chemistry lab, with me as their worthy assistant.

"Hey." Hedgehog jerks her head in greeting and returns to a microscope. No one else in here today. Strange.

"What do you know about the Secret Hunters?" Trixy asks.

"Not much. Santa told me a little one time—how they're vampires searching for him because they hate his power and witchery. Can't say I blame them. So they're the Van Helsing Vampires. Which is a more clever name than stupid Secret Hunters. Anyone could be secret hunters, even the humans who still crusade after vampires. If you're going to be vampires going after vampires, figure out a kick-ass name. I suppose we don't know who named them. So maybe someone slapped it on them and they got stuck with it."

We both laugh. Hedgehog glances over. "Will you shut the fuck up so I can concentrate?"

"Concentrate on what? That's what I'm trying to figure out here." I go over and get a licorice stick out of the candy jar. "When did you get this candy in here?" I twirl it in the air.

"Yesterday. Made a special request for it." Trixy grabs one for herself.

"Isn't it strange, the nice things we get? Think of the slaves in America, eating shitty cornmeal mush every day. You kind of expect shit food from slavery, you know? Not candy. Or Santa beers. Wonder why he treats us nice?"

Hedgehog looks up again. "It never dawned on him to do it a different way. He lets us take care of feeding ourselves, stocking the place, and all the amenities. Don't mention it to him, or he'll change it up on us."

"Or—" Trixy holds a finger up. "—he patterns this after the myths of the elves. So he attempts to make it a genuine Winter Wonderland. In his sick and twisted way. So he wants happy elves, despite enslaving us and the evil things he does."

I scratch my head. "Well, Hedgehog's right. Best not to ask him. What would the jock elves do if Santa stripped them of watching sports?"

Trixy punches me in the arm. "What would the jocks do? Please. What would the lesbians do?"

Hedgehog returns to her microscope again, bringing me back to the fact I am still clueless. "So what's our mission?"

"Your mission, if you choose to accept it," Trixy lowers her voice to a mysterious male kind of sound, Mission Impossible—Elf Style, "is to go after the Secret Hunters and exterminate them."

"Are you serious? How did that become our job? Isn't it Santa's responsibility? What the fuck can we do against them?"

Trixy grins. "He came here to assign us this task this morning. Picked us special for it."

"Truth be told," Hedgehog adds, "I kinda enjoy this one. We get to go after other vampires, instead of innocent humans. I know it's in league with Santa, which is never a good thing. Still, at least this pits evil against evil."

Trixy runs over and bear-hugs her partner from behind. "Good point! That's why I find you so sexy."

"Um, no foreplay in the lab." I take a bite of my candy. "Did he explain any more about our special mission?"

Trixy nods. "Don't talk with your mouth full of food. No wonder you don't have a boyfriend."

"I don't have a boyfriend because my one option up here is a demon-possessed animal. Explain."

Trixy laughs. "Here's the scoop. A small group of vampires know about him and resent his power. Like he told you. But they're getting bolder. They don't know magic, however, or have any means to get him. Yet. So he wants to get rid of them, in case. Problem being, at least in his eyes, if he goes out and slaughters them all, it would signal to other vampires the Secret Hunters were right, he exists. See, they try to recruit others to their cause, but even other vampires don't believe the Santa-as-vampire myths. He wants to keep it that way. Move in, kill them, any way possible, but get out as soon as possible."

"And what does this have to do with us?" Still a little foggy. Sometimes, because Trixy and Hedgehog are brilliant—not Santa and Rudolph self-proclaimed but false brilliance; I mean genius—which was true when they were humans, too; they forget they talk to Simon the Simpleton.

"We're supposed to create a means to eliminate them without it appearing as a vampire attack. He wants it to look natural."

"Interesting." I raise my hand in the air.

"Yes, Simon?" Trixy points at me.

"I think this task goes above my pay grade. Now I see why he came to the two of you. But what, pray tell, does this have to do with yours truly?"

Hedgehog laughs again. "We thought you'd like to be the assistant. We asked for one so we could add you to the mix. Otherwise, Santa doesn't want anyone else in on this project. Wants to monitor it up close in case we do come up with a way to eliminate vampires."

"Cool. So I'll entertain the mad scientists until you tell me what to do. Or whatever."

"Great." Hedgehog removes the slide and adds a drop of clear liquid to it. "Get me a beer."

"A task I actually can do!" I head toward the door to go retrieve it.

"Wait!" Trixy calls me back. "We may be here for a while. Get a whole cooler full, and bring appetizers."

I bow before her. "At your command."

I close the door real fast behind me, before the wad of paper hits me in the head. I grab a cooler and fill it with our favorite beers, hit the elf kitchen and load up on a bunch of bar snacks and bad-for-you food.

I roll the cart full of stuff into the room and start organizing it. "In line with getting candy and a few good things about being an elf slave, I would add the fact we can eat anything we want without getting too fat or sick."

"Right. A perk, if one must live for eternity as a vampire helper." Hedgehog rolls her eyes.

Trixy and Hedgehog work pretty hard throughout the afternoon on this potion, mixing shit together, blowing a few things up, staring into microscopes, and attempting to ignore my inane and never-ending chatter.

"Fuck!" Hedgehog explodes and throws a petri dish across the room, where it shatters against the wall with a puff of orange smoke.

I fetch a broom and dustpan to clean it up.

"Whoa, there, Silver. What's gotten into you?" Only Trixy could ask such a thing with the horse reference without getting her throat slit.

"I'm frustrated. We do this all the time to kill innocent humans, but nothing overcomes whatever reaction transforms them into vampires. We get close, but it fails because they can heal themselves."

"Too bad we can't toss them in the sun." Oops. I forgot to remain silent.

"That's it!" When I first heard Hedgehog yell, I flinched, figuring she prepared to eat me for lunch.

"It is?" I ask, hesitation in my voice.

Trixy snaps her finger. "Of course!"

Hedgehog and Trixy scurry back to their business, even faster than before.

"Um, before I sweep up this orange powder, can you assure me it's safe? It won't turn me into an Oompa Loompa or anything?"

Dead silence as they focus on their task.

"I'm leaving it here for the North Pole mice if you don't answer!"

"It's fine." Hedgehog waives her hand in the air to dismiss me. "Clean it up. Be a good little elf bitch."

At least she still has her sarcasm intact. The floor sparkles like new when I finish mopping, so I sit on a stool to watch them toil away. Boring.

"You-hoo, guys? You wanted me in here. So explain. What's up? Why is my comment so exciting? I know I'm gifted and all, but too smart for my own good, and it flies over my head, Santa in his sleigh soaring by."

Hedgehog returns to ignoring me, which I expected. But Trixy never gets so absorbed she fails to answer. I go over and knock on her head.

"I think I know why Santa puts you in the dungeon so often." Trixy brushes my hand away.

"We should have requested permission to punish him at will," Hedgehog adds.

"You're no fun. I'm just angling to know what's up."

Trixy finishes mixing a concoction and hands it to Hedgehog, who nods and smiles. Trixy washes her hands in the sink, finished with her project and free to speak.

"The element we needed. Sun. We think sunlight will break up the molecules and force the potion to work, if Santa can energize it with more powerful magic."

"You have parts of the sun in here to use?"

Trixy and Hedgehog both laugh again, making me feel stupid.

"No." Trixy pats me on the back. "The chemical mix can mimic the intensity of the sun's heat, which breaks apart the vampire's immune system that gives them the power to live forever. It acts kind similar to AIDS in a human."

"Vampire AIDS?" I scream. Makes me giggle.

"Essentially. Which is why they keep to the night. Not from a curse. It's the science of the transformation and how it interacts with the light. So we developed a compound to blast them with the intensity of being in the sun. Should kill them."

I scratch my head. "Why didn't anyone ever try this before? I mean a human, to get rid of vampires? A mad scientist must have thought of it. Work on a good project like this, instead of creating Frankenstein or a new bomb."

Trixy shrugs. "Hard to say. Maybe because it wouldn't work. We can't produce that kind of energy. Unless someone detonates a nuclear bomb, which would destroy the planet along with the vampires." Trixy boosts herself up on a counter, as Hedgehog puts the finishing touches on their experiment. "Plus, by the time humans gained the ability to even think about creating such an energy source, they stopped believing in vampires. The science to combat them came at the same time as disbelief, so vampires still had a perfect hiding place."

"But now you two invented a power source?"

"Nope." Hedgehog moves a vial of stuff into a contained glass enclosure, where I've seen them explode shit all the time. "Santa has to do it with his magic. Heat this fucker up. It acts as a conductor of energy until it reaches the power of the sun's rays. We can do it in miniature here, on the vampire cells Santa provided for the experiments, but that's it. Doing away with an entire vampire body will take more force. He wants it this way, so we can't turn it on him instead."

"I think I made a connection on my own." I grab a Santa beer to celebrate. "At least, regarding why Santa wanted it this way. If this works, he kills them and poses them as if they got trapped in the sun. Natural vampire death, and no one suspects Santa."

"Bingo!" Hedgehog announces and pushes a button. A second later, a brilliant flash of blinding light beams from the container, melting the glass into a mushy mess before it disappears.

Hedgehog jumps up and down and claps, while Trixy hoots and hollers.

"Did I witness an exploding vampire cell?"

"You got it!" In celebration, Hedgehog races over and slams me to the ground, a linebacker coming for a sitting duck quarterback. Hurts like hell, and she tickles me.

Our celebration winds down to sitting and drinking in the lab, waiting for Santa to return.

TOO SOON, I find myself riding along in the sleigh between Trixy and Santa, with Hedgehog on Trixy's other side. They told Santa about their success when he came to check on their progress, and he ordered preparations to leave at once.

The silence kills me. Trixy and Hedgehog always avoid any engagement with Santa unless necessary. I try to honor their tradition at their request, but it gets so fucking boring.

Okay, I admit it, I never saw the point in it. Giving Santa the silent treatment helps no one but bores the crap out of me.

"Regarding Frosty," I say.

Hedgehog glares at me. "Don't. Just enjoy the scenery."

Trixy shoots a dagger look my way.

"What?" I hold up my hands, trying for innocent.

"Ho! Ho! Ho! Let him talk. It passes the time."

I smile at the lesbians, feeling smug. "What the fuck is he?"

"A fucking snowman, Sherlock." Trixy spits her answer at me, to which Hedgehog gives a loud snort of approval.

Santa laughs too. When did they get in league with Santa?

"Seriously." I frown at my friends to keep them quiet. "Did you enchant him into being? To help with the sadistic side of Christmas?"

"No. And that's all I'm going to tell you. I already explained it's Frosty's story to tell, not mine. So enough about him."

"Did he give you a—" Before I finish my question, Trixy clamps her hand over my mouth.

"You saved your friend from flying overboard right into the Atlantic Ocean, like those baby Jesuses he's tossed out over the years."

I try my hardest after my near miss to ride along without speaking and take in the scenery as Hedgehog suggests, but how many times can one stare at black sky and stars, while hurling through the air in a sleigh pulled by reindeer and a bright red glow up front?

"Where are we going?" I ask.

"To the Vampire Hunters," Santa answers without any annoyance in his voice, despite the smart-ass nature of it.

"I know. I mean, where the fuck are they?"

Trixy starts laughing, the church giggles get to her. At first she stifles it. But it grows, and her jiggling body next to Hedgehog makes both of them start laughing out loud. I turn my head to see if Santa gets the joke, but he stares straight ahead at the reindeer butts.

"Can I join the hilarity?"

Trixy nods, begins to speak, but snot and spit come flying out as she laughs even harder. What got into these two tonight? They detest helping Santa even more than me. How many times has Hedgehog scolded me for finding any humor in our lives of elf enslavement?

Finally, Hedgehog gets it under control. "There's this right-wing nut job church hosting them. See, it's a conservative church in St. Louis. Goes around all holy and better than thou. The president worships these vampires in secret. Gains privileges and power from them. I'm not sure what they get out of it. Santa promises Trixy and I can expose their church and fuck with them as a reward for figuring out how to off his enemies."

That explains a lot. They can ignore Santa this time around because of their plans to fuck with another evil force in the world. And I get to tag along and watch both Santa and them, as well as see what happens with these Vampire Hunters. Not Abraham Lincoln, mind you, but super dangerous motherfuckers coming at us.

We swoop down toward Saint Louis, Rudolph leading the gang right past the arch and downtown skyline, until we land a short distance away in a suburb.

"Good thing we work so hard to stay inconspicuous, since twinkle toes the reindeer over there guides us right over the scene everyone gawks at when they come to St. Louis. We did the same damn thing in Paris, flying low over famous landmarks. So much for hiding the flying sleigh.

Plus, the glowing red ball of a nose on Rudolph, blipping away. Don't you think someone is always glancing at the arch over there, no matter what time of night? You're getting careless. Santa the Careless Christmas Legend. You've been hanging out with Rudolph too much and growing stupid."

"Shut up. Now is not the time. And maybe it's intentional." Santa points his finger at me and lifts it to his lips for silence.

"Intentional?"

Bam! Santa slaps his hand over my mouth with full force.

"Ouch."

"Nothing else. Got it?" He removes his hand as I nod.

Santa hops out of the sleigh, followed by Trixy and Hedgehog, so I go along too. We creep away as Rudolph commands the troops to fly into the sky. I decide to take a better accounting of my surroundings, but nothing stands out in what looks like a pretty typical middle-class neighborhood of houses, one little restaurant on the corner, and across the street a big church with several outbuildings.

Santa gathers us in a huddle and whispers his instructions. He barely starts when the giggles seize hold of me. I stifle them but burp up an even louder laugh.

"What could possibly be funny?" Santa's eyes turn black. Not good.

"Well, you know. We're walking in silence, whispering, but here we stand in the middle of a yard, you in your red outfit, big as snot, with three tiny elves. I mean, if we aimed for inconspicuous, we missed it by a mile."

"Why did I even risk the extra time to listen to your nonsense? Not another peep from you." To ensure I obey, Santa clamps a hand over my mouth again. I resist the temptation to bite him. "You have about ten minutes with the pastor before I should be done. Meet me at the base of the bell tower."

Santa twirls around and walks away.

When I turn to ask Trixy and Hedgehog what's next, I find them already running fast in the other direction. I sprint to catch up but do so after they stop outside a house on the church property.

"Who lives here?" I ask.

"It's a parsonage, Stups." Hedgehog acts like Santa, motioning for me to shut up.

"What's that?"

Trixy impersonates Santa by slapping her hand over my mouth. "Where the pastor lives. Shut the fuck up."

We climb through the window and snoop around the living room for a second. In a study, filled with books, a huge desk, and a couple of chairs, Trixy pulls out a zip drive and inserts it into a computer. It takes a minute for the thing to download, then she types around on the Internet, sending a bunch of files to people. I muster all the reserve in my power to remain quiet, because I want to know the plan here.

We move along and climb the stairs before storming right into the bedroom.

A woman sits up and screams, while the balding fat man next to her fumbles for a nightstand drawer but misses it and falls out of bed instead.

Before he regains his composure, Hedgehog hurries over, opens the drawer, and grabs the gun herself.

This time I laugh out loud, because the moderate-sized pistol she holds is closer to the look of a bazooka in the hands of a tiny elf.

"You'll want to listen to me before you do anything else." Trixy goes over and kicks him in the stomach.

Probably because Hedgehog aims the gun at his head, the dude gets up and crawls back into bed next to his still screaming wife.

"Shut the fuck up, NOW!" Hedgehog even gets me to quiet down with her scream. "Good." Her voice returns to normal volume. "I'm going to explain everything to you. You don't have any choice in these matters. No options. But I'm an honorable person, so giving you a fair warning seems the appropriate thing to do. Understand?"

Both people nod their heads.

"Good. Here's the scoop. I sent a packet to the press, with proof of the embezzlement, blackmail, and sexual escapades, all coming out of this church. Some you did. Some your followers. Other things your employees accomplished. So, yes, I know you did those things. My little release entails an entire expose on your church and everything going on under your watch. We kept the vampire thing under wraps, because no one would believe that fucked-up shit, anyway. This will ruin you, nonetheless. Only one thing you need to do going forward. No crying apology about your sin and going back into the ministry. Stay the fuck out of organized religion, and stop ruining people's lives with your warped theology, you only use to make a buck. Got it? Otherwise we come back."

The man nods, holding the bed sheet up to his chin as if it might protect him.

His sobbing wife stutters a louder yes as she clutches his arm. "What are you?"

Good question. I imagine the bewilderment in their little minds right now. They slept, masters of a kingdom of self-righteous hate, exploiting the people for their own gain and empowerment, when three fantasy creatures saunter into their bedroom, threaten them with their own gun, and destroy their lives.

Trixy laughs. "Angels from hell, bitches!"

Hedgehog fires the gun into the ceiling three times before we sprint for the door, run down the stairs, and go into the night, laughing our fool selves into crying. We slow down when we get outside the church, right at the tower where Santa instructed us to meet.

When we catch our breath, I take out my flask and pass it around. "In reality, that was kind of lame."

"What was?" Trixy wipes where she missed her mouth.

"We fuck up one pastor's life, but thousands of others out there continue spewing their hate-filled bullshit. The rest of them will dismiss him as a charlatan, a wolf in sheep's clothes, and carry on with their self-righteousness. Hurting people. Making themselves feel better with their flawed reading of the Bible. Forcing gay people to try to go straight, which ends up in suicide and depressed people. Or worse, failed marriages, unwanted kids, and complicated miserable lives."

Hedgehog and Trixy grow quiet. Hedgehog grabs my flask and drains it before throwing it into a bush. "You're a downer. Like we didn't know already. At least we killed one bird. Give us one victory before you piss on our parade."

"That could be a song!" Trixy begins a loud song, an impromptu one about crazy stuff and a parade, deflecting the anger and disappointment, getting our little band back on track with surviving the Santa enslavement as best as possible, given our realities.

It takes longer than ten minutes for the Jolly Dude to return. "You're late." I tap my wrist, despite no watch on it.

"No one listens to you." Santa motions with an arm. "Come. I need your help, Trixy and Hedgehog. Tweedle Dum can tag along if he insists."

We enter the church, which Santa defiled, because the cross above the altar lays on the ground in pieces, wine drips down the stone steps toward the pews, and Santa smeared a bloody substance all over the walls. Oh, literally blood. Gross.

"What's up?" Hedgehog asks him as we hurry downstairs into a crypt.

"I incapacitated them temporarily, but need help with the potion. Any minute now they'll move again. Which would spell doom for us."

I slap my hands to my side in anger. "It was easy? I thought this was supposed to be a huge match between you and the other vampires? This sucks. No action whatsoever."

"You imbecile." Santa hits me upside the head. "It's a vampire battle for the ages. Sure, I incapacitated them, because I walked right into their midst as if I wanted to negotiate. I had to get inside, risking everything. They tried to imprison me, but I expected it so instead threw a spell on them. A difficult spell to handle, one I practiced for years to master. And one I could do once inside their domicile. Even with that, here's the problem: I could do something very temporary because their healing power and other abilities will force it to wear off fast. Under typical circumstances, this means they could come after me soon and know how to follow me no matter where I went or how fast. So what's different this time? Before it happens, we can burn them to a crisp with Trixy and Hedgehog's invention. And why I wasted all this time telling you is beyond me, because now we need to hurry. If my spell ends before we get there, we're doomed."

I halt and turn around, scurrying back up the stairs. I know nothing about the potion, have no role here, and in no way want to confront an army of pissed-off vampires. Santa grabs my collar before I get up three steps and hauls me along with him.

In a cellar-type location, which makes me wonder why the church has a dungeon in the first place, we find a dozen or so vampires, suspended in midair but wiggling and struggling against the unseen forces holding them captive. They say nothing but grunt and groan, their activity growing more frantic when Santa enters the room.

One by one, he, Trixy, and Hedgehog go around to the vampires and force-feed them the potion. Well, they do more to trigger the chemical reaction or whatever, but I don't understand it. I can see each vampire gain a little more control of their functions with each passing second, and I can almost sense Santa's captivity potion wearing off.

"Now!" Hedgehog screams at the top of her lungs and points at Santa.

Whoa. Serious stuff. Hedgehog issued an order to Santa, which no one does, and more than that, he obeys instead of lashing out or punishing her.

Santa squints his eyes, claps his hands together, and a blinding light fills the room. Like someone took a thousand flash pictures at once, or twenty lightning bolts struck at the same moment.

When my eyes clear and the little white lights stop floating in front of my face, I glance around to see the damage. Santa stands in the middle of the room, laughing his ass off with Hedgehog and Trixy close by, their arms wrapped around one another.

"I assume those piles of ash represent each of the now incinerated vampires?" Again, I sound a little down because I expected a lot more grandiose story, and since my lesbian pals involved themselves, I expected even more.

"Ho! Ho! Ho! Right indeed! No more Vampire Hunters after Santa! And special treats for Hedgehog and Trixy when we return."

"What about me?" Santa kicks me in the balls as an answer, doubling me over on the floor.

Pissed, I sit and refuse to help while Santa and the elves shovel each pile of ashes into a separate bag. Finished, they gather everything and lead us back outside.

In no time, Rudolph flies to us with the sleigh; we get in, and head for a beach, I think in California. There, Santa stages the ashes seconds before the sun rises and we race toward the North Pole, arriving before daylight.

Safe inside the confines of this magical realm, I speak again. "Why the beach?" I impress myself with how long I maintain my silence from being hurt and pissed. But fuck being quiet. No one cared. Back to the questions.

Santa answers, no smart-ass comment or anything. "Vampires often go to such places to commit suicide, because of the intensity of the sun. Maybe because of the beautiful scenery as a last view. It looks authentic."

"To whom? Not the passing humans, who may wonder how piles of ashes ended up all over the place but not much else."

I watch Hedgehog and Trixy head away back to their room to enjoy the night off and a steak dinner he promised them. Trixy waves as she turns the corner.

"To other vampires. I still have a hard time believing you're so daft." Santa leads us down an icy hallway, past Mrs. Claus's door before he stops at the base of the turret leading to my room. "Now, to bed with you."

"Don't I get anything special for helping out?"

"You didn't do anything but annoy everyone."

I scratch my head. "I thought that was my job?" I say it funny-like, but in truth mean it.

"I suppose it is. Now go."

Santa slaps me upside the head for at least the fiftieth time in one night, so I turn around and run up the stairs to record this latest episode, knowing I gathered enough dirt now to expose the man and his empire. If only I knew a way to get the story out there.

Epilogue

LET ME BEGIN this final thought by pointing out I never claimed the status of mental giant. No ivy league education for me. No supreme intelligence guides a damn thing I do. I don't even wear the false mantle of calling myself brilliant, Santa and Rudolph ego style.

And go ahead and laugh your fool heads off, assholes.

Because I sit here writing this part in Santa's study, at his behest, needing his final approval before I tag it onto the end of this here little Santa ditty.

You guessed it. Add Simon the Elf to the list of Clement Clark Moore, L. Frank Baum, and the others who helped Santa spread the Santa word to create the myths and legends that still make him one of the world's most renowned figures.

What the fuck, right? I mean, how did I end up with those literary and artistic legends? Believe me, it has nothing to do with matching their eloquence or brilliance. Nope. The short answer: my name appears on the list because Santa duped me.

I feel so shitty, like a total moron. Duped by the Jolly Ole Fucker. Well, I'm not the first. The entire world seems duped by him, so maybe I should cut myself some slack. Still, who didn't see this coming, except me? Moral of the story: never ignore lesbian advice. Trixy and Hedgehog tried to warn me. Sure, they worried about my well-being, but all the same, heeding their advice would have averted this humiliation.

I'll cut to the chase and explain this here epilogue to what I thought was my secret file on everything Santa the Vampire. If you'll indulge another flashback to get this into your brain faster than anything else. Don't worry. I'm not using magic on you, the kind Santa and Mrs. Claus employed on me. Only a written flashback signaled by the upcoming extra line break.

I FINISH THE part of my secret journal where we stage the ashes of the Vampire Hunters in the California desert, ready for a long sleep, when I hear footsteps pounding up the ice stairs. Heavy steps. As in, Santa steps, not little elf or prissy reindeer. Not good. I throw the diary under the bed and leap in as Santa appears.

Whew, I stare into his jovial blue eyes and at his enormous smile, not the coal pits of anger. "Ho! Ho! Ho! Little guy, no need to hide the journal. Get it out. Let me see it."

I freeze. My mind spins, trying to figure this out, while Santa chuckles, even grabs his belly and rubs it.

"What?" I ask. Lame but buying time for the slow computer in my brain to crank up.

"Bring it to me. Come." Santa motions for me to get out of bed. "Let's return to my office and discuss this here little project of yours."

"I thought you ordered me to go to bed. A few minutes ago, in fact, you sent me up here."

"Because I knew you'd finish your journal."

I sit up, bewildered. "You know?"

Santa utters a hysterical laugh. "Simon, you complete and utter fool. Of course. Now, grab it and come along. If this goes well tonight, I'll give you the old green boots back.

I might even add a steak dinner like Trixy and Hedgehog earned."

Stunned, I creep out of bed, still dressed since I got in to hide from him, and crawl underneath to grab my manuscript. I hold it tightly to my chest as I wander down the stairs, traverse several hallways, and walk behind Santa when he marches right through an ice wall and into his study. Didn't even bother to smack me into the wall for the pleasure of hurting me; I just walk in as well.

I glance at the Santa memorabilia, scan the room for a torturous device or sign of the evil about to befall me, but Santa sits in his desk chair and motions me into a seat across from him.

"Let me see." Santa holds his hand out.

I hesitate before reaching over to place my precious journal in his hand, then scoot back and twiddle my thumbs and wipe sweat from my brow as he reads it.

I wince for the first couple of pages, nervous as hell, but grow more comfortable the farther he gets because the dude laughs the whole time. Twisted fuck. Time up here at the North Pole goes differently than anywhere else, so I sit without any sense for how long it takes him to finish.

He closes the book, chuckles again, and hands it back to me before sitting back in his chair.

"Marvelous! Ho! Ho! Ho!"

I stare at him, realizing after a moment I need to close my gaping jaw. "You're not pissed?"

More merry Santa laughter. Not the fake, Santa is supposed to be happy shit he gives people before offing them, but a genuine sense of bemusement.

"Did you drink something funny today? Giggle juice?" I search for an explanation, but nothing comes to me. See? Dense. I think the elf enslavement dulls my ability to think.

Seems obvious in retrospect. "Could you have a vampire fever? Are there vampire doctors to take care of you?"

Santa grins again. "Nothing whatsoever."

"Really? Because your reaction makes no sense. I figure I got at least a month in the dungeon coming, if I'm lucky."

Santa shakes his head. "You wrote this at my command."

Well, Santa, at last, did it. He at long last came up with a means of rendering Simon the Elf speechless.

My bafflement, of course, sends him back into hysterics. "You complete simpleton. I detected your trope after the first entry. You think my magic limited? Don't you have a sense for the complete power I yield over this place? When you went to sleep the first night, I crept up here, read the diary, and went back to my study to contemplate. I first thought of murdering you. But you amuse me too much. I thought of destroying it, punishing you, and moving on. Instead it hit me! I wanted this exposé written. You were the perfect author for the next step in my career."

I clear my throat. "You think you have a career?"

"We're not discussing a career."

"I'm attempting to avoid embarrassment. Okay, so you wanted me to write this all along?"

"What else explains my facilitation of you learning my story, your access to Mrs. Claus, to Rudolph, and everything else you learned? You amuse me, but you achieved such special status as a way of doing my bidding."

He got me there. And here I thought my charm and sense of humor got me this far. "Makes sense. Still, I don't get it. Why did you want me to write this? I figured it might undo you. Expose you to the world. Create a major hunt for you from the humans. I even think Mrs. Claus figured the same thing or wanted it released to the world for a reason to help her."

Santa nods this time. "I have no doubt. I know that's what you thought. And she figured getting it out there might lead to her release too. Not on your life! Ho! Ho! Ho! Nope." He shakes his head. "Never. You will remain my amusing slave, and she'll stay in custody to ensure my protection. Of course, I let you two believe whatever you wanted so long as it kept you on track, gathering the stories and putting words to them. She told you her story with the hope it might bring me down and protect herself in the process. And you kept churning it out, thinking it would expose me to the world and lead to your freedom."

"True dat." Fuck. He's such an asshole. "Any chance I could get drunk right now? Before we continue?"

"Be my guest." Santa motions toward his fridge, so I hurry over and grab three beers, popping them open at the same time. I chug one in seconds.

"Good thing elves don't need to worry about their livers." I hold up a second beer and tilt it toward him. "So, do I get to learn why you wanted this story released? Do I at least get a little satisfaction?"

"I cultivated this myth of Santa almost two centuries ago, building it to such a grand scheme by the middle of the twentieth century the legend went on cruise control. Once we established Rudolph, it went into commercial overdrive with nothing more for me to do. Most people view Santa as a harmless myth to delight children, hardly anyone thinks I exist outside of myths. I achieved what I sought from the beginning, a world beholden to me without even knowing it, and total domination of the vampire world, also without many of them realizing I exist. The few who hunted me, well, now I've conquered them too." He stops, stroking his beard, deep in contemplation.

"Knock on Santa's head! Where did you go?"

Santa clears his throat. "Excuse me. Where were we?"

I scratch my head, as confused as he. Did he have a stroke? "No clue. You recapped the legend thing, when I thought we were supposed to be learning why you want to reveal this shit."

"Ho! Ho! Ho! Of course." Santa nods but goes silent.

I arch a brow. "So are you continuing, or what?"

"Oh, right!"

Bad sign. Early onset dementia or vampire Alzheimer's. That's all I need to deal with. "Good. Because spending the energy to complete a ruse seems incongruous with turning around and telling the whole world the truth."

"Correct you are, in many ways. But here's the thing. I'm bored. It gave me a challenge for so long to build this up, but what now? Centuries ahead of the same ole, same ole, year after year? Something else calls to me."

I drain a beer and half of the next one. Wiping my mouth, I roll my eyes at him. "Are you fucking kidding me? You concocted this whole thing about letting me complete the journal and letting it out there because you got bored?" My turn to laugh pretty hard at him.

Santa shrugs. "What else?"

"Isn't this risky?"

"That's the point!" Santa claps his hands together.

"What is?" He loses me again, but I admit to not being the sharpest knife in the drawer since this whole conversation began. Because I should be getting my beauty sleep now. And it's getting worse as the buzz turns into a full-blown, drunken stupor.

"It takes the myth and this crap to a new level. Gives me new ideas to try. They'll search for the North Pole. They'll watch those fake Santas to see if the real one shows up. Will people dress up as me for Christmas anymore, or reserve it for Halloween? Will they lie to children, or clamp down on the legend? Hell, it could spark a culture war when those right-wing Christians begin spewing forth how they knew from the beginning not to worship false idols! And we haven't even gotten into the fact it reignites across the globe the debate over the existence of vampires! A few will shun it as complete fiction. Others will take up a crusade. All in a reinvigoration of the importance of me! All Santa story, me, me, me!" Santa pounds on his chest in emphasis.

Makes me giggle again. "At least you kept your healthy self-esteem." I almost think the next thing to myself, but instead keep going. "Or, your batshit crazy narcissism. I don't think anyone likes himself more than you. You're a complete nut job, from the moment you popped out of your mother's womb. Your inadvertent stumbling into vampirism exacerbated the problem. Who buys statues of themselves and puts them around the house? I'll answer. Psychopaths. The insane, or to be exact, criminal insanity. You know Louis the XIV from France? He used to travel around and give people portraits of himself as a gift. Can you imagine? But get this: you make him look humble and sane. Adolf Hitler wanting everyone to display a picture of him, hanging them everywhere in Germany. Saddam Hussein commissioned big statutes of himself. What do they have in common? Complete bonkers and total dictators. You're no different!" More beer. I've lost count at this point.

Problem being, Santa sits over there laughing. "Your jealousy of my situation astounds me."

My eyes grow wide with shock and I spit beer out, blowing it across the room. "Wow. Delusional too. So are we done? You want to release this information to the world to make life more challenging. Or at least you're sticking to your story. In reality, you desire more fame, accolades, or infamy. All of the above? So you take my journal—it's all yours—and we'll be on our merry way. Oh, wait. One more thing."

"Yes?" Still with his stupid Santa grin on his face, the Santa in the Coke ads staring back, who looks either sweet or like a lunatic.

"You're not pissed? I mean, you read my report there. Not a flattering portrayal. Pretty cutting, if you plan to use my tale to announce yourself to the world."

"People will see through your own jealousy and get right to my genius. Or begin those debates. Whichever, it serves my purpose. Besides, that's why I had you write it. I could have done this myself. Or picked another author or storyteller to do it, someone established, successful, and with talent, like Moore or Baum. But no. Your way of telling it makes it authentic. Real. Believable."

"Of course. Right." Two more beers out of the fridge, one half down the hatch, and now I can barely stumble toward the exit as the alcohol replaces the blood in my little elf veins.

"Oh, no. You're not going anywhere yet."

"We're not done?"

"Not even close."

"More revelations? Something else nasty coming my way? What's next?"

But the answer to these questions is the end of the flashback. Now you know how I learned the truth. So what now? Besides feeling no pain in my drunken stupor. Well, I sit here in Santa's studio, drunk, writing this here epilogue at his command. He wants me to update the story to this very minute. So I do.

"Done?" he asks when I start tapping my pen on the table, humming "Frosty the Snowman" and staring into space.

"I suppose. Here. Look it over."

Again he reads it and laughs most of the time. "Good." He hands it back. "A couple more things, and we'll be set. Keep this and continue updating until this gets into the hands of the author."

"An author?" I ask.

He nods. "Yep." He gets up. "Come."

"Wait a minute." I scratch my head underneath my little hat. "I thought I was the author."

Santa rolls his eyes. "You are. And will be. But we need a new person to get it into the hands of a publisher. So we'll have a coauthor."

"So it *will* be like Moore. And this person gets to fuck with my words?"

Santa shakes his head. "No and no. We don't need anyone as sophisticated as Moore. Just a run-of-the-mill author because this is already written. So he won't need to edit or mess around with it either. In honor of you, we'll pick a gay one."

"Wonderful. Such a favor you're doing for me."

"Can we get going now?" Santa twirls his finger around to signal his impatience.

"Where to?"

"The sleigh. We're off to an author I think will do the job."

"Isn't it daylight?"

"Not where we're going. You've been at this for a while and the sun went down."

"You mean I don't get any sleep at all? You know I get even more crazy and chatty when sleep deprived."

"You'll be fine. I think you'll enjoy this."

"Where we headed?" I ask as I trot after him, clutching my journal to my chest.

"Chicago."

"Chicago? What's in Chicago? I thought the publishing industry was in New York? Does the Center on Halsted have a wild and crazy liberal pro-gay press? Wouldn't it be hilarious? To publish this under their imprint?"

Snapping back to our typical behavior, Santa ignores me as I hustle after him, hop into the sleigh's passenger seat, and notice the reindeer hooked up, Rudolph's nose glowing up there, a big red dildo guiding the way. No other elf slaves. No Santa magic bags.

"No gizmos? No backup elves to help out? Where's Bobby? I thought at least you'd want him along, since tonight is pissing me off night."

"Nope. Unnecessary." Santa chirps for the reindeer to fly.

We shoot through the sky, even faster than normal, and soon enough I stand next to Santa in a little home office with a dude with long hair staring in amazement at us.

"Um, who are you?" His voice trembles and he scoots his chair back toward the window.

"Ah, of course this might surprise you. Happens every time. Permit me to introduce ourselves. I am Santa Claus and this here is Simon the Elf. We need a favor from you."

He sighs and runs a hand through his hair. "Either I drank way too much wine tonight, or this is a twisted home invasion and I'm about to die. What happened to my dogs?" Another random, odd question from a dude in complete danger. People are so stupid.

"Sleeping under my spell safely, I assure you." Santa sounds so calm and normal. Weird. He always likes to scare the shit out of people, and this dude would make a perfect victim. Probably scream his ass off. "Don't be alarmed."

The author nods. "Good. Because Akasha and Chewbacca don't deserve to be hurt. Go after me, not them."

Funny dog names. "Akasha. Cool dog name. You're an Anne Rice fan?" I ask him.

"Yeah." He looks at me, maybe confused by the sudden chatty question, given the nature of the situation. I always forget how warped my reality became as an enslaved elf.

Santa motions for me to shut up. "Enough with the dogs. They're safe."

"I don't imagine you'd just leave, would you? Let me live? I'd go back to my writing. I won't call the police. Unless, of course, I go back to my drinking theory, and this is a hallucination because I work too damn hard."

"Ho! Ho! Ho!" Santa holds his belly and it jiggles around. Gross.

Santa stops the stupid charade and turns those eyes jet black while his fangs descend.

The man shakes in his chair but makes no move to run. Must feel trapped. Destined to die. Poor guy.

"So you gonna off me?" he asks. "Figures a vampire would do me in. Since I write their stories. And here I thought it was make-believe. You know, I have a husband. And those dogs. They need me. Chewy's super sensitive. Something tells me you don't care about my dogs."

I laugh out loud, and even in his vampire form, Santa smirks. I feel guilty, because I'm laughing at the irony, but our merriment makes the guy start to cry.

"Stop crying." Santa, returned to normal now, reaches out and places a comforting hand on the author's shoulder. "I have no intention of killing you."

"Could've fooled me. What do you want? I'd rather die than experience an awful rape scene or torture."

Again we both laugh. I still hate I seem like a Santa crony here, but he's funny. I mean, not really, terrified and all, but his no-nonsense comment in the face of the ultimate danger is unique. No pleading, just laying out the facts as he sees them.

"Here's the deal. I've come to ask a favor of you. Do it for me, for us—" Santa points over at me and back at himself. "—and no harm will come to you or those you love. One rather simple thing that would help me."

"I'm not a part of this," I interject before Santa punches me in the side of the face to shut me up.

"Ignore the elf. Listen to me. Shall we discuss what I need?"

"This is getting stranger and stranger." He shakes his head. At least he stopped crying, even though he continues to shake. "But sure." His voice cracks. "Can't imagine I have much choice at this point. What would your special favor be?"

It hits me as I scan the room. Painting of a skeleton on the wall. A Dracula print. Gargoyles. I examine the titles of the books on a little shelf. *The Vampire's Angel. The Vampire's Protégé. The Vampire's Quest.* Santa told me he wanted a gay author. So he's gay. And does speculative fiction. No Christmas shit, but horror. I know, Simon the Slow Elf, given his reference to a husband. Makes him pretty gay. His horror titles could explain his reaction here, and on some level, he's used to diving into the world of vampires and scary shit. I decide I like him. Plus, I'm gay, so I'm glad a gay author will take up my journal. Huh, Santa was right. I appreciate how he picked a gay author to release his sordid tale.

"Simon, tell him."

I whip my head up and stare at him dumbfounded. I have no idea what he wants. "You, um, uh, you tell him."

"Are you afraid?" Santa squints his eyes at me.

"Hey, guys? I know you're in charge here, but, uh, I'm still freaking out a little. Any chance you'll get to the point?" The man interrupts our quarrel, again looking afraid and yet working to participate in a situation where a lunatic vampire dressed as Santa and his elf minion stand in his presence. "I have a lot of work to do if you decide to keep me alive. Plus, when the dogs wake up, they need to eat."

"I agree with your impatience." Santa grins. "It will get this accomplished fast. Simon has a manuscript he needs to publish. I want you to do that for him. Under your name. His name is Simon the Elf."

He rubs his forehead and frowns. "You want me to publish a strange memoir by an elf? Why not go to the publisher yourselves?"

"Not his style, to be direct." I point to Santa. "And, I'm an enslaved elf." I step forward and duck to avoid Santa when he swings at me. "Make sure you understand that part. It's important. Not doing any of this of my own free will."

"Okay." He draws out the word looking from one of us to the other. "So an enslaved elf wrote it. Still, how does this involve me?"

Santa tilts his head, thinking. "I understand your confusion. But see, you write about vampires, so it will make more sense coming from you. Let's do this. Coauthor it. You have to put Simon's name on it too."

Santa reaches over and picks up a book. I glance at the cover, with a blood red sky and the silhouette of a sexy male. Hot picture. *The Vampire's Protégé*. Nice title. I catch the guy's name on the book. Damian Serbu. The poor gent sitting there, I assume. In his other hand, Santa picks up *The Vampire's Angel* with a cathedral and angel wing on the cover. "See. This stuff relates to my story." He hands the books to Damian. Santa grins. "Yes. This will do. You publish them under your name, with Simon."

"You want me to whip this out, using my name, despite my having had nothing to do with it?"

Santa takes a deep breath, his impatience rearing its nasty head. "Listen, you're a random hack author. A gay niche guy, writing gay vampire stuff. How many people even read such crap? This will help you. You can even keep the royalties."

"Okay." Again Damian prolongs the word and scans the room, as if searching for an escape route.

"Do you mind if we use your desk for a moment?" Santa points to an antique school teacher's desk across the room in the other corner.

"It's Paul's."

"Is that a yes or a no?" Santa frowns his questions.

"Sure." Damian motions toward it with his shaking hand. "Go for it."

"Sit there, Simon. Catch up the story for us."

So I saunter over, climb into the big desk chair, and start writing away in my journal again. As I add this latest event to it—our interaction with poor Damian—Santa chats away.

"I want it out by Christmas. Doable?"

"Maybe. If my publisher agrees and has room for it. But I'm not sure my press will want this. And what about editing?"

"I don't care how you accomplish it, and it won't require editing. Can this be done?" Santa's voice grows stern toward the end of his sentence.

"Sure. Why not? I mean, I'll give it my best shot."

"Good. What I want to hear. And here's the title: *Santa is a Vampire*, with Damian Serbu and Simon the Elf as the authors."

I slam my pen down. "What a stupid title. You are so lame."

"Quiet, Simon."

"He kind of has a point." But Damian, too, gets quiet when Santa glares at him.

"And it kind of pisses me off, a stooge in Chicago gets partial credit for my work. Whatever. You're an ass. At least give me top billing."

Santa sighs. "You'll be listed as author, and we'll tag Damian Serbu on as more of an assistant."

"You're still a shithead." I feel better expressing my last curse.

Santa grabs me by the collar, lifts me out of the chair, and I scribble this last bit before I know he will hand this to Damian and we'll skedaddle out of here.

So, I'm signing off. Time to give this to Damian Serbu and hope, for his sake, it gets published. If you're reading this, well, watch for me. Never know when Santa and I will tumble down your chimney and fuck up your holiday cheer. See ya around.

If you enjoyed Santa and Simon, you'll love this excerpt from:

Santa's Kinky Elf, Simon

I amble down the hall, taking as much time as possible before getting to Santa's little chamber. Delay, delay, delay. Not that my reticence will change reality or get me out of whatever he wants. No, here at the ole North Pole, Santa reigns supreme. He's a vampire, see.

Crap. I realize you may not know the story yet. I spelled it out in *Santa Is a Vampire*. I wrote the book, though they put some hack named Damian Serbu on the credit line with me. Fuckers. Anyway, you can check it out to get the whole scoop once it comes out, so I'll cut to the chase here. Santa is a nasty-ass vampire, of the evil variety, and a warlock to boot, with a wicked form of magic.

"Simon, now!" I hear Santa bellow down the icy hallway. Remember, we're up here at the North Pole in Santa's castle, which he hides from the whole world with a powerful concealing spell.

Instead of hurrying me along, the edge in his voice slows me down. Foul mood. No telling what he wants this time. I mean, for a while he called me all the time while he told me his story, but we finished up with our little game once *Santa Is a Vampire* was finished. So I'm back to being just another one of the elves up here, enslaved against my will, forced to do Santa's bidding, no longer chumming around with him.

I stop in front of a big cardboard cutout, life-size, I'm telling you, of Santa holding a can of Coke and winking. Ugh. In addition to being a witchy vampire, dude is seriously narcissistic. He collects all sorts of Santa memorabilia and displays it around the ice palace, like this here thing. He finds it hilarious they always depict him smiling and happy with a twinkle in his eye, when really he kills people without regret—innocent people—all the time.

Shit. Here he comes. I dillydallied too long. "Hey, buddy!" I smile, tilt my head all funny, and wave like I spot my best friend in the world coming down the hall toward me.

Santa grimaces. "We're not buddies. Never have been. Never will be. I thought I called you? No, let me correct my statement. I did call you." He grabs me by the back of the collar and lifts me into the air, then spins around and proceeds to carry me the rest of the way to his hidden office chamber. To get there, we walk right through an ice wall. "It doesn't take long to get from one end of the castle to the next, let alone from where you were. You don't think I know you were in the lab with Trixy and Hedgehog? Well, I do."

I scratch my head, my pointy little hat almost tipping off. "Well, according to most labor laws, I should get a break sometimes. I've been cleaning shit up for them all morning. I needed to take my time getting here in order to rest. My rights, and all."

Santa leans back in a rocker, his eyes still a pleasant blue, but glares at me. "First, if you act this way again or continue with this attitude, you'll really be cleaning up shit. I don't mean figuratively, but right out there in the reindeer stalls. I haven't had to punish you that way in a while and I miss it. Second, you have no rights up here. You point it out to me rather fondly on a regular basis. North Pole labor laws merely stipulate you do what you're told, when you're told, how you're told. Nothing else to discuss or consider."

I jump into a bright-red beanbag and lean back. "Wait! Before we settle in for our latest little chat, can I have a Santa beer?"

Santa rolls his eyes but reaches over to the little fridge and pulls a bottle out.

"Sweet." I twist off the cap and take a big swig. Dealing with Santa is a lot easier with a good buzz. Actually, I prefer to be completely shit-faced, but sometimes alcohol loosens my tongue too much, and I get into way more trouble than I want. Leads to sessions in the ice dungeon. Not good. My ass is still sore from the last time, and not in the good kind of way.

He rocks back and forth, like a kindly gentleman, while I slam my beer, get up and replenish it, then sip this one more slowly as I wait for him. *Odd. Usually we get right to business. WTF?*

"Um, this is uncomfortable to me."

Santa squints his eyes together. "What is?"

I shrug. "Sitting here silently with one another. Like, if we were lovers, you'd expect a contented silence. Something pleasant as we enjoy each other's company. But that's not us. So what the heck's up?"

"Oh, Simon. Ho! Ho! Ho!" Great, fake Santa. Sometimes he delights in putting on the whole Santa show like he really embodies the loving-children-happy-jolly-fat-man stereotype. Annoying, because we know the truth.

"Oh, Santa, Fuck! Fuck! Fuck!" Oops. I mocked him. Went too far.

Santa's pretty blue eyes transform to black pits, leaving me staring into oblivion: his fangs descend, and he reaches over and smacks me upside the head. "Your imitation isn't even close to how I really am." As he likes to do, he snaps back to happy dude with no warning. Freak.

"It's not too far off, actually." If I do say so myself. "Anyway, enough with the pleasantries. What's up?"

"You're right. We should get right to it. I don't want to waste any more time with your nonsense. It's about the book."

He pauses, as if he explained everything. "The book?" I ask.

Santa nods. "*Santa Is a Vampire*. I'm figuring when and where to publish it as we speak, and then the grand exposure of my true nature to millions and millions will be complete. But I've been thinking about it."

"It's never good when you think," I interrupt.

Santa clears his throat and continues. "Specifically, about publicity and getting people to believe it. Or maybe to find a way to entice a press or someone to publish it, without having to threaten them. So I figured they will love me. Or at least be intrigued by me, as they should. Even if I just terrify them, I will get exposure. And they'll enjoy learning about the missus and Rudolph, all the legends and stuff being debunked and the truth revealed. All well and good. I think, however, I made a mistake in getting the story out there through you. I'm afraid you're too one-dimensional. I think they need to get to know you a bit better. The real Simon. What makes him tick? Why should they read what he has to say? We need a human interest story about you."

Santa rocks back and forth, his hands folded pleasantly in his lap, a look of complete satisfaction on his face. Makes it seem like he's a totally with it and brilliant CEO who explained a rational strategy for the company to follow.

Except this sounds batshit crazy. "Um—" I almost tell him exactly what I think, but visions of the ice dungeon pull me back. "—interesting. But really, they want to know about you, not me. I don't have much to do with it, right? You wanted it focused on your story. Me, secondary to the whole thing. The fly on the wall, telling it like it is. The ole voice-over narrator you never see."

He shakes his head. "Nope. I've already decided. They need to get to know you a little better. Human interest is the way to go. Buying into your elf story, into you, will help them believe the much more important story about me. It will get people to demand *Santa Is a Vampire* comes out soon. It's all about reality TV these days. I even have the idea sketched out. You'll need to execute it. Easy"

I'm too afraid to learn the story, so I sit quietly and stare at him.

"Don't you want to know the plan?"

My turn to shake my head. "Nope. Nadda. Nein. No. No. No fucking way. No."

"You're going to anyway. Actually, I think you'll enjoy it."

"Because you're always so concerned about my enjoyment? Right."

Santa leans forward, a broad smile on his face. "No, seriously. You'll get some pleasure out of it along the way. Not because I want to reward you. Like you said, I don't care about your happiness or contentment whatsoever. You'll nonetheless experience some pleasure because it fits the story."

I scrunch my brow. "Don't you think I should concentrate on helping Trixy and Hedgehog?" They're my best friends up here. Brilliant chemists. Spouses. Slave elves like me. And badass lesbians. Mostly, I get to spend my time assisting them. "I really don't think a human interest story about me will help your cause, in terms of people learning about your story. I'm incidental."

Santa pounds his fists on the rocker arms. "No! This is brilliant. It will help facilitate my story. You don't have a choice, so embrace it."

About the Author

Damian Serbu lives in the Chicago area with his husband and two dogs, Akasha and Chewbacca. The dogs control his life, tell him what to write, and threaten to eat him in the middle of the night if he disobeys. He has published *The Vampire's Angel*, *The Vampire's Protégé*, and—also by Simon the Elf, *Santa's Kinky Elf, Simon* with NineStar Press, with *The Vampire's Quest* coming February 2019. Keep up to date with him on Facebook, Twitter, or at www.DamianSerbu.com.

Facebook: www.facebook.com/Damian-Serbu

Twitter: @damianserbu

Website: www.damianserbu.com

Other books by this author

The Vampire's Angel
The Vampire's Protégé
"Professor Ghost" within *Teacher's Pet, Volume One*
Santa's Kinky Elf, Simon

Also Available from NineStar Press

Connect with NineStar Press

Website: NineStarPress.com

Facebook: NineStarPress

Facebook Reader Group: NineStarNiche

Twitter: @ninestarpress

Tumblr: NineStarPress